Chapter One

"Do you want a banana?"

It seemed like an innocent question. An innocuous one that held no meaning other than the offer of a banana. And Andy was hungry. A banana wasn't what he was after, he just wanted a bag of chips, but it was better than nothing. It would help until he got to the chip shop.

"Banana?" Andy muttered.

There were things on his mind. His girlfriend, Ali, had left for a work trip two hours earlier. She'd dropped some monster hints about marriage. Andy was not, by nature, a great picker-upper of hints, but these were as subtle as a Game of Thrones battle sequence. There was no question what she was after. Not that he didn't want to get married to Ali. It just seemed so grown up, and he'd just spent the last two hours playing computer games.

He stroked his beard. He'd grown and coiffured it in the hipster style and he was rather proud of it. It was red, the colour of his hair, and it was almost part of the uniform of the Clerkenwell based advertising company for which he worked. Ali had stopped hinting about that too. Her last words were 'lose the beard'. That wasn't hard to interpret.

"A banana," the man confirmed.

Andy was not very fastidious when it came to his five a day, which was why he was heading for a chip shop, although Ali had left some prepared meals for him. She'd also said 'don't go to the chip shop.' But he was starving. Ali had often said that Andy was not the most observant of people. He certainly didn't notice the padded jacket the man holding the banana was wearing. He also didn't notice the three other men walking swiftly towards him. They were almost on their toes, as if they were required to sprint at the drop of a hat, or even a banana. Andy hadn't noticed that, but he had seen the slight dark vein on the edge of the banana. It wasn't so dark as to suggest it was overripe, but it was on the cusp of it, as if it should be eaten immediately. He wasn't one for overripe bananas, and couldn't get on with barbecued ones either. But bananas were his favoured fruit, although some part of that was laziness. An orange took too much deconstruction for his liking, and a carelessly eaten apple led to a mouthful of pips.

"Thanks," he said, and took the banana.

And then Andy's life changed.

Chapter Two

All Jeremiah McGuffin had ever wanted was to make money. He'd had brief, fleeting moments, but his two dalliances with property development had coincided with two monumental market crashes. His publishing business went the same way when print was surpassed by the internet and, when he gambled on bad weather in Britain with a string of children's indoor adventure playgrounds, it heralded the longest rain-free period since records began. He got into timeshare just as the clever money went south and invested in a French holiday complex after which the weather turned, and it rained every summer. Jeremiah was no stranger to the bankruptcy courts.

The odd thing was that Jeremiah remained resolutely upbeat, convinced that one day his efforts would be rewarded. His time would come. It had to happen, he reasoned, as it was a matter of odds. It wasn't possible to be that unsuccessful that many times. But this time he'd pushed the odds in his favour. This time he was going to be the gambling house and not the gambler. He'd stolen a banana.

In the course of running his business there had always been an imaginary line, which defined the lawful. He was frequently on the wrong side. Sometimes by some distance. But his enterprises were fundamentally legal and honest. This one wasn't. This was very much illegal, although not in his mind immoral.

It wasn't that he had a strong sense of morality. He just wasn't averse to the occasional narcotic. And the banana he'd stolen wasn't any ordinary banana. His most recent enterprise involved the installation of burglar alarms. He'd been called into a strange loft apartment with an unusual smell. A smell Jeremiah recognised as cannabis. He'd wondered why it had required so much security and then, while fitting a movement detector, he'd overheard something.

"That banana, my friend, is worth a hundred grand."

That had focused his attention. The owner of the flat was a biochemist. He stopped installing and listened.

"It is a kind of sensual cousin to MDMA, with a longer hit, a polite nod to LSD with a soupçon of the hallucinogenic, and a leaner come down."

The biochemist was capable of out-talking a wine connoisseur when it came to describing the relative merits of a narcotic. While a wine connoisseur could taste gooseberries, he might actually see them.

"All bananas have identical DNA except this one."

Jeremiah hadn't met the biochemist - he'd only seem him from a distance - and everything he said was confusing. But the next thing he heard was relevant.

"This is the seed banana. The daddy."

Jeremiah froze. A narcotic banana worth a hundred grand seemed far fetched. But, he could hear, the biochemist knew his stuff.

"The banana ripens as the skin releases ethylene."

Jeremiah didn't know why this was relevant. The biochemist's voice became muffled. Jeremiah moved around the room until he found an air vent which ran between the two rooms. The biochemist's voice was louder and clearer.

"And this banana has unique DNA. It is a one off."

Jeremiah concentrated. This was like a Rubik cube which had been jumbled up, but he'd only ever completed the Rubik cube by cheating and pulling it apart. The biochemist was tall, ginger and wore a big bushy and unkempt beard and seemed to spend most of his time stoned. He was from a different world. But Jeremiah listened, and listened again, until finally it came together.

"The ethylene is the catalyst. It's not until the banana ripens that the narcotic forms."

It had been a little difficult for Jeremiah to understand the biochemist after that as he'd evidently celebrated with a cocktail of narcotics which had rendered his speech intermittent. But he was thinking. He had the codes to the alarm and he had a copy of the keys. He had work to do. This was the greatest opportunity that had ever fallen at his feet. Not that it had actually fallen at his feet. He'd have to do a bit of tackling and dribbling to keep it there, which was another way of saying he had to do a bit of stealing and kidnapping.

Jeremiah had stolen the banana and the biochemist wanted it back. But that wasn't the full genius of Jeremiah's plan. He knew someone who grew bananas.

Chapter Three

Andy's dad was on the train home. It normally took ages, but today it seemed to be in a hurry. It wasn't, but this time nor was he. A man had appeared from HR. Except he seemed more like a boy to Andy's dad. He'd talked to him and at the end they'd both agreed it would be better if he took early retirement. But he couldn't remember agreeing. It had been phrased in such a way as to suggest he'd won a prize, but now that he was digesting the conversation, it didn't appear that way at all. The weird thing was that he'd been pushed, but it felt like he'd jumped on his own accord.

Andy's dad had taken the same train for thirty-two years and he'd spent some of his time hating it. But now he was missing it already. The line had been upgraded and the trains were new and modernised, and it took longer every year. That was progress for you, he often thought. Except today when the train drew into Cobham it felt like it was minutes after it had set off. He was a bit shellshocked, even though he should have seen it coming. Andy's mum was pushed into retiring two years earlier, but he'd fooled himself into thinking he was too senior and critical to the operation of the bank. He should have known everyone was expendable. He got off the train and walked in the direction of his house.

It was the same house they'd lived in for thirty years in leafy Surrey. He'd not been long at the bank when they'd bought it, but now it was worth a fortune. He was staggered at the size of Andy's mortgage and the cost of his flat in Hackney. Andy had mentioned it was more of an apartment than a flat, although Andy's dad had no idea what the difference was, except he couldn't see them bringing up children there. Not that Andy was ready for children, in his view. But marriage wasn't far off. In his day people bought property together after they got married. Not that that was always the case. It was just what Andy's dad had done. He liked to do things properly. He turned a sharp left.

He'd walked the same walk for over thirty years and he'd never taken a sharp left, but today he felt he wasn't ready to go home. He needed more time to ruminate. Not that rumination would change things. But his mind kept returning to the same thing. What the hell was he going to do? He'd got up after the alarm at 6.45 every day and he couldn't think of one thing he wanted to do in the house. He wasn't a man who'd acquired a number of hobbies. He thought about golf and tennis and bowls. The list of things he didn't do, and had no interest in trying, was very long. He did a bit of gardening, but he wasn't sure if he enjoyed it. It was more out of necessity. If he didn't do it no one else would and the garden would look a mess. And what would the neighbours say about that?

Did he care what the neighbours thought? The problem was that on balance he did. He'd always cared about what the neighbours thought, although not in the specific sense, but as a general group. He wanted to conform. He was made to conform. But that wasn't what was worrying him. He was going to be at home, all day long, with Andy's mum. It wasn't as if they didn't get on. They did. They never argued. But, and this was beginning to stress him, what were they going to talk about?

Chapter Four

"Are you going to be alright without me?" Ali had asked earlier.

Andy pouted his lips in a dog-like expression. This would be the first time they'd been apart for over five years. But it was the domestic arrangements which had concerned Ali.

"You know how to operate the dishwasher?" she asked.

"Of course I do," Andy said.

"And the washing machine?"

"No problem," Andy said.

"And I've left instructions for dinner, and there's food in the fridge, and in the freezer," she said.

"I'll be fine," Andy said.

"You won't just go out and get chips?" she said.

"No, I'll follow your instructions," he said, crossing his heart and his fingers behind his back.

"Don't forget your inhaler," Ali said.

"I won't," Andy said, although he always forgot his inhaler.

"Okay," Ali said. "Then I'll go."

Andy got up, hugged her, and wheeled her case to the door.

"Be good," he said and kissed her.

"You too, And," she added, "remember to call your parents."

"Will do," Andy said.

"Oh," Ali said, leaning over to kiss him. "Lose the beard."

He ran his hand appreciatively through the growth. Despite his twenty-eight years it had only completed its coverage of his face a couple of years earlier and just in time for the beard fashion revolution. Originally he'd grown it in what he'd called an ironic way, which was his excuse for doing things that Ali didn't approve of. The problem was he was growing to like it.

"No problem," Andy said.

He'd doubted he'd shave it and so did Ali, but it didn't stop her asking. But there was something else she really wanted him to do and she wasn't confident that was going to happen either. But that didn't stop her laying the trail.

"And there's something you might want to tell your parents," Ali said.

This, they both knew, was the marriage hint. Except it had become less of a hint and more of a sledgehammer. Despite that, Ali was convinced Andy hadn't got it yet. It wasn't as if she expected the whole bended knee proposal, but she'd have liked something. It was time.

"Okay?" Ali asked.

"No problem," Andy said.

Andy was on his own and he knew exactly what he intended to do. He grabbed a beer, threw himself on the sofa, and turned on Top Gear. It was a gender specific guilty pleasure, as Ali hated everything about it. He watched the middle aged boys thrash around in Ferraris, which didn't mean a great deal to him, as he had only driven once since he'd passed his driving test. He assumed he could pick it up easily enough should he need to.

Once he'd had his fill of Top Gear, Andy switched to the next phase. He plugged in the appropriate leads, grabbed the controls, and played Gran Turismo for a further hour until he felt he hadn't shot enough people, and switched to Call of Duty. An hour later he'd massacred enough people to gather a bit of an appetite.

"What's for dinner?" he asked himself.

Andy wasn't used to be being on his own. The silence was a little unsettling. He checked the fridge and grabbed another beer while he read Ali's instructions. This cooking malarkey looked like hard work.

"Chips," he said.

He was fairly sure she'd mentioned something about chips. He finished the beer, grabbed his coat, and left the flat. Their flat was on the sixth floor of a newly built block, which sat above an underground station. They'd just bought it and the mortgage payments were pretty hefty, but it suited work, and had great access to the centre of town. It was also one of those areas which used to be run down, but had undergone a revolution of chicness. It was another reason to keep his beard.

Andy took the lift and walked to the chippy, unsure what he should do with his new-found freedom. It was an area with many pubs and he could feel the temptation, the lure, of the crowded, noisy social places. But he was going to have his chips first. A moment later he arrived at the chip shop to discover it was undergoing a renovation. Then he remembered. He'd had a conversation about this with the oil-stained man who ran the place. He'd said it was part of their program of works, which they carried out every twenty years. The man was deadpan and Andy wasn't sure if he was joking. Annoyingly, he'd set his heart on chips. Andy's palate wasn't a sophisticated one. As he couldn't think of another chip shop he took out his phone. It lit up with potential options, but all required a walk. Andy didn't like to walk very far if he could help it.

He had a think. Wasn't there one in King's Cross? He remembered staggering back at about four in the morning and grabbing some chips. King's Cross was only a couple of stops away.

Ten minutes later Andy found himself on the concourse at King's Cross. The chip shop, as he far as he could recall, was the other side. He hadn't got far when someone stood in front of him.

"Do you want a banana?" the man said.

Chapter Five

"It is pronounced Low-Bow," Barry said slowly adding, "as in the bow or bow."

Barry made a shape with his hands to illustrate an archer's bow and a knot. It wasn't helping. He stood tall. He was one of the tallest men in his African country, a country which he considered compact, but which others referred to as small. Often they chose terms which were more derisory than merely small, particular when he was dealing with the British who had ruled at one time, but had barely remembered the event.

"I dare say," Sir Bernard said.

Prior to the meeting, which Sir Bernard was reluctant to take, he'd described Lobo as a poxy, suppurating zit of a country, which was so small that if one person farted the whole country would smell it.

"Lobo," Barry said with pride.

Barry came from a long line of Barrys, all of whom had been king and sole ruler of his country. He often wore jeans and a teeshirt but, more recently, as he was making his way through his fifties, he favoured a tailored suit. But he'd been reading the Daily Mail and it had told him that British officials tended to genuflect to the ethnic minorities. Consequently he was dressed in colourful tribal robes which he'd bought in a tourist shop on a trip to Nigeria. He looked, by any standards, pretty splendid, but they were itchy as hell. Barry had been educated in England, although not at Eton, as his father had hoped, because he had neither the connections nor the qualifications, and the general thinking was that at least one of those criteria should be fulfilled. But instead he went to a small, sporty school which constantly spoke about its all-round education, rather than its dismal academic record. Nonetheless he had acquired quite a plummy accent, but today he had chosen to opt for his African accent, as he knew how much the English liked their stereotypes.

"But these things aren't that simple," Sir Bernard said rising to his feet.

Sir Bernard had both the qualifications and the connections, and he *had* been to Eton. He too was wearing his tribal clothing of a Saville Row pinstripe suit, and he even stooped he stood as tall as Barry. Were his accent to be any plummier it wouldn't be possible to decipher.

"Your people owe my people," Barry said.

"Are you sure?" Sir Bernard asked again. "What was the country called?"

"Lobo," Barry said.

"And you're sure we ruled it?" Sir Bernard asked again.

"Absolutely," Barry said through gritted teeth.

"Well, if you're really certain, but I suspect it's a jolly long time ago and we did, how shall I say..." Sir Bernard paused. "Rule most of the world."

The muscles in Barry's face tightened. Despite spending a lifetime attempting to emulate it, he hated the British arrogance. He had hoped for a subsidy, just a little bit of money thrown their way, now he was struggling to achieve a trade deal. He couldn't believe it. He thought of himself as almost an Englishman. He'd even studied geography at university – not, as his father had hoped at Oxford or Cambridge, but at Trent Polytechnic – where he'd achieved a perfectly respectable third.

"We need to trade," Barry said, pronouncing each word in his full African accent.

Trent Polytechnic had been quite a fun experience, but it hadn't garnered the contacts he'd have liked. His friends Mick, who ran a small wine bar in the pleasant market town of Saffron Walden, and Jeremiah, who tottered from one business to another, were not of much use when it came to running an African country. What Trent Polytechnic had given him was a taste for alcohol, light narcotics and women of easy virtue. While this gave him some pleasure, it also wasn't of much use when it came to running a country of any size. And things weren't going well. They had been exporting peanuts to neighbouring countries, but Barry had made a strategic change, and now they were in bananas. They were all in. The worse thing was they were being paid peanuts for the bananas. It had been a bit of a disaster. There was starvation, and a bit of an uprising, but worse than that his presidential Mercedes was now not just the model before the model before the current one, but it was the one before that. It was very unpresidential. All he needed was a trade deal with a rich country.

"Indeed," Sir Bernard said, although he thought he'd wrapped the conversation.

And the British, as far as he could see, were stinking rich. He'd hoped to upgrade the embassy, but there had been a confusion with postcodes when he'd bought it, and he'd ended up buying a flat above a chip shop in Lewisham. Despite that the cost had been crippling.

"I do not ask much," Barry boomed.

He'd spent the morning in a place called Sloane Square and the streets were lined with six figure Range Rovers, each rather more than the crippling cost of the embassy. And there had been Maseratis and Ferraris and Porsches, as if they were given out with cornflakes.

"And we are old partners," Barry insisted.

What annoyed Barry was that he didn't, in his view, want for much. If he had a more up to date Mercedes and a stable of supercars, he'd be perfectly happy. Was that too much to ask for?

"Right," Sir Bernard said.

Sir Bernard sighed. He'd got a first from Oxford in PPE and had considered a career in politics rather than the Foreign Office. It was at times like this he regretted it. He didn't want to waste any more of his time, but he could see that Barry was likely to be persistent. He'd have to fob him off with something.

"Are you in London for long?" Sir Bernard asked.

"A few days," Barry said.

Things had got so bad Barry was behind on the payments on the presidential jet and, as it was financed through a particularly dodgy outfit related to British royalty and the son of a former prime minister, he didn't want to stay in London long. It might get repossessed.

"Excellent," Sir Bernard said in as genial manner as he was capable of. "I'll get back to you."

Chapter Six

Andy reached out for the banana. There was a flurry of activity around him, but he hadn't registered that it was related to him. He had the banana in his hand. And then people were all around him.

"What's the matter?" Andy asked.

The men around him were tall and their faces were expressionless. They surrounded him. He was moving. Andy couldn't tell if his feet were on the ground. For a second he thought it was a practical joke, the sort that would be filmed, but the faces of the men said otherwise. He tried to complain, but his voice didn't travel, as if the noise of the concourse at King's Cross had been turned up. He was close to the edge of the building when a door he'd never noticed before opened up, and they were through into a dark room. The men moved away.

"What the fuck?" Andy said.

He meant to say more, but this was all he could manage. He felt as if he'd stepped into a computer game. The kind which involved a lot of killing. It was quite surreal but, unlike when he played on the computer, he was shit scared. He looked around.

"Don't even think about it," a voice growled.

Andy hadn't even thought about it. Escape seemed impossible and foolhardy. The room looked like a store room. The question was what was he doing there and what did they want?

"Who do you work for?" the same gruff voice asked.

He wasn't certain who'd asked him, but he was happy to answer.

"Pyjama Case," he said.

There was a silence. A menacing silence. And then someone hit him in the stomach. The fist had travelled so quickly and returned to its owner with such stealth he couldn't tell who had delivered the blow. Andy crumpled. He would have fallen to the floor, but someone seemed to be propping him up.

"It's true," he spluttered.

Andy had gone to a very nice primary school. It was multicultural and there were many children from tough backgrounds, but no one had ever laid a finger on him. After that he attended a large comprehensive, which was considered to be up and coming but had a reputation as a rough place, yet not one person even raised their voice in anger at him. University was a place of beer and occasionally cannabis and the worse thing that happened to him was when he'd tripped over a kerb and broken his ankle. It would have been painful were he not so extensively anaesthetised by the seven pints of cheap lager he'd just consumed. He'd never even received a Chinese burn in jest. This was quite easily the most painful thing that had ever happened to him.

"That really hurt," Andy said.

He looked at the expressionless faces of the tall men around him. They were not exuding empathy. He had to start talking.

"It's a digital advertising company based in Clerkenwell," he said.

As far as Andy was aware all companies of this sort were based in Clerkenwell. It was hipster central. It was why he'd grown his beard. Beards were virtually essential for the role. They were part of the uniform. He wasn't sure he'd conveyed the message.

"I'm on the client liaison side, but I'm more of a creative," Andy explained.

He looked at them look at each other. Somehow he sensed that this wasn't the answer they were looking for. He didn't have much more to give.

"We specialise in the ergonomic interface between the spoken and the written," Andy said.

This was one of the most prominent claims on the company website and Andy had never, until this point, questioned the voracity of this sentence. But right now, like the men around him, he had not the slightest idea what it meant. Foolishly he decided to elaborate.

"We question..." Andy began, and then he decided to keep quiet.

He didn't think it likely that the men around him required the services of the digital advertising world.

"Why did you take the banana?" one of the men asked.

He couldn't say who'd asked, although he thought the answer to the question was obvious. Nonetheless he had to say something.

"I was hungry," he said.

Another fist flew. Again he couldn't see who'd thrown it, and its retraction was so rapid he wouldn't have been surprised if one man had thrown it and another taken it back. Was that possible? He didn't think so, but he was beginning to lose the plot. He slumped. The banana was still in his hand and he'd accidentally squeezed it slightly.

"Good," one of them muttered.

They'd carried out their roughing up as planned. One of the men threw a hessian bag over his head.

"Move," another said.

Andy held the banana out, but no one seemed interested in it. The minor pang of hunger he'd felt had been relegated to the back of a long queue of pains, but he didn't have time to think about them. The men surrounded him and he was on the move. They went through a further door which took them out into the open. There was a fresh wind which he could feel through the hessian bag and which brushed the mat of perspiration on his forehead. They were moving across the street. Traffic was stopped. Andy was thrown into the back of a van and someone slapped the side of the van.

"Go! Go! Go!" someone shouted.

Andy could hear the squealing of wheels and a thump as they'd evidently hit something.

Chapter Seven

Jeremiah had been forced to bring in some help. He couldn't kidnap someone on his own. It made him a little nervous, not least because he intended to lift the biochemist at King's Cross. They were a team of security experts he'd once hired for an installation. They were a little scary, but they'd exuded competence and had insisted on Kings Cross because they had the keys to a maintenance cupboard. Their job was to grab the biochemist, rough him up a little, bag him and throw him in the van. Jeremiah's job was to drive the van and take him to a secure place.

Jeremiah was waiting in the van. That had also been a new enterprise. He knew he couldn't buy or hire a van in case it was picked up on CCTV, which left him only one option. He had to steal it. He'd googled it and was surprised how forthcoming the internet had been on the theft of vehicles. He'd invested in some equipment and he was ready to go. And then he'd come across a van with the keys hanging temptingly in the ignition. It was bright yellow and filled with flowers, but he only needed it for a few hours. He was tapping the steering wheel. This was a very distant stretch from that imaginary line of legality, but this was his moment.

"Oh shit," he said.

He was on a double yellow line and he could see a traffic warden walking towards him with some purpose. He didn't want to get out of the van. He had a baseball cap on. He pulled it down. The traffic warden tapped on his window.

"You can't park here," the traffic warden said.

The traffic warden used to be in advertising until a misplaced comma, which suggested that his client enjoyed anal sex, terminated his career. He'd become a minicab driver until he'd suffered a Touretteical outburst which his passenger had interpreted as sexual harassment. He was lucky to get this job.

"I won't be long," Jeremiah shouted.

Jeremiah didn't want to open the window and stand a greater chance of identification. The traffic warden looked persistent. Jeremiah was sweating. He checked his mirrors. He'd left the back doors open and the engine was running. Wasn't that enough?

"You can't park here," the traffic warden repeated.

Jeremiah tried to remain calm. He needed to be calm. But his nerves were on a knife edge. It wasn't, he reassured himself, as if the parking ticket mattered. He was about to kidnap someone. It wasn't his van either.

"Fuck off!" Jeremiah shouted.

And the parking warden fucked off. He fucked off in the direction of a police car which had just parked at the end of the road. The traffic warden had now attended every known seminar on inappropriate behaviour and was an expert in the field and, in this regard, was a poacher turned gamekeeper. He wasn't having anyone telling him to fuck off.

"Oh shit," Jeremiah said.

He was pretty certain he could see a police car at the end of the road. It prompted a sweat tsunami. He'd looked at this from every angle and now he realised that King's Cross was a stupid place to have chosen. But he had no choice. The security team had insisted. Worse, had the biochemist called the police?

"Be calm," he told himself.

Of course the biochemist hadn't called the police. He was fabricating an illegal substance. He was as bad as Jeremiah. Worse, possibly. This thought reassured him. He relaxed. And then someone smacked the side of the van with the flat of his hand and it made such a loud, and resonating noise, that Jeremiah very nearly crapped himself.

"Go! Go! Go!" someone shouted and slammed the back door of the van.

The bundle had been delivered. Despite anticipating this moment, Jeremiah did nothing for a second. His mind froze. What was he thinking? Then he was back. He threw the gearstick into first, whipped out the clutch, and floored the throttle. It wasn't an ideal starting procedure and it certainly hadn't included mirror, signal and manoeuvre. But, as the wheels squealed, there was quite a bit of manoeuvre. It took him a fraction of a second to realise that people were scattering in front of him, and a further fraction to notice that helmets were flying. That, he knew, was not a good sign.

Chapter Eight

When Ali got on the plane she realised she wasn't entirely relaxed. She wasn't frightened of flying, she rather liked it. Andy always shuffled about nervously. She wasn't concerned about the bonding exercise that her company had organised, although she wasn't looking forward to that either. The only good thing was that it was in New York and that was great. It had to be in New York otherwise no one would have agreed to go. She wasn't *that* fond of her colleagues. But the company had a sister office. She hadn't looked into the company structure, but she suspected it was more a second cousin twice removed. There was a lot of overstatement in the company ethos which, each time she read it, sounded more like bullshit.

They were a digital magazine business run by Miles, who claimed to have done everything. Except, within the first two minutes of meeting him, Ali had him down as a bullshitter. She had yet to decide whether he'd done half of what he claimed, or whether the figure was much lower. But she was an editor of an online listings magazine and she had quite a bit of freedom. She suspected it was because Miles had not the remotest vision, but he also paid her well, so she wasn't complaining. It looked good on her CV, and she might stay a year or so, and then head for something more exciting. Ali was ambitious. But it wasn't her job that was making her feel nervous. It was Andy.

They'd met at a party in Clapham four years earlier and had never been apart for as long as a week. It wasn't that she thought he was going to run out and cheat on her. She suspected he would spend most of his time on the sofa playing video games. It wasn't a very edifying image of the man with whom she wished to spend the rest of her life. But it was the second part of that sentence that was causing a problem for her. She *did* want to spend the rest of her life with him, and she'd been dropping hints to that effect. She wasn't the kind of girl who had planned out her wedding as a child with specific views on the church, the bridesmaids dresses and the reception. But the important part of that sentence was the first part. She wanted to get married. To Andy.

She also wasn't the kind of girl who'd thought about how she'd like to be proposed to. It didn't have to be on a golden beach, or in an expensive restaurant, or even on bended knee. If she did think about it, and she wasn't prepared to admit to herself that she was, a bold declaration would be nice. A single table set for two, perched on a cliff overlooking the Caribbean, would be good. The waiters would be formally dressed and would move in a blur around them, as they were too busy looking into each other's eyes.

"Bollocks," Ali said to herself.

She was going mad. She'd never been to the Caribbean and, now that they had pretty hefty mortgage payments on the flat in Hackney, it wasn't going to happen anytime soon. Worse, she suspected that Andy's best effort would be 'how about it?' Not that she would complain. She knew who she wanted to marry and bold statements weren't his thing. There were many things that weren't his thing, which made it amazing that she was so certain that he was the one. But she was certain. And she'd expected him to say something before she'd left. She was itching to tell her parents and it was time to tell his. She might have to stop dropping hints and tell him outright.

"Anything to drink?" the stewardess said.

"White wine?" Ali asked.

She was given a small bottle with a twist cap. Ali poured it into the plastic beaker and wondered whether there was a hint that she could drop that even Andy couldn't miss.

Chapter Nine

The steering wheel was spinning hopelessly in Jeremiah's hands. He'd mounted the kerb. He hadn't intended to, but he was struggling to control the van and, although it didn't look like it, he was attempting not to run over the traffic warden and policeman that had stood in his way. Then he saw the bus stop. There was a lengthy queue despite the late hour, and he was in danger of ploughing them all down, and turning a discreet kidnapping into a terrorist attack. He grabbed the steering wheel and yanked it to the left.

"Oh shit," Jeremiah screamed.

There were obstacles in the way. Jeremiah was unaware that the van was the florist's pride and joy. It was a highly specified Mercedes, and Jeremiah had just driven over a high kerb ensuring that the van would never again drive comfortably in a straight line. The good news was he'd made it onto a small side street, but a large iron bollard was the remaining obstacle. It took out the left light and most of the wing and pushed him to the opposite side of the road where he collided with a refuse truck which took out his right headlight and gouged a deep mark across the entire right side. The side door would never open again.

"Oh shit," Jeremiah said again.

The bad news was that it was a one way road and Jeremiah was travelling at speed. The wrong way. He was also unaware that the florist had been suffering from all the economic factors that prompt people to put buying flowers at the end of their list. Except today. Today had been a bumper day which would have made up for a terrible month. At least it might have, had someone not stolen his van. Flowers were flying everywhere. He narrowly missed a cyclist hitting a parked car instead. And now he could hear noises. Sirens.

"Oh shit, shit, shit," Jeremiah said.

He'd meticulously worked out a route. And this wasn't it. He turned into another road. It was narrow and the van was wider than he was used to. He just missed two parked cars, but took out a rank of bicycles, and the back end came around and hit a parking meter. It was the only remaining panel that hadn't been dented and Jeremiah was unaware that one of the economies the florist had been forced to make was his van insurance. One half of the bumper was trailing on the ground describing an arc of sparks. He turned again and this time he was travelling the right way down a one way road, but there was a stationary car ahead of him. It was an Uber Toyota Prius waiting for his fare. Jeremiah hit it with some force.

The Prius shot forward into the main road. It landed in the side of a passing bus, forcing the driver into instinctive corrective action, and taking the bus into the path of a lorry travelling in the opposite direction. It was a lorry laden with Calor gas cylinders, which would have remained in their cradles, but the bus had caught the lorry at an angle which turned it. It tipped and the bottles flew out. One of the bottles landed on its valve and the valve gave way.

"Oh fucking shit," Jeremiah said.

He floored the throttle. He'd seen a gap and he went for it. It was between the scattered cylinders, the lorry on its side, and the stricken bus. He was through in less than a second and down the road and back on his planned route. He was fifty yards further on when the combination of leaking gas cylinders and a sparking bumper united or, more accurately, ignited. It was a deafening explosion. Jeremiah floored the throttle and snaked down the road. He took his planned turns until he arrived at a darkened place.

"Shit," Jeremiah said.

He couldn't believe it. There was someone there. Why would anyone park their car in such a remote and darkened place? Then he noticed that there were people inside the car. His headlights lit them up. He could see a middle aged man apoplectic with panic. The naked woman in his lap was the explanation, as the man had not long been selected to represent the constituents of Loughting and Bunterhouse, and the woman was not his wife. She wasn't even a young researcher. She was carrying out a service for which he'd been paid. The man wrestled with the steering and steered the car out of the little alleyway, while guarding his face with his right hand. The woman threw something out of the window.

A used condom slapped on the windscreen. Jeremiah parked the van and turned the engine off. His heart was thumping in his chest. He could hear a cacophony of noises. There were sirens and he was pretty sure he could hear a helicopter. But noisier still was the wheezing noise coming from the back of the van. It sounded as if the biochemist was having an anaphylactic shock.

"Oh for fuck's sake," Jeremiah muttered.

He heaved himself over the seat and into the rear of the van. The biochemist was heaving in an alarming way. Flowers were scattered everywhere. Jeremiah knew that a dead biochemist wouldn't be much good to him and would elevate kidnap to murder. But he didn't want to be recognised either. He shook him.

"What's the matter?" Jeremiah asked.

It was an odd question to ask of someone who'd just been kidnapped, roughed up, and who was wearing a hessian sack on his head, but he was aware that the biochemist was attempting to say something. He put his ear closer.

"Inhaler," the biochemist said.

But it wasn't the biochemist, it was Andy. He also didn't know that, despite a reminder from Ali, Andy had left his inhaler on the kitchen table. Jeremiah panicked and punched Andy in the face. Although not a generally approved method of dealing with an allergic reaction, it seemed to work and Jeremiah bundled him out of the van and through a hole in a fence and onto a building site which was unattended for the weekend.

Chapter Ten

Andy's mum could see Andy's dad at the end of the garden. She didn't know what he was doing there and suspected that neither did he. She'd digested the news of his retirement and now they moved about the house uneasily. It was as if the natural order of things had been disturbed. Things were no longer in their rightful place. She'd adapted to her own retirement by concentrating on the house. She'd cleaned every corner of it. At times she'd felt a bit like Lady Macbeth, so it was possible she hadn't adjusted *that* well. Then she'd painted the spare room. It should have been finished in a couple of days, but she'd just completed the task. It had taken five months. And she'd taken up yoga.

The friends she'd had, the friends they'd had, had mostly moved away. She realised now that those friends had been slightly older, and retirement had involved moving anywhere except Surrey where they'd lived for the last thirty years. But she'd made a new friend at the yoga class. Lydia was glamorous and fashion-aware in a way that intimidated Andy's mum, but she was doing her best to keep up. She knew she was what used to be called 'square'. Not that there was anything wrong with being square. If square meant straightforward and honest, then she was happy to be square. She couldn't wear the clothes Lydia wore and wouldn't want to. She wouldn't dare go out in public clad only in the leotard that Lydia favoured for the yoga classes. The thought made her shudder.

But, looking out at Andy's dad thrashing about in the garden, she wondered what was ahead of them. She wondered if she should bring it up, but they weren't the kind of people who revealed their souls. They were, she reminded herself, square, which meant they kept all that mumbo jumbo to themselves. She had no idea what Andy's dad was doing but she did, for a second, wonder what he was thinking. It wouldn't have helped.

Andy's dad had put on some work boots he'd been given as a retirement present. They had deep soles with a thick tread and he intended to clear the end of the garden, which was a bit of a wilderness. But a sort of philosophy was emerging in his head. If he cleared it today, then he would have completed the only job he could think of doing. Completing it today would be a mistake. A big mistake. Then there was the rhubarb. Andy's dad didn't like rhubarb, but he'd never mentioned it to Andy's mum who liked to make crumble with it. He had done his best to ignore the rhubarb, then he'd moved it to the dry, stony soil, and then he'd surrounded it by taller, thirstier plants that would eventually seal its fate. He'd tried hard to make its environment as inhospitable and arid as possible. And the stuff had thrived. It was everywhere. He'd hack it all down but Andy's mum would notice.

But, as it happens, he'd acquired a new task. Next door's dog had got through the fence again and he'd just stepped in dog shit. Andy's dad had stamped and wiped and dragged and still not managed to get the shit out of the deep tread of the sole of his right shoe. He didn't want to have to take them off, and do it by hand, so he continued to drag, wipe and stamp until the job was done.

"Get out," he said rather angrily.

He'd never been angry before. He'd just gone to work and come home like everyone else. He hadn't hankered after more, or thought there was more to hanker after. The shit really was stuck deep in his sole. He was going to have to take them off and clean them by hand.

It occurred to him that a shed would be useful at the end of the garden. He'd use his new iPad and have a look into it. For a second he pictured himself sitting in that shed. It was a comforting thought and it would delay the clearing of the garden, aside from a small section where the shed might stand. Of course he couldn't clear *that* until he knew the size of the shed. He decided that sourcing a shed would be a good task for the afternoon. Although looking at the dog shit on his shoe he wondered if he'd have time today. He walked back to the house. He'd found an order. Today he'd get the shit off his shoe, tomorrow he'd do the shed-sourcing and the day after he'd clear the space, or do whatever was required, for the shed. That would take him up to the weekend, and Andy's dad knew what to do at weekends.

Chapter Eleven

Jeremiah had a pint in front of him. His doctor had mentioned issues with his blood pressure. It was sky high now. His hands were shaking with nerves. He'd slipped into a busy pub and, as far as he was aware, he was unnoticed. He needed to get the pint in him fast. It was a little tricky getting it in his mouth. Quite a bit lay on the table. He attempted to steady one hand with another. He should have started with a brandy. But then he shouldn't have made the pick up at King's Cross station. In his defence, it was his first kidnap.

"London is in lockdown as we assess the impact of the latest terror attack," the newsreader said.

There was a television above his head. He was a terror suspect, which meant that the full extent of the police's resources would be deployed. He ordered another beer. This was a disaster. He'd tied the biochemist to some reinforcing bars, which would be the foundations for a development which claimed to be exclusive. It had been a bit of an obstacle course, but he was confident he was secure. The problem was picking a moment to collect him.

"In other news," the newsreader said, "Fingers Marvin, notorious for removing the fingers of PPI workers at a call centre, has escaped from prison."

Jeremiah was grateful that the news had shifted from the terrorist attack, but the pub was alive with people talking about it, and he could hear a helicopter outside. He'd moved away from Kings Cross and wasn't so far from Hoxton, but he needed to stay still for a while and calm his nerves. He had more self medicating to do. By the third pint his hands had steadied. He drank it a little slower and, by the time he'd finished it, the pub had begun to empty and he could no longer hear the helicopter.

When he'd finished the fourth pint his blood pressure had fallen from close to a coronary to the merely alarming. It was a measure of the adrenaline flowing through his body that he felt disturbingly sober. But he was ready for the second part of the plan. He took out his phone and texted the address of a pub in Hoxton. He had to make his way there and, when he left the pub, the world had almost returned to normal. Public transport was functioning again and, with his baseball cap tipped down, he dropped into the tube. He'd chosen a stripper pub as he knew his mate Barry liked strippers. He hadn't told him it was a stripper bar.

Jeremiah was so desperate to get away from the scene of the crime that he travelled for two stops in the wrong direction. He got on another train and, by the time he'd arrived at Hoxton, he was feeling a little more relaxed. It felt like the plan had fallen apart and now it was coming back together again. He had to keep calm. And then something occurred to him.

"Bugger," Jeremiah muttered.

He'd forgotten the banana. He'd left the biochemist holding the banana. There had been too many things going through his head. It didn't matter, he reassured himself. He had the biochemist and that was the most important thing. He approached the pub. Two large bouncers stood menacingly outside, but he entered unnoticed. He'd also chosen the pub because it was noisy, full of distraction, and they were unlikely to be overheard. It had been smartened up since he'd last been there and there were girls in lingerie walking around with beer glasses full of pound coins. Barry was not difficult to spot. He'd positioned himself as close to the stage as was possible without actually being on it. He was clearly very preoccupied. Jeremiah sidled up to him unnoticed.

"Hey, King Bazza," Jeremiah said.

Chapter Twelve

Barry had time to kill. He often did. He wondered if Sir Bernard would actually get back to him. He doubted it. He walked into Sloane Square and saw something that got him very excited.

"Oh my god," he said.

He uttered the words as if he'd just witnessed the parting of the sea, but for him it was rather more than that. Something he'd read about, but had never actually seen in the flesh or, more accurately, the metal.

"Lamborghini Aventador," he muttered in awe.

It was more than awe, it was excitement which bordered on the sexual. It wasn't entirely uncommon for men in his country, those that hadn't had the benefit of an education at Trent Polytechnic, to masturbate in the street if they should see a woman, or occasionally an object, which excited them. Trent or no Trent, Barry was tempted. He had to have one of these. The need, the ache, was too great. He turned away. But he couldn't. He took out his phone. It was an iPhone which was becoming a little elderly. It would have made an uncomfortable lump in his ceremonial robes, but he was wearing jeans and a jacket. The robes were just for the Foreign Office and they might have been a mistake.

He checked his phone. His mate Jeremiah had a business proposal and Barry really needed some business. He'd hinted that it involved bananas. He was waiting for Jeremiah to confirm the venue. Barry hadn't decided where he was going to stay the night either. He'd checked the flat above 'Gary's Chips' in Lewisham and it was worse than he remembered. There was mouse shit everywhere. He'd seen mud huts which were cleaner. He wasn't going to sleep there. He wondered if he should sell it and buy a Lamborghini. He wouldn't mind sleeping in that. It might even make him too excited to get any sleep. He suspected the flat wasn't worth enough. He took a picture of the car and started to walk away when his phone chimed.

"Excellent," Barry said.

He said it in the style of an African king, which he was. His grandfather had been a bit of a moderniser, and had talked about downgrading their status to president, but an unfortunate accident with a marrow had terminated his life and his reign. Barry wasn't going to change it. He liked being a king. He often put the accent on to amuse himself. They were meeting in a pub in Hoxton. It was the other side of London, but he had plenty of time. He was about to descend into the tube when something caught his eye.

"Oh my god," he said.

Barry was actually bidialectual and normally his English accent would return as soon as he encountered his first Englishman, but there was something primal about the object in front of him. He gave it the full African accent.

"Maclaren," he said.

It was astonishing to look at. The bodywork flowed back and forth like the surf on a sea, fixed for all time. It was quite majestic. Barry realised that if he didn't get the hell out of their quickly he risked being arrested. He turned round and walked down the stairs into the safe haven of the tube in which there were no cars. He tried to think about his accommodation. He could sleep on the plane. It was a Boeing 737 and was, he liked to say, state of the art. It was actually state of the art in 1973, when a Saudi prince had purchased it and kitted it out. He was the eleventh owner, although the finance company looked like it would be the twelfth. It remained a very comfortable place to be, with a leather-lined sitting room and a large bedroom with an ensuite bathroom. Some might describe the decor as tacky. He would happily have stayed there, but the landing fees at City airport were outrageous, as were all the major airports. It was parked in an airfield in Essex and the cab ride had cost him a fortune. That left a hotel in London, which was what had taken him to Sloane Square, where the streets were lined with pornographic cars. And the hotels were eye-wateringly expensive. His plans for the evening might become a little less king-like. He might crash out on someone's sofa.

Half an hour later Barry was in Hoxton. He was an hour early but he was thirsty for an English beer, although it was more likely to be a beer branded as Austrian or Spanish, and brewed in Rotherham. It didn't matter, as he was drinking it in England, and it didn't taste the same as the beer at home. It was his dream, once he'd assembled his garage of supercars, to install an English style bar at one end. He wasn't familiar with Hoxton and the men seemed to wear tribally similar beards in a weirdly fashioned shape. He found a pair of doors which seemed to frame the opening to a pub, and entered. It wasn't very traditional and it didn't have any windows. There was a large stage at one end. He bought a pint and sat down. Two minutes later he discovered why there was a stage and no windows. It was a strip bar.

"Excellent," Barry said in full African dialect.

Barry really liked strip bars, and he sat himself close to the stage. He would have gone closer, but this wasn't his country. A girl came on the stage and was now occupying all his attention.

Chapter Thirteen

Ali hadn't taken advantage of the free wine on the plane and had only consumed one of those little plastic bottles. They were like scale models of the real thing. She had a suspicion the week was going to be a nightmare. When the plane came to a halt and the door opened, she could feel a little blast of hot air. Another part of her was excited about going to New York and she would have liked to have gone with Andy. She checked her phone. She wasn't particularly expecting a text from Andy, but it would have been nice. But her phone was text free and she made her way to passport control.

An hour later they were in a bar of overwhelming chicness, as if it had been stolen from the set of Sex in the City. That would be before the Sex in the City films when, in Ali's view, it all turned a bit uncool. The bar was set in a building which seemed to stretch to beyond the sky. It had more storeys than it was possible to count and she'd nearly fallen over trying. It *was* exciting and, if she wasn't in a committed relationship, she would love to go a little mad. There hadn't been much madness in her life.

"Cocktail?" Miles asked.

He'd said it with a strange emphasis on 'cock' and Ali thought it best to pretend she hadn't noticed. Miles might have been cast in the films of Sex in the City, as he was the kind of man who was dedicated to the cool, but somehow fell short. She wondered if there was a law which says that the more someone works at being cool, the less cool they are. A little like extreme politics which travels so far in one direction it arrives at the other side. Ali really felt she should have a column.

"Sure," Ali said.

Sometimes Miles fell short by quite a long way. His every possession which, unknown to Ali, included his underpants, was bought to say something about him. His suit, his watch, his sunglasses, his car, his shirt, his shoes. They all said he worshipped at the altar of designer names. It was also an attempt to disguise the undisguisable fact that Miles was getting on. Ali suspected there wasn't much to Miles.

"Mojitos?" Miles said.

But in thinking that, Ali thought, how much was there to Andy? The answer, she knew, was plenty. He wasn't governed by the need to have stuff. He didn't say things he didn't mean. He was without guile and, yes, there was plenty to him. She couldn't believe she'd even thought it.

"Why not," Ali said.

Miles snapped his fingers in a way which she found rude and irritating, but he felt was masterful and kind of cool. He'd often talked about opening an office in New York, but she doubted it would ever happen. He just liked to name drop. Although if they did, and she was invited over, she'd have to decline, which would be a pity as she could imagine herself with that imaginary magazine column. It would be pithy and poignant and would make observations that would give an insight into living in the city. That only suited someone who was single. She checked her phone.

"Are you expecting someone to call?" Miles asked.

Not that she wanted to be single. She really enjoyed the whole coupling business and knowing that if she wanted to eat out, she'd know who it would be with. But if she was the Sex and the City version of herself, she'd have views on a number of things. She'd probably have to know a bit more about fashion.

"No, just keeping an eye on social media. You know, like young people do," Ali said.

Miles struggled to find an answer, although he was certain he'd think of one the following day. Life was a bit irritating that way, and Miles was sensitive about his age. Sensitive to the point that he lied about it. He saw a man every four weeks who skilfully, and subtly, kept his hair quite close to the colour it used to be. At least he hoped it was skilful. It cost a fortune. The mojitos arrived.

"Cheers," Miles said.

"Cheers," Ali said.

She wondered where the others had gone, as she didn't entirely welcome the one-to-one attention that Miles was giving her. She really hoped he wasn't hitting on her as that would be awkward. Even if she wasn't betrothed to Andy she wouldn't be interested in Miles.

"So what have we got to look forward to?" Ali asked.

She realised she'd thought 'betrothed' when there had been no sign of said betrothal. It reminded her of that Neville Chamberlain speech. Perhaps she should give Andy an ultimatum. As of noon today, she thought, no such undertaking has been given.

"We've got workshops and nightclubs," Miles said with a smile.

Ali smiled. On the inside she was groaning. She did not want to spend more than one evening in a nightclub and, if she was alone with Miles, then one would be too many. She didn't, if she was honest, want to be there at all.

"Great," Ali said.

Chapter Fourteen

"Mister President," Glot said.

Barry couldn't believe it. The stripper had removed her minuscule underpants and revealed a crotch that was entirely bereft of hair. Not even a suggestion of it. There was nothing to imply, or from which someone could infer, that hair had ever grown there. How could it be removed so absolutely? One of the strange genetic characteristics of the women from Lobo was that the women were, in general, pretty hairy. Barry had slept with a lot of women, but he only had the vaguest idea what a vagina actually looked like. That was until now, which was why it was bloody annoying that Glot had called.

"Your almighty highness," Glot continued.

"What, Glot?" Barry asked.

Such was the power that Barry yielded in his own country – he was practically a deity – that he could have made it illegal to phone anyone watching a woman take her clothes off even if the caller had no idea that was happening. He could even impose a penalty of castration. The stripper moved to his side of the little stage. She stopped, turned and bent right over. His view was positively gynaecological. He had no idea there were so many bits to it. It made the distraction all the more irritating. Glot was his pilot.

"Some people were here." Glot said.

The ‘t’ in Glot wasn’t just pronounced, it was emphasised by a click in the throat. It was a tiring name to say and Barry would have found another pilot for that reason alone, but Glot was the only person in the country qualified to fly the Boeing.

“There are people everywhere,” Barry said. “This is London.”

Glot could also be a cheeky bastard and that irritated Barry.

“This is Essex,” Glot said. “And they were here to repossess the plane.”

This caught Barry’s attention, despite the many folds of the stripper’s vagina.

“What did you tell them?” Barry said.

“I said you’d make a payment in the morning,” Glot said.

They both knew what that meant. They’d have to get the hell out of there before dawn, regardless of Sir Bernard. This was a real problem. If he didn’t generate some money soon he’d be very deeply ensconced in the shit. He needed a plan. He needed to flog those bananas, or he was going to be left with his ancient Mercedes and, worse than that, he’d have to downgrade the jet. A Cessna wasn’t very presidential. It almost preoccupied him to the point of missing the strangely wobble-free nature of the next stripper’s breasts which was confusing as plastic surgery had yet to arrive at Lobo. He also didn’t notice someone standing next to him.

"Hey, King Bazza," Jeremiah said.

There weren't many people who he allowed to refer to him as 'Bazza', but his friends from Trent Polytechnic received special dispensation. They hugged each other and followed it with the traditional greeting.

"Beer?" Jeremiah said.

"Beer," Barry confirmed.

It was a more a Trent Polytechnic tradition than that of Lobo, but it was always a good start. Jeremiah returned with two beers and they topped up the strippers' beer glasses with pound coins.

"I have the solution to all your problems," Jeremiah said.

It was enough to take Barry's eyes away from the stage. This was what he wanted to hear.

"Is it legal?" Barry asked.

Barry was not concerned by the legality, particularly as he made the laws in his own country, but he was anxious to find out how dangerous it might be, and what kind of profit margin it might yield. On balance, illegal was probably a good thing.

"At the moment," Jeremiah said.

Barry was getting a tingle of excitement but, as a stripper from Bulgaria had just parted her legs, it wasn't entirely clear what had prompted it.

Chapter Fifteen

Ali professed exhaustion, and illness, as she wasn't having another mojito with Miles. She dragged herself away and across the road to the hotel. The hotel was well located and claimed to be 'boutique'. This, as far as she could gather, was modern speak for small. Small, but with highly perfumed and stealable bottles of hair and body product. She sniffed them all. The walls and carpet had a black and white Art Deco theme running through them, which she guessed was the final part of boutique. The bed was oddly high and she climbed up, arranged the pillows and grabbed the remote for the television. This was part of the ritual of a new hotel and would involve running through the channels until finally turning it off, or settling on the music channel, and putting the sound on low. Except in Italy. She'd once gone to Pisa with Andy and they'd got back late to discover hardcore pornography on broadcast television. That had been a memorable evening.

But tonight she settled on the music channel and looked at her phone. She was wondering where Andy had got to. She would have expected a text by now. It occurred to her that he might be wondering why she hadn't texted him. She could change that. 'Arrived safely in the Big Apple' she wrote, adding an 'x'. She pressed send and waited. She didn't expect an immediate response and she grabbed her laptop.

"Ali," she wrote, "had made it to the Big Apple."

She paused. She had the need to express her thoughts, although perhaps not exactly her thoughts. She needed an alter ego, a version of herself. She could be the narrator character in Sex in the City. The English version, which is not to say that she would be any less sophisticated. She'd sound more sophisticated with her English accent. Although that too would be a version of her English accent. Now that she thought about it, her alter ego would be a good deal posher too. Her family would be distantly related to royalty and she'd have gone to one of those posh girls-only schools like Roedean. She'd heard that they cheer 'Ra-Ra-Roedean' at matches. And her name would be Jemima.

'Was the Big Apple big enough for Jemima?' she wrote. 'Mummy and Daddy's estate was over a thousand acres and the ancestral home had forty-two bedrooms'.

The narrative would involve a lot of rhetorical questions, which would imply that rather than asking about the relative merits of Jimmy Choos over Louboutins, she was actually exploring the human condition. Although Ali had never referred to her parents as Mummy and Daddy, and their home was not remotely ancestral, and the garden wasn't quite a hundred feet long. She wondered if forty-two was too many bedrooms. She'd come back to that later.

'And now she was in a hotel room on fifth avenue in a nice room, although a long-tailed cat would challenge its dimensions. Jemima was here to have fun.'

Then she realised that Jemima would probably speak in the first person. She tried again.

'Dandy, the cook's cat at home, would have too long a tail were she to be twirled in this room'.

It did, Ali thought, make Jemima seem a bit cruel, but posh people with their hunting were a bit cruel. They probably did measure rooms by inflicting something unpleasant on an animal. She needed to bring it back down.

'But it was big enough for shagging.'

Ali looked across the room. Because it was small and boutique there were a lot of mirrors, and she wished Andy was there for reasons she struggled to put into words as Ali, but had no problem as Jemima.

'With a flick of my head I could see Dan's pumping arse, and from another mirror I could see...'

Ali stopped. This wasn't the human condition, this was pornography. She couldn't remember what kind of comments the narrator on Sex and the City had made and hadn't quite settled on the appropriate tone for Jemima. She'd decided that Jemima, in common with posh people, would be rampantly promiscuous. She'd arrive in New York for a shag-athon. But she wasn't sure about Dan. It didn't sound American enough, although she liked the use of the word 'arse' as it distinguished it from 'ass'. This was harder than she thought. Maybe she should bring it closer to home.

'How long should one have to wait for a boyfriend to text? Was it hours or days? Was the time difference a reasonable excuse?'

Jemima would probably have an occasional boyfriend, but he'd either be from a well connected wealthy family, or a distant cousin with a title. Either way the family seat would be maintained. But in the meantime Sebastian, as Ali decided to call him, would be shagging away in Monte Carlo while Jemima was shagging in New York. It was amazing the upper classes weren't more riven with sexually transmitted diseases, Ali thought. Although perhaps they were.

'When is it reasonable to expect your boyfriend to propose?'

This didn't sound remotely like Jemima. It needed more spice.

'There's only one thing better than a black man and that's two.'

It was back to pornography, but Ali had decided that was safer ground than exploring the business of being proposed to. Although Jemima was more likely to do the proposing. She worried that Ali would have to do that too. It was while she was thinking about whether Jemima regretted not inviting a third black man into her room that she fell asleep, waking briefly at four in the morning to find the lights on and the music channel playing Dire Straits.

Chapter Sixteen

"And you said it involved bananas?" Barry said.

Jeremiah smiled. He knew he needed to hold back the killer line. He needed to feed the information gently as if he was catching a fish. But he also knew that Barry's attention span could be a little unreliable. He had to get to the point.

"Very valuable bananas," Jeremiah said.

The light was low and mainly directed at the stage where Branka from Lithuania was removing the small strips which made up her bikini top, revealing her seven thousand dollar breasts. They were breasts which were very resistant to movement, but Barry hadn't noticed as now he was focussing on the possibility of shifting a harvest of bananas. Valuable ones would be even better.

"What does it do?" Barry asked.

Jeremiah tried to remember what he'd heard the biochemist say.

"It is a narcotic, a blend, like MDMA, cocaine and LSD all rolled into one," Jeremiah said.

Barry was more a beer and wine man, although his son Barry junior was something of an expert when it came to drugs. It didn't mean much to him and he was more interested in the economics than the chemistry. Drugs were a bit of a mystery.

"A banana is a drug?" Barry asked.

"Yes," Jeremiah said.

"Do you smoke it?" Barry asked.

"No," Jeremiah said and drank a bit more beer.

"Do you inject it?" Barry asked.

"No," Jeremiah said, drinking a bit more.

Barry thought about this. He was fairly sure that someone had once told him about a narcotic which was smeared on the genitals. He didn't want to suggest it, and recognised that genitals might have been playing on his mind, but he couldn't think of another way it might be ingested.

"Do you smear it on your genitals?" Barry finally asked.

"No," Jeremiah confirmed.

"What do you do then?" Barry asked.

"It's a banana. You eat it."

"Oh," Barry said and they watched as a stripper lifted her left leg until she could kiss her knee. It almost revealed her internal organs.

Barry's train of thought concerning narcotic bananas disappeared. He wondered if he could institute some sort of decree in which all women were required to shave their pubic hair. Although he was virtually a sole monarchy, there weren't many ministers through whom he could put through such legislation, and sensed they might be a little reluctant.

"Very valuable," Jeremiah said again.

He needed to get Barry on board. He needed to help him pick up the biochemist and the banana. Once they were in the jet they would be safe. He tried to think of a few other things he'd heard.

"All bananas have the same DNA," Jeremiah explained.

"Do they?" Barry said.

Branka's act was coming to a very satisfying conclusion and Barry couldn't keep his eyes off her.

"It's something to do with changing the DNA," Jeremiah said.

Barry's raised his eyes. On the stage Branka had been replaced with Dubravka, who was competing for his attention with her comprehensively lasered nether regions in which every follicle had been annihilated.

"And it provides the finest experience in a legal and transportable wrapping," Jeremiah said.

Dubravka had finished with a flourish and been replaced by Chardonnay who came from Bradford and, rather shockingly, had pubic hair. It wasn't a huge great bush like the girls from Lobo, who actually lived in the bush, but it was a well coiffured strip. It seemed a bit of a shame to Barry. Jeremiah could sense he was losing Barry and then something else that Leon had said came to him.

"The thing is," Jeremiah continued. "When you first grow the banana the new chemicals are undetectable. And then it ripens."

Barry managed to take his eyes off the girl for a second.

"Then what?" he asked.

"Then pow," Jeremiah said. "Blows your head off."

He wasn't sure if 'pow' was better than 'bang' or if it was helping reel Barry in.

"Pow?" Barry asked.

"Pow," Jeremiah confirmed.

Of the many things that Barry liked to have blown, his head was not one of them. He'd never understood drugs when alcohol did the job so well. He would have turned away and looked at Jeremiah, but Chardonnay had left the stage and a fresh stripper, in so far as a stripper could be thought of as fresh, had arrived. He couldn't tell what her pubic condition might be, but was anxious to find out. He would have left it there, as he couldn't immediately see the benefit of a narcotic banana, but Jeremiah had something else to say.

"A hundred grand a banana," Jeremiah said.

"What did you say?" Barry asked.

"It has a street value of one hundred grand a banana."

Chapter Seventeen

The yoga class was over and Andy's mum rolled up her mat. She had her own mat now, and walked along the high street with it like it was a placard. It was declaring the new slightly bendier her, and her entry into a club of women. She knew it was a certain kind of woman, even though she knew it wasn't really her.

"Fancy a coffee?" Lydia said.

Andy's mum was delighted. She'd not had a coffee with Lydia before and she hoped that a little of the Lydia glamour might rub off on her. This was further entry into the club.

"That would be lovely," Andy's mum said.

Andy's mum wasn't sure, but it felt as if Lydia's eyes had flared in a way that suggested that she found her turn of phrase amusing or quaint, but not necessarily in a good way. She'd have to be on her best behaviour. They wandered in the direction of the coffee shop. Andy's mum was dressed in her baggy tracksuit and Lydia in a slightly shocking nipple-revealing leotard with a makeshift wrap skirt slung round her. The woman was disturbingly chic.

"The Green House?" Lydia suggested.

"Great," Andy's mum said.

She'd not been to the new coffee shop either, as she'd looked at the prices and thought it odd that anyone should want to pay over three quid for a coffee, when they could have one for practically nothing at home.

But she didn't point that out. When they arrived Andy's mum immediately felt as if she were personally raising the average age. She cast her eyes over the clientele. She didn't want to be judgemental, but there were an awful lot of young people with those weird sculpted beards like Andy now wore and quite a few tattoos. Lydia seemed at home.

"What would you like?" Lydia asked.

Andy's mum really wanted a cup of tea, although she thought that wouldn't be cool. Or it might be if it was sufficiently obscure, fantastically expensive, and farmed by Tibetan monks. Andy's mum could be a bit cynical about the coffee shop revolution.

"What are you having?" Andy's mum asked.

"I'll have a skinny latte," Lydia said.

It seemed as if the responsibility for payment had passed to Andy's mum and she ordered the same thing. She didn't seem to get back much from a tenner but then that was the price of fashion. Andy and Ali would have known what to order and wouldn't have been remotely surprised by the exorbitant cost. The coffees arrived and they looked for a table.

"Might have a fag," Lydia said.

They ended up with a table that was half inside and half outside and Lydia took a seat, and removed the paraphernalia for rolling one of her own. Andy's mum took a sip of her coffee and found the resulting milky drink to be pleasant enough. It didn't take long for Lydia to get to the point.

"So, do you work?" she asked.

"No, not anymore. I guess I'm what's called retired."

"What did you used to do?" Lydia asked.

Andy's mum explained about the bank and about Andy's dad and his recent retirement. She didn't mention his strange moods, as she thought that was normal, and would work its way out. She didn't want to make a fuss. That was another way of defining what kind of person she was. She didn't make a fuss.

"Me?" Lydia said, although Andy's mum wasn't sure if she'd got round to asking what Lydia did.

"I'm a journalist. Women's issues, mostly," Lydia explained.

"That sounds interesting," Andy's mum said brightly.

"It can be," Lydia said earnestly. "The pay gap is a disgrace and women's rights are still ignored."

That sounded like making too much of a fuss to Andy's mum, but she thought it best to agree. It was a bit of a hobby horse for Lydia who had personal issues of her own.

"It is as if we are not allowed to age, when men can," Lydia continued.

Andy's mum only read women's magazines when she went to the dentist and, as she'd inherited strong teeth, it wasn't more than once a year.

"And then there's sex," Lydia said.

Most of the magazines seem sex obsessed to Andy's mum and she found them too embarrassing to read in a public place. Sex was not a subject she'd discussed much, and even less so with the person she'd regularly had sex with. Not that it was that regular anymore, but she assumed that was normal at her age.

"Oh," Andy's mum said.

Andy's mum looked around. People could hear them. This was a fashionable coffee shop but it wasn't *that* fashionable. This was Surrey. Andy's mum hoped desperately that she'd change the subject.

"There should be constitutional rights," Lydia said.

Andy's mum relaxed. She didn't know about her constitutional rights, but she didn't mind discussing them in a public place. Although the ones she could think of were American and Andy's mum knew that Britain didn't even have a written constitution. Not that any of that helped. She tucked into her skinny latte, although she hadn't the slightest idea what made either it a latte or skinny.

"A woman," Lydia said, "should have a constitutional right to an orgasm."

Andy's mum choked on her skinny latte and, if the people around her weren't listening before, they were now.

Chapter Eighteen

Andy would have had a blinding headache, but there were too many other parts of him which were competing for his attention when it came to pain. He wasn't even sure he could put them in order. His wrists hurt, because they were bound together with something which had been applied without much concern for his comfort. Then there was his nose. It might well be broken, but as he couldn't raise his hands to check, he couldn't be certain. But he could taste blood. Then there was his stomach, where he'd been punched with some force, and lastly his head which hurt, probably as a result of everything else. And he hadn't packed his inhaler as Ali had suggested, which made him feel there might be some good news. It seemed as if the punch in the face had cured him of his allergies. He could smell the flowers, but it wasn't prompting a seizure. The worst thing was the bag over his head.

Not that the bag hurt. It was just a little frightening. He was trying to figure out what he'd done wrong. He must have done something wrong otherwise he wouldn't have been repeatedly punched and held hostage. For some reason he was still gripping the banana. He had no idea why, but it felt reassuring. Like a child with a blanket. Then something occurred to him. His mobile phone was in the front pocket of his jeans. All he had to do was get his body close to his hands, which were tied around something. He lent down and attempted to get his hands as close to the knot securing the bag around his neck. His fingers scraped the edge of something. Gaffer tape. It was securely taped. He picked at it. Half an hour later he was still picking at it. Twenty minutes after that he was ready to give up. Then he tore a long strip. It was quite satisfying. Ten minutes later he was able to pull the hessian sack off his head.

"Oh my god," he muttered.

He was tied to some reinforcing bars with what looked like half a reel of gaffer tape. He would have to bite though it. He lowered his head, but when he bumped his nose onto the steel bar a spike of pain went through him. He tried moving his head about as if he were a teenager attempting what might be thought of as a sophisticated snog. It didn't lessen the pain much. But he had no choice.

"Fuck!" he shouted.

He'd bitten his hand. Now he had an additional pain to contend with. He tried to gnaw from the opposite side of the tape and ten minutes later he was free. It gave him a little high. A genuine sense of achievement. All he had to do was untie his legs. He wondered if he should phone the police first. If he could untie himself he may not need the police. He took his phone out to see if he could establish where he was. It was dark with black shadows cast from the moon. It was so dark that the bright light of his phone made him jump, which would have been fine, but his legs were still bound together. He tripped. As he tumbled his phone fell out of his hand. It bounced on the hard mud and would have come to a halt were it not for a deep pile which had yet to receive concrete. The phone tottered on the edge like an Essex girl in high heels. Then it fell. Andy could hear it hitting the sides of the shaft until it finally arrived, with a plop, at the evidently water-filled bottom. He stood for a few seconds, and just felt angry with himself, and angry with life. It was the latest iPhone too. It cost him forty quid a month and he couldn't remember if he'd paid the extra for the insurance. He feared he hadn't. Finally, when he'd finished admonishing himself, he bent down and attacked the gaffer tape around his legs. This time he managed to find the end and unravel the sticky stuff.

"Right," he said to himself.

He turned and saw a tall black man who punched him in the face. Andy went out like a light.

Chapter Nineteen

Barry had summoned for the first time, with the use of his iPhone, an Uber cab. Amazingly it had arrived in seconds with a quoted cost of four pounds. It was remarkable.

"Stop here," Jeremiah said.

They got out. It was pitch black and they were alone in a rather desolate part of King's Cross. But Barry was salivating at the thought of a hundred grand banana. It might have been the beer, but Jeremiah had convinced him that this was a sure fire thing. A safe bet. A certainty. He followed Jeremiah as they wandered along a main road. Barry could see large, recently constructed buildings, looming near to them. They turned a corner and arrived at a small alleyway. There was a stationary car which seemed to be rocking.

"What's that?" Barry asked.

"Ignore it," Jeremiah said and led the way to a hole in the fence and into a building site.

"Down here," Jeremiah said.

Now that they were the other side of the timber hoardings there was even less light, and Barry placed his feet carefully. Jeremiah was altogether more reckless, and he swayed from side to side, as he lost and found grip in the mud. He had consumed rather significant quantities of alcohol. After a few minutes he realised he needed light. He took out his phone and waved it around.

"Where is the little bugger," Jeremiah muttered.

He'd been in a bit of a panic when he'd dumped him and there hadn't been much time. He looked around. The absence of light made it hard for him to find any landmarks which would help locate the biochemist with the banana.

"What's that?" Barry said.

They froze. There was a distinct groaning noise. Jeremiah changed direction and followed the noise and three minutes later Barry saw a cowering figure.

"There he is," Jeremiah said.

Barry looked down at the possible solution to all his country's problems. He had originally hoped to do business studies, but he hadn't made the grades and geography seemed like a good opportunity to put Lobo on the map. He found it irritating that people had not heard of his country and had not the slightest idea, or interest, where it might be.

"And this man can create a hundred grand banana?" Barry asked.

Although Barry hadn't studied business, or economics, he wasn't having any difficulty multiplying a hundred grand by a few million bananas. Or rather he was, but it just didn't matter, as every time he came up with a bloody great figure. A figure large enough to house the biggest collection of supercars in the world. There would be Ferraris and Lamborghinis. In the back of his mind, the very distant part, there was a thought that his people wouldn't starve and the rubbish would be collected. They were having a bit of a rat problem. Although as the people had taken to eating the rats, perhaps it was more a solution than a problem.

"That's the fella," Jeremiah said.

The cowering figure didn't look like much. Barry looked around. It wasn't that tidy, or orderly, a building site and he was just sober enough to realise he had to tread carefully. Jeremiah was approaching the biochemist fast.

"Give me the banana," Jeremiah said.

Although Andy was cowering in a section of strip foundation, most of the building was designed to rest on piles which were thirty feet deep. There had been an argument a few days earlier as to which order the foundations should be dug and concreted, and some piles had been dug and concreted, some had been dug, and a few had been dug and a reinforcing cage had been lowered in. There hadn't been enough time to add the concrete. As Jeremiah took a further step and said 'give me the banana," he was unaware that between him and the biochemist lay a deep cylindrical hole. 'Give me the banana' were the very last words Jeremiah uttered before falling down that deep shaft and, in the blink of an eye, all his optimistic dreams of a prosperous life disappeared with every other thought, as he was fatally skewered on the sharp edges of a reinforcing cage.

"Ouch," Barry said.

There was a sudden and eery silence. Barry got down on his hands and knees, took out his phone, and used the torch to light up the shaft.

"Oh my god," Barry muttered.

It wasn't a pretty sight. He very nearly threw up. He looked up. There was no point in attempting to hoist his friend out of the hole and seek help. The reinforcing cage and Jeremiah appeared to be permanently united. Jeremiah was unquestionably dead.

"Jeremiah," Barry said.

It was a final salute to his friend. For a second he felt he owed it to Jeremiah to ensure that the narcotic hundred grand banana thrived. It was his duty. He looked around for the biochemist and found him. He wasn't just cowering. He was shivering. Barry sat down for a second. He had to keep it together. Jeremiah had been his friend. But now he was stuck in London with a biochemist, a dead man and a jet that was about to be repossessed. Could he do this on his own? He needed to get him to the plane. How difficult could that be? Barry had only taken one Uber and he could see that the drivers were not entirely engaged with their passengers. He also knew that England was a place full of eccentrics who wore weird clothes. He picked his way very carefully down to the cowering man. He realised that the biochemist was preoccupied and hadn't noticed him despite the noise that Jeremiah had made, although most of that had been lost down the deep shaft.

The biochemist was almost free from his bindings. He turned to face Barry. Barry didn't have a gun, or any other means of threatening him, but he knew in an instant what he had to do. Barry punched him the face.

"Fucking hell," Barry shouted.

Barry could see stars. As he'd never punched anyone in the face before he had not the slightest idea it would be so painful. He'd practically broken his hand. Wasn't the object of hitting someone to inflict pain on them, and not the other way round? He had to sit down to let the pain subside. It was then that he noticed that the man lay crumpled in front of him. He needed to get a move on. He removed the remaining restraints and attempted to pick him up.

"Fucking hell," Barry said again.

He was bloody heavy. He'd have to drag him. Barry grabbed a foot and heaved, but there were further issues with this. His right hand was in so much pain it was useless and he couldn't get a good enough grip with his left. How did people do this sort of thing? It would take too long to get Glot down to help him. He'd have to do it on his own. Barry looked around and found the solution. A dumper. While Barry had never hit anyone before, and would never hit anyone again, he had hot wired the odd car as a child. It was a form car share, and how many people travelled in his country. He picked up lump of wood and bashed the ignition until it came to pieces and, with a spark, he touched two wires together and the dumper fired up. It was unbelievably noisy. He switched it off.

It took a further half an hour to get Andy into the front of the dumper but, once he had, he got him across the site and to the boundary in about two minutes. It took a further two minutes for the Uber to arrive. The driver, who'd once worked in the film industry, but had lost his job when he'd groped a Hollywood actor known for groping others, glanced at Barry and the man he was propping up. Barry smiled and, in his full African accent – the English really do like their stereotypes – said, "My friend. He drink too much."

Chapter Twenty

Ali was surprised to discover there really was a New York office, and it was well located with a distant view of Central Park. A frisson of excitement ran through her, she just couldn't help it, and everything about the operation this side of the Atlantic sounded more exciting, prescient, urgent, relevant and chic than the London base. Given the chance she'd have thought of more adjectives, but everything was moving too quickly. It was like the difference between a British and American hospital drama. In Britain the trolleys wouldn't crash into anything, there were no gunshot wounds, and everyone would talk in a calm whisper. The American version was quite different with people running around, talk of gurneys, blood spurting everywhere, and a lot of urgent shouting of acronyms. It seemed to be the same in publishing.

"Can you hold that cover!" someone shouted.

"I've got Jay-Lo on the line," another said.

"George is going to be a father again," someone else said.

People were whizzing around in an impossible fashion and Ali felt a mixture of intimidation and excitement. This was the environment she wanted to work in. This is how it should be. The office was long and narrow and located in the pitch of the roof with dormer windows either side. At the end was a glass wall, behind which was the editor. She was moving, gesticulating and talking. The kind of multitasking which only a woman could do, in Ali's view. It was then that she noticed that the office was almost entirely staffed by women.

Ali was here to introduce herself and she walked from desk to desk quietly doing so. They nodded and shook her hand and smiled, but they were all too preoccupied to chat for long, and Ali didn't expect them to. It was quite a cosmopolitan office, although most of the accents were American, and everyone seemed intimidatingly beautiful. She was making her way towards what looked like the queen bee. Ali hadn't taken Miles very seriously, and consequently she hadn't researched the New York office, and was unaware of any of their names, and surprised to see the titles they were working on. This was real publishing, not internet listing, and she'd give her right arm for a go at it.

She might have paused to think about the sacrifice of a limb and a relationship, but who had time for that kind of reflection? Hearts were beating faster here. Ali hadn't dreamed about a proposal, or selecting a wedding dress and something that wouldn't make the bridesmaids look too pretty, but she had dreamed of a work environment like this.

As she approached the glass-walled office she sneaked a peak at the Editor-in-Chief. She had long blonde hair which was tousled, yet organised. The disorder in her hair was planned. She held the phone with her delicate well-manicured hands. She had a short skirt from which long elegant legs of a perfect hue emerged. Her blouse fell open in precisely the way it was designed to giving just a hint, like the trailer for a film, of what sublime sexiness lay beyond. Ali realised she was developing an unnatural crush. When she got close to the glass door in the glass wall the blonde editor looked up at her, and made a signal for her to enter with her slim fingered elegant hand. A part of Ali jumped. As she approached the glass door she noticed that the elegant legs came to an end in an impossibly tall pair of high heeled shoes. It was a mystery to Ali as to how anyone could endure a day's work wearing them, but they looked fantastic.

Ali had never once looked at another woman and thought lustful thoughts, and was finding the experience alarming. Then she thought about Jemima. Jemima would obviously be bisexual. It would be offensive to make her otherwise. And Jemima would know precisely what to do. Ali, on the other hand, hadn't the slightest idea. She pushed open the door.

"Hi," Ali said. "I'm Ali."

She could see now how tall the Editor-in-Chief was, although the heels were part of it, and Ali looked up and smiled. She was alarmed to find a steady piercing stare.

"Hold on for a second," she said.

It wasn't clear whether the instruction was for Ali's benefit or whoever was on the other end of the phone. She suspected everyone obeyed her regardless. But she'd uttered the words with a preciseness and clarity that said two things. One was that she was English and the other was that she was cut-glass posh.

"I don't care," she said to the phone. "Fuck 'em."

She slammed the phone down and turned to Ali.

"Fucking lawyers," she said.

Ali didn't know what to say, although she felt she should agree.

"Don't I know it," Ali said.

Ali had never once knowingly had a conversation with a lawyer and Andy had done all the negotiations when they'd bought the flat. But she had read that lawyers were a pain.

"Nice to hear a Brit voice. My name's Jemima," Jemima said.

She said it too quickly for Ali to process.

"You've got to be kidding," Ali said.

Chapter Twenty-One

It was fair to say that Andy's mum had never thought, not even once, that she had any kind of right, constitutional or otherwise, to an orgasm. She'd nipped into the village to buy a few groceries and she found herself in the newsagents. She couldn't bring herself to pick up the kind of prurient, sex-obsessed woman's magazine she'd been too embarrassed to read in the dentist's. She tried to read the front covers, which were at eye level, while simultaneously looking at the front covers of a knitting magazine which was lower down. She wasn't sure what she was looking for and wondered if she'd be too embarrassed to buy it. She'd dithered for just a shade too long.

"Can I help you?" the newsagent said.

Andy's mum panicked. She grabbed a magazine and picked up a Daily Mail which she intended to sandwich it in on the walk home. The newsagent didn't seem to notice or care, and she wondered what he'd say if she said 'I have a constitutional right to an orgasm'. But she didn't say anything and it wasn't until she got home that she discovered that she'd bought a Marie Claire. And it wasn't short of precisely the kind of articles she was secretly looking for.

She checked the house to see where Andy's dad was and then saw him at the end of the garden. He seemed to be thrashing about again. She went straight to the guts of the magazine, although now she thought about it, that wasn't the correct body part. She went to the genitals of the magazine and read with a mixture of horror and excitement.

"Oh my," she said. "Oh my, oh my, oh my."

The worse thing was that since her coffee with the impossibly glamorous Lydia, she'd been thinking about it, and she realised that at her core she still felt quite young. Or she certainly didn't feel old. She read on.

"Oh my," she said again.

Andy's mum was not a woman who swore, but she'd have felt like a navvy if she'd read this out loud. It was quite shockingly explicit. She only had the vaguest idea that she possessed a clitoris and she couldn't be sure that Andy's dad knew much more. She looked at him hacking about at the end of the garden. This was the time when they should be together, yet they seemed further apart than they'd ever been. It was prompting Andy's mum to think about her relationship with Andy's dad and the future, and she'd never done that before. She was a woman who didn't like to make a fuss. She read on.

After a while she'd run out of 'oh my, oh mys'. She couldn't read anymore. This was the world of the Lydias, and not the world she inhabited. She should accept it as it is. She hadn't been as strong as she should have been on women's rights, and there was a moment when she too could have taken the same management course Andy's dad had. But the bank hadn't been very supportive when it came to women at that time and she'd just accepted it. But that didn't bother her.

What did bother was more primal. She'd struggled all week to acknowledge it, but it wouldn't go away. It was hanging in the back of her mind like a chorizo in the larder. Her mind kept returning to it. Andy's mum had decided she'd like to have the occasional orgasm.

Chapter Twenty-Two

They'd only just managed to get the plane in the air in time. The loan company really was quite insistent that he make the payments. Barry thought it impertinent. Didn't they know he was the president of Lobo? He was practically a king. It was bloody annoying. Why was life so difficult?

Once they were out of British airspace he relaxed a little more and grabbed a beer from the fridge and picked a magazine from his considerable collection of supercar literature. It reassured him to read about the Ferrari P1. He'd definitely have one of those in his collection along with a few classics, like an F40. He'd read they were only a million pounds. That didn't seem like much. Although it was a lot of bananas. But not so many narcotic bananas. Such was Barry's facility for mathematics it took him a while to arrive at ten. But it did sound very illegal.

Barry had once received a caution for urinating in a public place. As he was in Hull at the time he didn't think it completely out of order, but the policeman clearly disagreed. He'd also incurred seventeen speeding violations and a little over a hundred parking tickets. He'd paid a few of them, and attended court a couple of times, and he was generally not welcome to drive a car on British roads. He had also told the occasionally untruth concerning his education, but what he'd never done before was kidnap someone. He wasn't a man of a particularly criminal nature. But needs must, as his mother used to say. Barry's hierarchy of needs weren't quite the same as those of his people but, top of the list, was the rather pressing need to make a payment on the jet. He'd love to pay it off but jets were quite expensive and, if he had enough money to pay it off, he'd either upgrade it or start on his supercar collection, which was the second item on his list.

He'd hoped to convince his government that the country needed to encourage tourism and one way was to construct a world class building in which the supercar collection would be housed. Annoyingly, they hadn't bought it. There had been some nonsense about food and shelter, but he hadn't listened to it all as his eyes had glazed over and he'd thought about a Maclaren F1. His proposal had been leaked to the press and the local newspaper had referred to him as the 'Bastard Son'. This wasn't because they questioned his parentage, but because they thought he was a bastard. He wasn't popular at home, which was why he'd jumped on the plane in the first place. His father had been the great reformer. He'd built roads and schools and apartment blocks to the point that Lobo no longer looked like the mudhutted third world country of his youth. His father had passed him the baton and everyone roundly agreed, without exception, that he'd dropped it.

Barry had told them that he was off to play a round of golf with Prince Andrew, but he'd never met him, and he couldn't play golf. He'd assumed it was the sort of game that anyone could play, but found it spectacularly difficult and couldn't for the life of him think why anyone should put so much effort into something of such little consequence. His assimilation into British culture, mostly via Trent Polytechnic, was a variable one. There were some things he understood completely, like beer and fast cars, but most sports had remained a mystery to him. The press knew this and had questioned whether he was actually seeing Prince Andrew.

While it was true that little white lies followed Barry around, at least he'd assigned them a colour, the kidnapping business was new and a little stressful. It was quite clearly a crime and involved stepping over a line he'd not breached before. He grabbed some ice from the fridge. His beer was cool enough, but his hand hurt like hell. He was never going to hit anyone again. He'd decided his best way forward was to suggest a partnership. It seemed a little late now, but it was better than having to hit him again. He'd thrown the man with the banana into one of the bedrooms.

He'd called his cousin. Barry's cousin, Gary, was the clever one. He'd studied biochemistry at Manchester and he knew stuff about chemicals. He could analyse the banana and with it, and a bit of luck, he could make a fortune. He thought about that for a second. It really helped. He took another beer and enjoyed a further thought about the relative merits of an F40 over the later F50. They were both about a million. The solution was simple. He'd have both.

Chapter Twenty-Three

Ali had nearly blown it with Jemima. She'd had to backtrack with the 'you've got to be kidding' and now she was back in her hotel room. She was supposed to be getting ready to go out, but she'd decided that she could do that in about three minutes. She'd checked her phone and found nothing from Andy. She'd reset the phone in case it was having a strop and, once it had blipped and groaned, it said the same thing. Nothing. Not a text or a call or an email. It wasn't as if there wasn't a large variety of ways with which they could communicate. She lay on the bed and opened her laptop.

She didn't think her alter ego could still be called Jemima. The real Jemima was something else. Ali hadn't stopped thinking about her. She was a complete vision of who she wanted to be, but feared it was asking too much. Every little part of her seemed so perfect. She couldn't stop herself looking at her hands and her legs and her skin. Then there were her eyes. She'd only dared look at them for the briefest of a millisecond, not least because Jemima looked right back. But, in that millisecond, she had managed to see a deep hazel-like greeness which was quite arresting. Then there was her attitude. Never before had she come across a woman with such an in-your-face, fuck you, get out of the way, take no shit, I'm the boss, are you still here? Shit-kicking attitude. And she did all that without saying a word. She was the kind of woman who could cross the road and stop traffic.

Ali realised she was getting herself more than a little flustered. This was quite a crush, although she assured herself that it was primarily professional. But Jemima was too busy to see them this evening, which meant another evening with her London work colleagues. Had she been seeing Jemima, then Ali would have started getting ready an hour earlier.

"Hold on girl," she said to herself.

That definitely sounded a little on the wrong side of a crush. But even if she did spend an hour, she couldn't compete with Jemima. She wondered what Jemima was doing that evening, which had meant they couldn't get together. For a second she thought of her covered in food and feeding two young kids.

"No, not a chance," Ali said.

Jemima was in a restaurant at the top of a hundred storey skyscraper that was so exclusive that normal people, people without the benefit of her hazel green eyes, would have to book a year in advance to get a table. It would be for a special occasion like a birthday, or anniversary, and it would be the place that both parties would have dreamed of going to ever since they were teenagers in the Bronx. And it would sink a month's salary. Ali had to think to give the place a name. It would probably be French, possibly La something. Ali realised she'd had have to come back to that – building a fantasy wasn't that straightforward –

but Jemima would say, in a whimsical manner, 'shall we go to La Something French?' Ali realised she was obsessing and the only solution to that was to take something from the minibar. She couldn't remember what Miles had said about the minibar, but she found a tonic and a gin and united them. She had plenty of time. She'd secretly bought a bottle of vodka at the duty free section. She thought she might have to anaesthetise herself from the boredom of her colleagues' company. She hadn't gone over the top and had bought the cheapest. It was one of those unknown Russian sounding names in a long cylindrical bottle. Perhaps she'd get to that later. She brought her mind back to Jemima.

Then there was the next question. Who had Jemima met? Ali wanted it to be Brad Pitt. Jemima was helping him work through his issues with Angelina, while at the same time shagging him senseless. These were secret meetings and they were in a lightless corner of the restaurant, almost suspended over the night lights of the city. Jemima knew the owner well and he was very discreet. Ali realised this implied that Jemima didn't have a conventional relationship. She wasn't the long term girlfriend of a wealthy industrialist. It sounded too conventional. The shocking part of that revelation was that, while Ali wanted to be like Jemima, she also wanted Andy to propose. Ali's phone beeped.

Finally, she thought, Andy had responded. She looked at the text and saw it wasn't Andy. She wasn't sure which emotion was greater, disappointment or annoyance. Instead it was one of her London colleagues. It read, ‘where the fuck are you?’.

“Shit,” Ali said.

She hadn’t been paying attention to the time, certainly not the time in New York. She got up and threw her clothes on. Three minutes later she was out the door.

Chapter Twenty-Four

Andy's head hurt. It had hurt before – he was no stranger to the hangover – but this was a more general pain. He could make out a noise. He'd been sleeping. It was a very deep sleep in which he'd pieced together what had happened, and he realised it was all a bad dream prompted by a bad joint, although he had no recollection of having smoked one. He would stick to alcohol in the future. He'd been tripping and in that trip he'd imagined people hitting him. And there was a banana. He wasn't sure if the banana was something embedded in his subconscious and was a metaphor for a distant part of him that was troubled. He wasn't one for analysis and he'd probably forget it. For a second it occurred to him that the banana might have some more obvious significance. His sexuality had never troubled him before, and the thought that the banana might represent a penis was troubling enough for him to think about getting up. He opened his eyes.

He didn't recognise the bed or the sheets. This had happened to him once before when he was at university after a drinking spree. He'd ended up with a woman he didn't recognise in a town he'd not heard of. Ali would kill him if he did that again. He didn't think it likely. The room was odd. It appeared to have a curved roof and, now he was properly awake, the sound he'd heard before was becoming clearer. It sounded like a brass band. That was strange. His face felt puffy. Puffy in a way that would be entirely consistent with someone having hit it. Repeatedly. It was then that he noticed the banana. Andy felt a rising sense of panic. It forced him to do some more piecing together and conclude that he *had* taken a banana and he *had* been kidnapped. And there was no question someone had hit him.

"Shit," Andy muttered.

There was a small square curtain. He pulled it back and was hit by the sun streaming through a curiously circular window. He was beginning to feel like Alice in wonderland and every thing he could see wasn't just curiouser and curiouser, it was weirder and weirder. The earth around the plane was parched, he thought. That stopped him in his tracks. He had to deconstruct the sentence. Was he in an aeroplane? It would explain the curved ceiling and the circular window. What it didn't explain was how he'd got on. And if he'd got on a plane, what about luggage and boarding passes and passports? He was pretty sure he didn't have any of that. There was a further issue.

He let his eyes adjust to the sunshine. There was a brass band and groups of people – black people – dressed in what looked like tribal clothing. There were huts with straw roofs. This didn't look like England, he thought. It didn't look like Ireland or France either. The door flew open.

"You," a tall black man pointed. "Stay there!"

"Where are we?" Andy asked reasonably.

"We are in," Barry said, applying his African accent, "Lobo."

"Lobo?" Andy said.

"Yes," Barry declared proudly.

Andy needed a little more clarity.

"Where is Lobo?" Andy asked.

He now recognised the tall black man as the man who had hit him. There were other men who had hit him and he had not the slightest idea why. He'd just gone out to get a bag of chips.

"Africa," Barry said.

Chapter Twenty-Five

Andy's mum found herself feeling nervous. The yoga class had come to an end and she wanted to speak to Lydia. But she couldn't quite bring herself to suggest a coffee. It was as if Lydia were above her station. She needn't have worried as Lydia smiled at her and said, "coffee?"

"Sure," Andy's mum said.

She'd been practising saying that all week and, though she might say so herself, it wasn't bad. It was certainly better than 'that would be nice'. She wanted to learn to talk in a way that didn't sound like she was always addressing a vicar.

"The usual?" Lydia said and they walked to the absurdly fashionable and expensive Green House.

But Andy's mum wanted to do more than that. She wanted to address the orgasm issue and, if it had to be done in public, then so be it.

"I could do with a nice sensual massage, right now," Lydia said.

Andy's mum had wondered how she'd work her topic of interest into the conversation, but she was to discover that with Lydia it was never far from the surface.

"That sounds nice," Andy's mum said, but it still sounded like she was having tea with the vicar.

Lydia raised a slight eye. It was just a flicker, and it might have been derisory in nature, but she put it away just as quickly.

"And I've been thinking about my constitutional right to a..." Andy's mum said, but she couldn't finish the sentence.

She'd also practiced saying that all week, but she just couldn't bring herself to say orgasm. She'd been struggling just thinking about it.

"Orgasm?" Lydia said loudly.

Andy's mum blushed. She looked straight ahead, but she was pretty certain she could hear heads turning.

"Yes," Andy's mum squeaked.

"Have you spoken to him about it?" Lydia asked.

'Him' was Andy's dad and Andy's mum had very much not spoken to him about it. There was no way she could casually weave it into their conversation. Did you pay the milk bill? Yes, and by the way... While Lydia's every sentence was peppered with sex, Andy's dad was rather more reserved.

"Not as such," Andy's mum admitted.

Andy's mum really wished she hadn't brought it up, but it had been on her mind all week.

"You've got to," Lydia urged. "Don't mess about, don't take hostages, grab him by the..."

"I get it," Andy's mum interrupted.

Lydia looked up at her. Now that the subject had been raised she hoped to have some fun with it.

“But firstly you’ve got to know how to have an orgasm,” Lydia said.

Andy’s mum would have been affronted by this, but it might have been one of the problems.

“You need to know your own body,” Lydia continued.

Andy’s mum could see the sense in this, but she feared where the conversation might go.

“When was the last time you masturbated?” Lydia asked.

Lydia had not lowered her voice and she asked it as if she were asking for instructions to the supermarket. Andy’s mum was too mortified to answer and just shook her head.

“Well, that’s your starting point,” Lydia said.

Andy’s mum didn’t know what to say, but it wasn’t a problem as Lydia hadn’t finished.

“Then you’ve got to show him,” Lydia said.

While Andy’s mum had been intimate with Andy’s dad on many occasions it had never stretched to expressing her needs in such an explicit fashion. Andy’s mum suddenly realised that Lydia was going to be more specific and Latin.

“You’ve got to show him your...” Lydia said.

“That’s great,” Andy’s mum shouted and now the whole cafe was looking at them.

Chapter Twenty-Six

"Africa," Andy muttered.

It didn't seem possible. He would have gently smacked his head to check he wasn't dreaming, but there was enough pain coming from his face, and he didn't want to add to it. There was no question he was fully conscious. And in Africa. The brass band was not the most tuneful and the music seemed to be a mix of genres. He wasn't sure if they were playing an anthem or the Beatles. They were terrible.

"Aren't they good?" Barry said with pride.

Barry had many qualities, but a musical ear wasn't one of them, and assembling a brass band in his country hadn't been easy. But it was one of his indulgences. He wasn't short of those.

"My name is Barry," Barry said. "But you may call me Your Excellency."

The brass band had finally finished. Some of the members of the band weren't very musical either and they frequently had problems bringing whatever they were playing to a conclusion. Occasionally it just petered out, as each member had a different view as to how it should end. Today they were almost together, aside from the tuba which pumped a couple more honks, like a wild goose.

"Andy," Andy said.

Barry offered his hand and Andy tentatively shook it. He wasn't quite sure why he was being greeted, but it was preferable to being hit.

"Why am I here?" Andy asked.

Barry looked at him. He didn't look like the mastermind behind a narcotic banana worth a hundred grand.

"Don't you know?" Barry asked.

"No," Andy said.

"I think you do," Barry insisted.

"I don't," Andy said.

Barry pointed to the banana. For some reason it was still in Andy's hand.

"The banana?" Andy suggested.

"Exactly," Barry said.

Andy looked at the banana. It looked like every other banana he'd ever seen. It was yellow and had a slight curve. It might have been less green than before, he couldn't be certain. But it was clear that he'd found himself in a place where such a thing is rare. He thought he should help fill in the gaps. He worked in advertising. How hard could it be, he thought.

"It's a fruit," Andy explained. "I guess," he continued, "it's almost unique in that it comes in its own easy to unwrap case, like a pillow case."

Barry stared at him. Andy sensed it wasn't enough.

"It has a sweet taste and is rich in potassium," Andy said.

But he was stumbling. He had no idea why a richness of potassium was a good thing. But, as his audience had evidently not come across a banana before, he thought he could be a little loose with the facts.

"Which helps to maintain a healthy heart," Andy bullshitted.

It didn't seem enough. He knew he must have missed something.

"And lungs," Andy added.

Barry's expression was getting darker, which did not seem like a good thing.

"And liver," Andy said.

He wondered if he should suggest that the banana also provided firmer erections, or if that was going too far. Then something else occurred to him.

"They grow on trees," he said. "In bunches."

That was it. He couldn't think of anything else to say about bananas. Then one further thought came to him.

"They were immortalised in the song by Harry Bellafonte," Andy said.

There was a pause. Andy couldn't discern the nature of the silence, and whether it was hostile, or an invitation for him to sing the song. He had no choice.

"Deo," Andy sang.

It was at this point that Barry grabbed his throat. He pulled him close to him. There were shades of Darth Vader coming to Andy.

"I'm not a fucking idiot," Barry said.

"No, of course not, Barry, your excellentness," Andy croaked.

Barry put him down.

"I know what a banana is. But that," Barry said pointing at the banana, "is not a normal banana."

"It isn't?" Andy said.

"No," Barry said.

"Oh," Andy said.

They both looked at the banana. It continued to look like every banana they'd ever seen.

"You have reengineered it," Barry said.

"I have?" Andy asked.

Barry looked at him uncertainty. Alarm bells were ringing somewhere in his head.

"Yes," Barry said firmly. "You are a biochemist."

Andy was beginning to get an understanding of where things might have gone wrong.

"No," Andy said, "I work in advertising."

"Advertising?" Barry asked.

"I work for a company called..." Andy stopped realising that the last time he'd said Pyjama Case he'd received a punch in the stomach.

"I did media studies," Andy said meekly.

"Not biochemistry?" Barry asked.

"No," Andy said.

"Shit," Barry said and wondered what to do next. Then he knew what Andy had to do.

"You're going to eat the banana," Barry said.

"I am?" Andy asked.

"You are," Barry said.

Now the banana looked like a loaded gun or a hand grenade. Andy peeled it as if it was going to go off in their faces. With the peel removed it still looked like a banana.

"Eat," Barry said.

Andy looked at the banana. His hand was shaking. He didn't have a choice. He took a small bite. He chewed. He swallowed. The banana tasted exactly like a banana. It began to give him confidence.

"Rich in potassium," Andy said.

"Sit down," Barry said.

Barry tried to remember the things that Jeremiah had told him. He'd said only a small quantity was required. A bit was ample. He didn't mention the time it took to take effect and Barry studied Andy.

"Feeling any different?" Barry asked.

Andy wasn't sure if he should mention the qualities that a richness in potassium brought and then decided that more bullshit would probably not be helpful.

"No, not really," Andy admitted.

"No sense of euphoria?" Barry asked.

"I can't say so," Andy said.

Barry checked his watch. It had only been a few minutes. He needed to be more patient. It wasn't something he was renowned for. Ten minutes slowly passed.

"Anything?" Barry asked.

"No. I'd have to say no," Andy said.

They waited a further ten minutes in silence when the brass band noticed that Barry hadn't left the plane and began their rendition of 'Tie a Yellow Ribbon Round the Old Oak Tree'. Although it sounded more like a cross between Britney Spears 'Toxic' and Beethoven's fifth. There had been some dispute about what they should play, and while it had been generally agreed that it should be 'Tie a Yellow Ribbon Round the Old Oak Tree,' a few were rebelling, and a few more couldn't read music, and one or two couldn't read anything at all.

"I'm hearing some crazy music," Andy said.

Barry looked at him sternly.

"Are you taking the piss?" he asked.

"No," Andy said.

"Glot!' Barry shouted.

The pilot walked slowly through the cabin in a sauntering kind of way which filled Barry with fury, but which he had to suppress as he couldn't fly the plane himself.

"Tell the band," Barry said slowly. "To shut the fuck up."

Glot wandered out into the sunshine and up to the band leader and delivered the order word for word. It took a while to disseminate the instruction, as the man on the tuba wasn't just tone deaf, he was completely deaf. With a bit of prodding the band faded and eventually stopped. There was silence in the plane.

"Anything now?" Barry asked.

But Barry was getting the feeling he'd been taken on a wild goose chase. Forty-five minutes later he gave up.

"Glot," he said to Glot. "Get rid of him."

Chapter Twenty-Seven

"So, is he going to pop the question?"

Ali's week of bonding had only just begun and already it was getting awkward. Andy hadn't phoned her and she'd been unable to reach him. That wasn't a good sign, particularly from the man she thought was going to take their relationship to the next stage.

"I'm not sure," Ali said.

She wasn't even sure that Andy knew that she was expecting him to pop the question. She knew men required a little prompting and she thought she'd laid out a few hints. She wished she hadn't mentioned it. It was another late evening and the evening had been reduced to her, Jess, Tony and the accounts girl. The accounts girl rarely said anything and looked like a frightened rabbit caught in the headlights of an advancing truck. Tony, they had all agreed, was in denial of his sexuality. Jess was something else.

"Not sure?" Jess said dismissively.

One of the things that Ali was learning was that Jess was, and she couldn't think of another way to put it, a bit of a cow. She made these little digs, which Ali hadn't noticed to begin with. Although it might have been because Andy hadn't called and she was feeling a little sensitive.

"No," Ali said.

It wasn't as if Jess's life was filled with marriage proposals. Ali had initially thought Jess was a buxom and sassy, but now she was feeling she was just fat and a bit bitter. In some respects the bonding trip was less than successful.

"But he will," Ali said brightly.

She got up to get more drinks. She didn't want to drink more, she'd rather have gone to bed, but she wasn't going to be defeated by Jess's bitterness. If she'd told them that Andy hadn't called and hadn't answered when she'd called him, she would have to field all sorts of unpleasantness. She wasn't going to do that.

"Same again?" she said.

The bar was far enough away for her to discreetly make a call as she waited to be served. She waved at the barman and looked at her phone. Bang. It went straight to voicemail. That wasn't normal. Andy always answered his phone. She'd called him when he was with clients' or at the gym, or on the toilet. Now she thought about it was most often the latter. But he always answered.

"Same again, please," she said to the barman.

They were running a tab which the company was foolishly paying for and it had become pretty sizeable. They may not collectively be in agreement about many things, but they'd all decided they didn't give a damn about the size of the bar bill. Ali took one quick look at her phone. Andy hadn't responded to her texts either. She wondered if he'd phoned his parents. She had mentioned it a few times.

"Cheers," she said to the barman and walked back to the table.

The discussion had shifted away from her, as she hoped it might when she left the table. Although she couldn't rule out the possibility that they were gossiping about her in her absence.

"You fucking bitch!" Tony shouted.

Tony stood up and, if he was defending his sexuality, he was not doing a good job as he positively flounced. He was quite red in the face. Ali had grown a little bored of him too, but she decided to defend him just to irritate Jess.

"Calm down, I'm sure she didn't mean it," Ali said, pulling him down onto a stool.

Tony hated any kind of confrontation, but had lost it for a second. Now he just felt embarrassed. He was in danger of becoming gloomy again although, to cheer himself up, he began to write his CV in his head. As soon as they got back he intended to get the hell out of this awful company.

"We don't care about your sexuality," Ali said.

She'd missed the conversation that had preceded his outburst and hadn't meant to say anything about his sexuality. It just came out. The problem was she just wished he'd do the same.

"I'm not fucking gay," he shouted, getting up.

"May I make a suggestion?" the accounts girl said.

They all looked at her and the accounts girl wished she'd remained silent. What was she thinking? Now she'd put herself in the firing line. Working at this company was like volunteering for a firing squad.

"Well?" Jess said.

The accounts girl panicked again.

"You've spent the whole time complaining about men and your sex life," she said looking at Jess.

"And you," she said turning to Tony, "have protested your heterosexuality."

"Look Doris," Jess said.

"It's Daphne," Daphne the accounts girl said.

They looked at her accusingly. No one knew why someone from accounts had been invited. Daphne hadn't wanted to join them, and had spent the evening building up the courage to do a runner. Now she wished she had.

"Well," Daphne said, hoping it was obvious. Clearly it wasn't.

"Get together," she finally managed to say.

Chapter Twenty-Eight

When Andy woke up he found himself in a ditch. It was a ditch, he knew, in Africa, which was something he was still trying to process. It could have been worse, as the instructions 'get rid of him' could be interpreted a number of ways, and Glot was not noted for his kindness. The car was still moving, moving at quite a pace, when he hurled Andy out, so he was lucky he didn't hit a tree or land in a swamp. While Glot hadn't attempted to kill him, he hadn't cared if he did. But Andy wasn't feeling as if this was his lucky day.

He was now no longer merely hungry, but positively ravenous. He got up. And then he got it. It all made sense. He'd stepped into a reality show. There were hidden cameras and an audience anxious to find out what he does next. The problem was he hadn't the slightest idea of what to do next. He checked his pockets. He had an Oyster card, with around twenty pounds on it, but of not much use outside the London transport system. And he had a fiver. A fiver with which he'd hoped to buy some chips. Not even a credit card and certainly not a passport. This was surreal, Andy thought. He wondered if Ali was watching and sniggering with the audience. What would they call the show, he wondered. It would probably have an exclamation mark at the end of it. Something like *In the Shit!* He certainly felt like he was in the shit. He couldn't see how things could get any worse.

Andy still had half a banana in his hand. Its skin had turned black and it looked a bit sorry for itself, as if it had curled up in sympathy with his own predicament. But he was starving. He ate the remains. It tasted just like a banana. For no particular reason he began to sing to himself. He wasn't normally inclined to sing to himself. It was remarkable how successfully the banana had assuaged his hunger. He climbed out of the ditch. In the distance he could see a building. It was a tall single storey building like a warehouse, and it looked as if it were clad in aluminium. It was painted with large swirls of colour in a style which either says street art or graffiti, depending on your point of view. The barren earth didn't look so barren, but more a patchwork quilt of vibrant colours. He felt taller too, as if he were looking down, and observing himself. He could hear music. It was the thumping bass sort that moves the air. He looked at his hands. They seemed a long way away. Ali always said he had nice hands. As he got closer to the building he could see it was moving with the bass, although it seemed to be rippling like the sea. He could make out faces in the graffiti. They were familiar faces. They too were moving as if they were interacting with each other. One was Mr Grebble. He was the headmaster who had tried to expel him. Oddly he was standing next to Paul McCartney, who was wearing a tall hat like the kind the short engineer wore – was it Brunel? He couldn't remember. Next to him was Elvis, who was kissing someone. Andy couldn't make out who. Then he realised it was his mother. His mother waved at him and then turned back. He could see tongues. Andy smiled to himself. The most extraordinary thing was that nothing seemed extraordinary. His earlier conception of the surreal had been supplanted by the truly surreal and yet it didn't seem surreal at all.

"Alright Andy?" Paul McCartney said to him in his distinctive Liverpudlian accent.

"I'm fine, thank you," Andy said.

"Feeling good?" another voice said.

It looked like the man from the chip shop. He wondered how he'd got here, but didn't seem surprised to see him.

"Not bad, thank you," Andy said.

Andy was walking through the album cover of Sergeant Pepper's Lonely Hearts Club band except for the addition of Mr Grebble, Elvis and the man from the chip shop. And his mother. John Lennon passed his mother a joint. Andy stumbled on the sea of dandelions under his feet and fell over. He got up. He was getting closer to the building, although at times it seemed as if the building was getting closer to him. He couldn't tell, but he was certain the distance between them was becoming shorter, which amounted to the same thing. A second later, as if the concept of the passage of time was no longer linear, he arrived at a pair of doors. He hadn't noticed the doors before. They were on the side of the building and also covered in swirly images, which looked like people he knew, and then didn't. They flew open and a tall man appeared.

"Welcome!" the man yelled.

It wasn't Paul McCartney, or Elvis, or Idi Amin, or his mother.

"Hello," Andy said.

"You're not from here," the man said.

"No," Andy said. "I need to get home."

"Home!" the man yelled. "Where is home?"

"England," Andy said.

The tall man laughed as heartily as he'd ever heard anyone laugh. He could see into the building. People were dancing, jumping and whooping.

"This is Lobo's finest rave," the man said.

"Oh," Andy said.

The concept of a warehouse full of drunk and stoned young people dancing to deafening house music and labelled a rave had spread across Europe and then died of old age. In Lobo it was the latest thing and most of the nation's young, many of whom were directly related, were present.

"What is your name?" the tall man asked.

"Andy," Andy said.

"Do you know who I am?" the tall man asked.

Andy had to admit he didn't. Right at the moment he knew almost nothing about anything. Although right at the moment he didn't find that troubling.

"Do you know who my father is?" the tall man persisted.

Andy had to admit he didn't.

"He is the king, Barry," the tall man declared.

The name rang a bell in Andy's head, but not a very loud one, as it was struggling to compete with the talking images on the side of ghetto building, and the noise that was erupting from inside.

"Do you know who my grandfather was?" the tall man asked.

Andy couldn't understand why he would and shook his head.

"The former king," the tall man said.

Andy nodded but thought he'd better say something to stay in the conversation.

"What was his name?" Andy asked.

The tall man beamed.

"Barry," he said.

"Oh," Andy said.

"Do you know who my great grandfather was?" the tall man asked.

Andy didn't but thought he'd hazard a guess.

"The former former king?" Andy ventured.

"Yes!" the tall man said with glee.

"And what was his name?" Andy asked.

"Barry!" the tall man said.

Andy was beginning to see a pattern emerge.

"Is your name Barry too?" Andy asked.

"No," the tall main said.

"So what is it?" Andy asked.

"Barry Junior," Barry Junior said.

With the introductions concluded, there was the small matter of the entrance fee. Barry junior put his hand out. Andy shook it.

"Entrance fee five Doolahs," Barry junior said.

"I don't have five Doolahs," Andy said. "But I've got five pounds."

Andy found the crumpled note in his pocket and gave it to Barry junior. Barry junior looked at it curiously and shrugged. He was very much the wrong side of sober.

"Enter," Barry said.

Chapter Twenty-Nine

"Hundred grand bananas," Barry muttered. "Bloody disaster."

He could see his chances of a world leading supercar collection evaporating quicker than a pina colada in the Lobo sunshine. His cousin wasn't making him feel any better.

"I hear Barry Junior is making a bit of a racket with his raves," Gary said.

Barry sighed. The boy was a great concern to him.

"I've tried to get him to study," Barry said. "But he's just interested in girls, drink and partying."

Gary looked at Barry.

"And drugs," Gary added.

"Maybe," Barry said.

It left a little pause.

"Have you ever wondered why that is?" Gary asked.

Barry looked at him bemused.

"You're not exactly the ideal role model," Gary pointed out.

"I graduated from Trent Polytechnic," Barry said indignantly.

They were in a small bar. It was a mud hut with a straw roof and was a throwback to a previous era. Barry's father had relentlessly covered the country in concrete which, he'd said, was the new modern material for the modern age. He'd demolished the mud huts, but they'd begun to reappear, and this bar would have reminded them of their youth, but they were brought up in an old colonial house made of brick and stone which had been imported at great expense.

"The thing is he doesn't have to work hard to get the top job. When you're gone he'll become president and he knows it. Why study?" Gary asked.

Barry knew this, as he'd felt the same as a kid. There had been a moment just after it was accidentally revealed to him that Father Christmas did not exist, that he realised that it was no coincidence that all his male ancestors had been the supreme ruler of Lobo.

"Things are changing," Barry said. "And who says my boy takes drugs?"

"Everyone," Gary said and waved to the bartender.

A couple of sizeable rums appeared dressed with sticks of fruit. Barry had a tab at the bar, which the state paid for, but which his ministers were becoming irritated by. They seemed to think he should be working harder. They had no idea, Barry thought.

"What did you do with the bloke with the banana?" Gary asked.

"Dumped him in a ditch," Barry said and took a gulp of the rum.

"That's a bit mean, isn't it?" Gary said.

There were very few people who could get away with treating Barry like that and there were occasions when Barry had to remind his cousin that he was the supreme leader. But chucking him in a ditch had been a bit mean. In his defence he was quite new to violence and abduction. It might have been something else he didn't have a facility for.

"What else did Jeremiah say about the banana?" Gary asked, moving the conversation on.

"I'm not sure," Barry said.

Barry tried to trawl his memory. It was quite extensive, positively encyclopaedic, when it came to 0-60 acceleration times of supercars but a little vague on most other matters. He thought. Then something came to him. He tried to remember.

"He said," Barry said slowly. "When you first grow the banana the new chemicals are undetectable. And then it ripens."

"And what then?" Gary asked.

"Pow," Barry said.

"Pow?" Gary asked.

"Pow," Barry confirmed.

"Anything else?" Gary asked.

That was as much as Barry was able to dredge up. He'd tried his hardest. He finished his rum and thought about ordering another. His father had introduced a drink driving ban and, astonishingly, even extended it to his son. But now that Barry was supreme leader it didn't matter, and normally Glot drove him around, although he was a little resentful about it. When they'd landed he'd said he needed some sleep. But Barry preferred to drive himself. He looked at his empty drink.

"How's the wife?" Gary asked.

Barry's wife, Junior's mother, never left the house and had not the slightest interest in where he went, or what he got up to. He was thinking of driving across the border to a very discreet whore house he favoured. But he feared that if he had another rum he might not be able to get it up. There was something not quite right with the supreme leader not being able to get it up. It had happened before and the girls had told him he was magnificent and damn near omnipotent. It wasn't a cheap whore house and they wouldn't let him run a tab. He'd have to drop by a cash machine.

"No idea," Barry said.

"So was it ripe then?" Gary asked.

"What?" Barry asked.

As far as he was concerned his wife was very ripe indeed.

"The banana," Gary said.

"I don't know," Barry said.

"He did say it had to be ripe, didn't he?" Gary pressed.

Barry fiddled with his drink.

"You waited for it to take effect, didn't you?" Gary said.

"Of course. I waited at least forty-five minutes," Barry replied.

"But you didn't wait for the banana to ripen," Gary said.

Barry shook his head.

“Where did you say you left the man with the banana?” Gary asked.

“In a ditch,” Barry said with irritation.

He didn’t want to go over the ditch thing and it’s meanness again.

“We need to get him and his banana,” Gary said urgently. “Now.”

“He’ll have eaten it by now,” Barry said.

It left a pause. Barry was watching Gary think. Nothing much was happening and then suddenly it seemed as if a light had come on.

“The seeds,” Gary said. “We need the seeds.”

Chapter Thirty

There had been moments when Andy had woken up and his head had been in a jumble. He'd once drunk for twelve hours at a stag do and the following day he could remember very little about anything, including the strippers. This morning was worse than that, and he was thinking about Ali. Before Ali there had been Penny and before Penny there was Eva. He had a brief dalliance with Claire, and a one night stand with a girl whose name he'd never known. That was the complete inventory of his sex life and, while it wasn't huge it always stood, he thought, on the right side of respectable. He wasn't a great seducer of women. It was why his initial thoughts that morning were a little confused.

He'd opened his eyes and he'd seen something a little shocking. There was no good way to put it. It was quite easily the hairiest bush he'd ever seen, and that included the occasional visits to the internet. It was so luxuriant it looked as if it could be combed into various directions, or worse still, pinned back. It took him a while to recognise it was a vagina. He turned over. He now found himself facing a large pair of breasts. Then he closed his eyes. He appeared to be in bed with two women. He opened them again. He *was* in bed with two women. How had that happened?

Andy remembered the fields of daisies, or they might have been poppies, or it could have been a paisley rug.

That wasn't helping. He remembered Paul McCartney and his mother kissing Elvis. He knew his mother wasn't the kind of woman who randomly kissed men. He wasn't even sure she kissed his father and, on top of that, Elvis had been dead for forty years. This was enough information for Andy to conclude that he hadn't just taken a trip. He'd been tripping. Something hallucinogenic had found his way into his system. Except all he'd eaten was a banana.

"Banana," Andy muttered.

That explained quite a bit, if not everything. It didn't entirely explain why he was in bed with two women. Then he remembered Barry Junior and the rave. He'd tumbled into the rave like a mosquito drawn to light. There had been dancing. Then someone had told him, it might have been Barry, that white men were a bit of a novelty here. They'd never seen a man with red hair. And no one had a beard like that. Then he'd danced. Despite his colour, upbringing and musical tastes, Andy was quite a respectable dancer. Although it wouldn't have made much difference.

"Morning Andy," one of the girls said.

Fortunately he was facing the breasts, as a talking vagina would have meant he was still in the grip of whatever he'd taken the previous night. He'd grown so used to the surreal he wasn't quite prepared for the real. The other part of real was that he was stranded somewhere in Africa with just an Oyster card and five pounds. Now he thought about it, he no longer had the five pounds. But there was another question.

"Did we? Last night..."

The woman smiled. Andy took an indiscreet fraction of a second to look at her a little closer. She was a girl around his age, although her body was certainly womanly, and she had immaculate light brown skin. She had a pretty face too.

"Oh Andy," she declared. "Don't you remember?"

Andy didn't, which at least made him feel a little less guilty. Ali would not be pleased. The more laddish version of himself would have said, 'what goes on tour' but he wasn't on tour. No one, as far as he was aware, had ever coined the phrase 'what goes on kidnap, stays on kidnap'.

"With Fullbush," the girl added.

Andy wasn't sure if he'd heard that right. He couldn't have. He turned to face the other girl and was confronted with the same sight that had disturbed him earlier. She got up and turned. She was slimmer than the other girl with little breasts that were pointing at him. It was quite distracting.

"Don't you remember me?" she said, and for clarity she repeated her name.

"Fullbush."

Despite the awkward and terrifying situation Andy found himself in, he couldn't help wondering to whom he was going to relate the story of Fullbush, and her luxuriant pubic growth. He certainly couldn't tell Ali, and many of their friends were joint friends, which would make the story a little dangerous.

"Pointer," the other girl said.

It took a couple of beats for Andy to recognise that was her name and a further beat, as he glanced at her breasts, although they might have been glancing at him, to see the significance of it. But he'd just realised something else. He was entirely naked. Not even a pair of socks. Ali wouldn't let him get into bed wearing just socks and it was absolutely forbidden should sex be on the cards. It really looked like he might have had sex.

"Pleased to meet you," Andy said.

The girls laughed. They weren't normally this wild, but they couldn't resist the rare opportunity of a white man and they'd argued over who should have him. Ordinarily their solution would have delighted Andy, but he was suffering from some very conflicting feelings.

"Pleased to meet you too," Fullbush said and playfully slapped his bottom.

He watched her get up, a little mesmerised. It looked as if her pubes may be platted. There was certainly enough of it to make platting a possibility. She walked slowly towards what he guessed was the bathroom. He turned to Pointer.

"Do you know if there is a British embassy here?" he asked.

"British," she said with a smile and pointed at the wall.

Andy followed her finger until he found a picture of Charles and Diana, which was faded with age.

"Prince Charles," he said.

"And Diana," Pointer said.

He was about to explain how badly wrong it had gone with Charles and Diana and then he decided against it, as he feared he might shatter an image.

"The embassy?" he asked.

"No embassy," Pointer said.

"One nearby?" he asked.

"Yes," she said. "Two or three..."

"Excellent," Andy said.

He could easily walk two or three miles or, better still, kilometres. He'd have to explain how he was kidnapped and didn't have a passport. The British authorities would know what to do.

"Thousand kilometres," Pointer said.

"Thousand?" Andy said, his panic returning.

"Two countries away," she confirmed.

Chapter Thirty-One

Ali had decided that it would be better if her alter ego was called Georgina, although Georgina wasn't a million miles away from Jemima. If Jemima had a sister that's probably what she'd be called. They would have competed with each other to bed the stable hands and also for the attention of their father who would be called something like Lord Fothergill. He would spend much of his time in the townhouse in London and attending the upper chamber. Not that the townhouse would be modest. It would be one of those Georgian jobs, at least three windows wide, with floor to ceiling windows and proper crystal chandeliers. Ali's vision of Jemima's upbringing had shades of Jane Austen about it. Jemima probably did the whole deb thing and attended balls with the young Conservatives or the young farmers.

Ali pondered the gap between loathing and envy. It wasn't a very distant one. She didn't much like the idea of the company of either the young farmers or the young conservatives, and just imagined them as pink faced and baying. Not that she'd met any. The house she'd been brought up in had been pleasant enough, but it was more characterised by paper Ikea light fittings than crystal chandeliers. And when she'd first read Jane Austen and Jane had referred to her love of 'balls', Ali hadn't immediately envisioned large parties. She hadn't been that young and she'd really thought

Jane had meant testicles. It suggested that the world she was picturing was unreal but, and this was the envy part, she thought people like Jemima led unreal lives. They were brought up to believe in their natural superiority and were never plagued with doubts of any kind. It was for that reason that Jemima carried herself as she did. Ali wondered if she might have a chip on her shoulder.

Ali pointed the remote control at the television. She was lying on the bed in her room delaying the evening with her London colleagues. The music channel changed for something about puppies. She couldn't really stop thinking about Jemima. There was admiration too, although she tempered that with the thought that Jemima had led a privileged life. If she too had grown up on a country estate and attended a posh school, would she be able to hold herself in the same manner as Jemima? Could she emulate it? Ali got off the bed.

She walked across the room. As it was a small room it didn't involve much more than three strides, but she watched herself in the many mirrors as she did it. She walked back. She tried again, but this time attempted to endow the walk with seven generations of wealth and standing and entitlement.

"Better," she said.

And then she sat on the bed and opened a box. She'd been shopping. It might have been something buried in her subconscious, but she had decided that she needed more of the Jemima equipment. She'd bought some Jemima high heels. They were quite expensive. She put them on and tried the same walk.

"Bloody hell," she muttered.

It wasn't easy. She needed to get herself into character. Ali stood tall, as if she was looking down at everything and everyone around her. This was better. She needed a further trigger.

"Balls," she said.

She didn't mean testicles. She meant a grand house with a vast, probably circular room, in which champagne flutes and polite conversation and Strauss-like waltzes all effortlessly mingled. It was as if she was holding her arse in. It worked.

"I take no shit," she said.

She walked a little more, grateful that the room wasn't vast as it was quite tiring. She almost didn't recognise herself in the mirror.

"How much shit do I take?" Ali asked.

She strolled a little more. She needed to get close to Jemima and observe her every move. Ali wanted to acquire that feline quality of power and authority.

"No shit at all," Ali said.

That was exactly how much shit she took. The problem was that Rome wasn't built in a day. She had to take it one step at a time. She sat on the bed.

"Fucking hell," Ali said.

Her feet hurt like hell. There was no way she was going out wearing those shoes. She took them off and lay back on the bed. Although she wasn't certain she could emulate Jemima's bearing, she was pretty sure she could be as good a journalist. Wasn't that the most important thing?

"Balls," Ali said.

This time she did mean testicles, as she realised that in the social whirl that was New York, style might have a greater place than substance. It was that and she'd just seen the time. She had to go and join her colleagues.

Chapter Thirty-Two

"Do you know where my clothes are?" Andy asked.

He'd covered himself protectively with the single sheet and looked around the room. He might have anticipated seeing a shoe by the door, his trousers near the bed, or his underpants hanging on a light fitting. He wasn't conversant with the protocol when it came to mad and hurried sex, as he normally had plenty of warning when sex was on the cards.

"Clothes?" Pointer said and laughed.

Andy did not find this very reassuring, as there was a limit to the things he could lose, and this comfortably exceeded it.

"Don't you remember?" she asked.

Andy's recollection of recent events was limited, although it might have been his system attempting to protect him. There was only so much he could take.

"I don't think I do," Andy said carefully not wishing to offend.

"Do you remember the pick up?" she said.

Andy's confused mind processed this and it prompted a memory. She didn't mean pick up, she meant pickup. She was referring to a vehicle. He'd been in the back of it. It was full of hay and he was lying on his back and looking at the sky. It was packed with stars. In London a star occasionally made an appearance, and in the English countryside there were decidedly more, but nothing like last night. He'd assumed that he'd been tripping, but the stars weren't a psychedelic fantasy.

"I do. And the stars. I remember the stars," Andy said.

This was helping. But he wasn't the only one in the back of the pickup.

"Look,' she said, pointing out of the window.

Andy got up. He wrapped the sheet round him and leaned forward. They seemed to be in the second floor of a modern apartment block. It looked like it could be in London, or Blackpool, or anywhere in Britain. The view outside did not look like Britain, but it wasn't so far away from Spain either. There was a large battered pickup parked below them.

"Are those..." he asked.

Pointer nodded. While he was hiding himself she was entirely naked and very comfortable with it. His trousers and teeshirt were strewn across the hay in the back of the truck. That meant he'd walked from the truck to the apartment without his clothes. Andy was not, by nature, an exhibitionist. He wondered again what he'd taken. He had smoked a little pot and he'd once taken ecstasy, but aside from that his experience of narcotics was limited. The alarming thing was that if he weren't stranded in the middle of nowhere with no way of getting back, he might have enjoyed it.

"Oh," Andy said.

He could hear a sizzling noise. In his current world he was reluctant to make assumptions about anything, but it was accompanied with a smell which was reassuring and very welcome.

"The smell?" Andy asked.

Pointer leaned over and picked up what looked like a long teeshirt. She did so in one fluid movement without bending her knees as if she were a yoga expert and she threw it over her head. It was more a dress than a teeshirt and Andy wondered if he was the only naked one who'd walked from the pickup. He did remember feeling that he was remarkably free of inhibitions.

"Breakfast," she said.

A minute later Fullbush appeared, also dressed in a teeshirt dress, and skilfully carrying three plates.

"Bacon and eggs," Fullbush said.

They were the two most welcome words Andy could wish to hear. He was starving. He ate them rapidly thinking that they tasted *exactly* like bacon and eggs from home. He wondered if he was back on the reality show, but things were too crazy for that. When he finished he felt a lot better.

"I need to get home," Andy said.

"You can stay here," Fullbush said.

"But," Andy said, "I have a job."

He was thankful that they didn't ask him what he did, as few people seemed to understand the advertising world when he described it to them. But they continued to smile at him.

"And I have a flat too," he said.

The girls looked around their own flat. It wasn't so different from Andy and Ali's, except he'd bought with him a sizeable hifi and a large screen television. This flat was a little less masculine. They smiled happily at him.

"And I have a wife," he said.

Ali wasn't actually his wife, although they had talked about marriage. Or Ali might have talked about it and he'd certainly listened. But it was easier to describe her as his wife than his girlfriend. He looked at the girls hopeful that they might help him, but the smiles had faded. The atmosphere had chilled a touch.

"You have a wife?" Fullbush said.

It wasn't quite a shout, but it was said in a tone which was distinctly hard edged and pissed off.

"More of a girlfriend," Andy said quietly.

He realised he had no idea what the moral boundaries were in Lobo, but he suspected he'd just tripped over one. The girls crossed their arms. A minute later they turfed him out of the flat.

Chapter Thirty-Three

Andy's dad had finally cleared a section of the garden and organised a shed. He still wasn't fully convinced he'd removed the dog shit from his shoes, but that would have to wait, as the shed had come in a kit of parts. As far as he could see from the drawings it looked like around a million parts, and he had serious doubts as to whether he'd finish it by the end of the summer. As it was May that gave him a pleasing amount of occupied time ahead of him. He could see he'd need it as Andy's mum was going a little crazy, in his view. She was walking down the garden with a cup of tea.

"Tea?" Andy's mum said.

"Thanks," Andy's dad.

"You should take your shirt off," Andy's mum suggested.

"My shirt? Why?" Andy's dad asked a little confused.

"To get a tan," Andy's mum said.

Andy's dad looked at her as if she was mad. What would be want a tan for? Who would see it? He turned back to the instructions and realised he needed to get some tools for the job. He would have researched it on his iPad, but he needed to get out of the house. He looked up and found that Andy's mum was still standing there. She seemed to be waiting for something, although he had not the slightest idea what it might be.

"I've got work to do," Andy's dad said gruffly.

It was a bit rude, but he couldn't help himself. Andy's mum walked back to the house. She quite liked the gruffness and would be more than happy to hear it issue a few commands of a distinctly sexual nature. It was a thought that confused her and made her blush.

"Right," Andy's dad said to himself with the same gruffness.

It was the voice that was appropriate for the job of shed builder and, after he examined the instructions a little further, and arranged the components on the cleared section of the garden, he walked back to the house. He grabbed the car keys and shouted, "I'm just going to B & Q."

He was up the road before Andy's mum had the time to digest this, which was a shame as she would have liked to have gone with him. But it was the first time for a while she'd found herself alone in the house. She went up to the bed and lay down. There was a thought floating in the back of her mind which she was trying to beat away like it was a hungry puppy that was pleased to see her.

Andy's dad had arrived at B & Q, parked the car and located the power tools section, and was finding the selection a little overwhelming. Although he had no long term plans for shed building – this would be his first and last – he wanted to buy some more serious tools, as building work seemed like a good way to spend his time.

"Can I help you?" a salesman asked.

He was less a salesman and more a helper, and he was part of a new policy of employing older people, which Andy's dad found reassuring.

"Yes, I'm looking for a cordless drill," Andy's dad said.

He asked this at the precise moment that Andy's mum had stopped battling with the thought in the back of her head and had decided to confront it. Lydia had told her she needed to know her body and now was as good a time as any to attempt that exploration. Some might say it was forty years later than normal, but Andy's mum had described herself as 'square' and that might explain it. She'd removed her clothes. Just the act of clothing removal was giving her a frisson, as it seemed very naughty indeed. She lay there for a moment wondering where to begin.

In B & Q the elderly helper – Andy's dad had decided he was rather older than him – was giving him useful directions in the power tool department.

"You might want something with more power," the elderly helper said.

Andy's dad had picked up a cordless drill that was light and fitted easily into his hand, like a handgun might. Not that Andy's dad had ever picked up a hand gun, but there was something a little macho about the process of buying power tools.

"Try this," the elderly helper said, passing him a drill.

It was much heavier and Andy's dad couldn't help noticing that the muscles in his forearm flexed when he held it. As he'd sat at a desk for thirty years they hadn't done a lot of flexing, but there was no reason why they couldn't make up for lost time.

Andy's mum, in the bedroom at home, was thinking the same thing. It had taken her some time to locate the Latin thing, she still couldn't quite bring herself to say the word, but after much searching, there was no question she'd found it. Her stomach flexed as if it was leaping away from something.

In B & Q Andy's dad was being seduced by the tools with the word 'professional' marked on them. His experience of builders was that they rarely turned up on time, or completed the job at the quoted price, so it was hard to say if marking something with the word 'professional' was a good recommendation. But it sat in his hand with a threatening weight and hardness.

In the bedroom Andy's mum was surprised, as the locating part of the exercise had been completed, to find the same thing. Now that she had it she wasn't entirely sure what to do with it and she started with a tentative rub.

At the same time Andy's dad had pulled the trigger of the cordless drill, its operation was fairly straightforward, and it made a pleasing well-engineered noise and turned appropriately.

"Of course," the elderly salesman said. "If you can afford it, this is the one to get."

The elderly salesman picked up another cordless drill and allowed himself a pause. He was a big fan of power tools. He read all the magazines and had driven many a screw into an unsuspecting block of wood although, as his wife would attest, he was pretty hopeless at DIY. But he was introducing this tool with some reverence, as if he were a chat show host who'd bagged Robert De Niro, and had yet to decide which words would be appropriate for his audience.

"This is the mother of all tools," the elderly helper said breathlessly.

He handed it to Andy's dad and the muscles in his arm flexed again, but this time they were made for each other. The perfect union of man and tool.

"Careful," the elderly helper warned. "It has a hair-trigger."

It was at precisely that moment that Andy's mum was regretting not having mounted the exploration forty years earlier and discovering that, she too, had a hair-trigger.

"Dear mother of god," Andy's mum groaned.

Chapter Thirty-Four

Andy scampered through the building with his hands covering his genitals and made it out into the morning sun. He had no idea of the time, but it was warm already. He hid in the doorway and looked along the street. It was a strange contrast of the normal – the four-floored concrete faced apartment block could have been anywhere in the world – and the palm trees. They weren't the sort that had been shipped in and planted at great expense. They'd grown there naturally and had grown tall chasing the sun. The street appeared empty.

"Now or never," Andy said, trying to reassure himself.

He stepped onto the street and, as he did so, it was as if everyone suddenly appeared. There was a woman selling chopped up pineapples on a stick. She looked at him a little surprised. She'd worked on the same street corner for three years and this was the first time she'd seen a naked white man. Two cars came down the road. A gang of children came rushing by, and a young woman on the way to her job at the bank, stepped out at the same time.

"Morning," Andy said.

At university he'd once stolen a bed and carried it, with a friend, to a large lecture hall. It was the bed of a student who refused to change his sheets, and his friend told him that the key was to pretend that what they were doing was perfectly normal. No on had noticed. He strolled to the pickup as if it was the most normal thing in the world. It didn't take long to recover his trousers and shirt, but his underpants were nowhere to be found. He was a man who held strong views about wearing jeans without underpants, not least because of the zip-related hazards that might arise. But right now it was the least of his problems. His feet were a little fragile, and he couldn't see himself getting very far without shoes. He searched optimistically through the hay in the desperate hope he'd find a pair of size nine and a half Adidas trainers.

"Shit," Andy muttered.

He gave up. His feet would have to toughen up with the rest of him. He stood up and got hit on his shoulder by a flying trainer. He looked up at the open window of the girls' flat and the second trainer hit him in the face. He landed on his back, but the hay cushioned his fall. Two minutes later he was walking along the main street. His head was clearing and his predicament was becoming clearer. He had to figure out what to do. The obvious thing to do was go to the authorities, and tell them what had happened to him, and hope they'd help him. The problem was that it appeared as if it was the authorities who had kidnapped him. Barry was the king.

He wondered who he could call but, without his mobile phone which he'd lost in the mud somewhere near King's Cross, he was a little lost. He had to figure out *how* he could make a call. Ali's number was programmed into his phone and he hadn't the slightest idea what the sequence of numbers might be. He only knew one number and, as he was so deeply in the shit, it was who he was going to ring. He was ready to return to the mothership. His parents. He'd not asked them for help of any sort for over ten years and not much before then. There had been a moment when he'd been cautioned by the police. He'd been more than a little drunk and he'd kicked a tin can. It had flown through the air and landed on the crotch of a policeman. His dad had been pretty good at dealing with that, much more so than the policeman.

The problem was how to make a call without a phone, or the means to either acquire one. He needed an embassy, but Fullbush had said that was two countries away and he didn't have a passport to cross borders. Or, again, the means to acquire one. He carried on walking until he found himself on a road bustling with people with huge colourful food stalls and markets. It was at least helpful that everything was written in English. There was a sign at the end of the road which caught his eye.

"Labour exchange," he said.

Chapter Thirty-Five

Ali was flagging already, but her London colleagues were determined to keep the evening going.

"Let's dance," Jess said.

The tensions had grown and they needed to do something before they killed each other. Tony seemed the most keen.

"It's this way," he said authoritatively. "In the basement."

"We need to take the lift," Ali said.

"Elevator," Jess corrected her.

It was a small lift and they were forced to stand close to each other while avoiding eye contact. Daphne was a foot shorter than the others, which made avoiding eye contact easier for her, although the lift was lined with mirrors, so she kept her eyes to the ground just in case. The doors opened with a ting and the sophisticated tinkle of the piano in the bar they'd just left was replaced by something more primal. Ali would have gone to bed, but she didn't want to be the first to retire. Jess led them onto the dance floor and Ali reluctantly moved to the music. Tony was a revelation.

"The boy can dance," Jess shouted, but it got lost in the noise.

Tony could dance but, again, it did not reinforce his insistence that he was straight. It was just further evidence to the contrary. But that didn't stop Tony, who'd evidently found his spiritual home. Daphne shuffled enthusiastically missing every beat, occasionally by a big enough margin to catch the next. Despite that she was enjoying herself, although she'd consumed more gin and tonics courtesy of Miles in the last three hours, than she had in the previous six months. And Tony was finding his groove.

"Shots!' he shouted.

He had timed it perfectly between the rise and fall of the music and pirouetted to the bar. The man, Ali thought, wasn't gay. He was a raving queen. Tony expertly lined the shots up and they each grabbed a glass.

"Cheers," Tony said, and they knocked them back.

There was a small pause when everyone wondered what to do next and Jess said, "fuck it," and made an action with her hand which prompted another round. Tony lined the shots up like little soldiers.

"Cheers," Jess said and they knocked them back.

They looked at each other unsteadily. There were many things they could resist, but a free bar was clearly not one of them. Daphne stepped up to the bar and attempted the same hand action, but the bar was tall and Daphne wasn't. The barman had moved on.

"Oi!" Daphne shouted.

The others looked in surprise and the barman returned for a further round of soldiers for slaughter.

"Cheers!" Daphne shouted and they knocked them back.

Tony led them back to the dance floor. Daphne had never felt quite so fortified and she threw off her jacket, a jacket she'd never been seen without, tugged her blouse and got stuck in. The freer version of Daphne was able to hear the music and move to it and jacketless reveal a hitherto unnoticed, and quite considerable, cleavage. If the others were looking at her she didn't care. She was becoming a soul woman with attitude. Tony took her hand and it was hard to say who was piloting who, but it looked quite expert, almost as if they'd rehearsed. It was a large dance floor and they moved around it with ease.

"Who'd have thought?" Ali shouted.

It put the evening back on a more upbeat footing and they danced and took shots until late enough into the morning for Ali not to clearly remember how she'd made it to bed.

Chapter Thirty-Six

"Welcome," a stocky man in a shirt and tie said.

Andy had not felt very welcome anywhere he'd been lately. He took a seat as instructed and waited.

"Robbie," the stocky man said and offered his hand.

Andy shook it. Robbie was a man who sweated a lot, but always insisted on wearing a tie, which he constantly fiddled with. The patches under his arms grew throughout the day but, as it was still early, were more like a gloaming moon than their final, almost to the waist, fullness.

"Andy," Andy said. "Andy Broderick."

"Welcome," Robbie said again.

He sat down and removed a card from a plastic box.

"Address?" Robbie asked.

"Hackney," Andy said.

Robbie looked at him curiously.

"Where's that?" he finally asked.

"In London," Andy said.

Robbie's face remained blank, as he evidently hadn't heard of London either.

"England," Andy added, but Robbie was none the wiser.

"Great Britain?" Andy said.

Robbie had graduated with a first in business studies, but very little of it included geography, or the history of his country, neither of which he was remotely interested in.

"I'll put your address as here, shall I?" Robbie suggested.

"Please," Andy said.

Andy looked around the room. It looked more little a police station. There were computers on desks with old screens, with no one else except Robbie manning the desks. But Andy needed a job. With a job he could eat and make a telephone call. He hadn't decided what he was going to say to his mum and dad, but if they could get into his flat, grab his passport and fly over that would be great. He needed to find a way of phrasing that in a way which didn't make it seem like too much to ask. He'd have to sell it to them, but that was his profession.

"What is your business?" Robbie asked.

"Advertising," Andy said confidently.

There was a pause, which Robbie eventually broke.

"What is advertising?" Robbie asked.

Andy had sat through a number of interviews, but no one had ever asked him this question. He was a little inclined to tell him that half the time it was a waste of his client's money.

"You know," Andy said. "Making advertisements."

Robbie looked confused.

"For companies," Andy added.

Robbie looked at him in a way which suggested more explanation was required.

"It's the business of promoting, through digital, printed and social media," Andy said.

Robbie's face broke into a smile.

"I know what advertising is," he said. "But we don't have any positions available in advertising at this time."

"Oh," Andy said. "Will there be any positions in the future?"

"In advertising?" Robbie asked.

"Yes," Andy said.

"No," Robbie said and looked down at the papers in front of him.

"What skills do you have?" he asked.

"I can write. I have good computer skills on Mac or PC," Andy said.

He hadn't operated a PC in years and, judging by the computers in the desks, he'd need to brush up his skills on ancient software.

"No vacancies," Robbie said.

There was another silence and the realisation that they were approaching this from the wrong direction.

"What jobs do you have?" Andy asked.

Robbie shuffled more papers and looked a little coy.

"Do you know how to operate a broom?" Robbie asked.

If Ali had been asked this question of Andy she would have replied in the negative and his Hoovering skills weren't much better either.

"Yes," Andy said brightly and, to illustrate the extent of his broom related skills, he made a sweeping action with his hands.

"Excellent," Robbie declared with a smile lighting up his face.

"Great, when can I start?" Andy asked.

He wondered what kind of package such a job would have and whether 'package' was the right word. He watched as Robbie picked up a list of names. It filled the page. He turned the page to reveal a further list. He turned a second time and then a third and on the fourth he added Andy's name to the end.

"Two or three..." Robbie said.

Andy looked at him hopefully.

"Years," Robbie said.

"Oh," Andy said.

His job prospects were clearly bleak and a sense of rising panic returned. It was then that he noticed the telephone on the desk.

"Would you mind if I made a call?" Andy asked.

"Be my guest," Robbie said.

Chapter Thirty-Seven

Andy's dad was at the end of the garden. He was suffering, he thought, a form of post traumatic stress. He'd begun putting together the shed with his new cordless drill. It had so much power it hurt his wrist. He was beginning to feel he'd been suckered into its purchase. But it was more a seduction. That was his other problem. Andy's mum had said, 'I've got something I want to show you.' He'd put down the drill and walked up to the house. And then it happened.

If he'd been on that game show 'Mr and Mrs', in which he was required to predict what his wife might do he would never, ever have guessed. Not if he'd had years to consider the question, and not if he'd been given clues of the most blatant nature. The woman had gone mad. He thought he was going to look at a drawing, or a water colour, or perhaps something she'd cooked. Or it might have been the new paintwork in the spare bedroom. Or something on the television. He'd even thought, for a moment, that something serious might have happened.

When Andy's dad had made it into the house he couldn't find her. She'd called from the bedroom, which was irritating as it meant he had to remove his boots. He still wasn't certain that he'd removed all the dog shit. The soles were very deep. He padded up to the bedroom. He wondered if there was a plumbing crisis in the ensuite. Although the words 'I've got something to show you' didn't quite suggest that. He was inclined to tell her that he didn't have time, he had work to do, but the more he dithered the slower the construction of the shed would be, and that would be a good thing. He didn't expect her to be lying naked on the bed.

"This," Andy's mum had announced. "Is my clitoris."

She'd been practicing the word for days and now it had just tripped off the tongue, which was an irony she was hoping Andy's dad would make less ironic. She'd had another coffee with Lydia, who was really quite animated on the subject, and these were her specific instructions. She was pleased with herself as each time she'd uttered the word she'd sort of swallowed the end of it, which was something else that might have been ironic. But she'd done it. She was buck naked and lying on the bed with her legs wide open. In that area the yoga had been most helpful and she was fairly certain she couldn't have parted her legs quite so far when she was a young girl. Lydia had also made an enquiry as to her topiary down below and it took some explaining before Andy's mum got the gist of her meaning. And, on Lydia's advice she'd taken a razor down there and with great care attempted a little tidying. But it was a bit high risk, as the focal point was awkward whether she had her glasses on or off, and it would have been a shame to damage something she'd so newly discovered.

The preparation for this moment had put her in quite an excited state, she couldn't help herself, and it might have been that that had stopped her thinking through the potential responses. Once she'd focused on the matter, and the advice that Lydia had so willingly offered, she didn't have room left to think about the consequences. Andy's dad had screamed. He'd run out of the house and into the garden nearly forgetting his boots. Next door's dog had crapped in the garden again and now it was all over his socks. He'd slipped and fallen over in a desperate bid to get away from his wife. He had to put his boots on without his socks as he daren't go back into the house. He could hear the telephone ringing, but he had no intention of answering it.

Andy's dad was shaking a little. He was attempting to trace, in his mind, recent events. It hadn't helped and now he was thinking about the previous thirty years and what might have gone wrong. In the Victorian era Andy's mum would have been sent to a sanatorium to deal with such madness, but he might be forced to deal with it on his own. Andy's dad was not equipped to do that. There wasn't a power tool available for such a problem. Although he was wrong about that, as Andy's mum discovered when Lydia took her on a shopping trip the following day.

Chapter Thirty-Eight

Andy dialled his parents' telephone number adding the international dialling code for the UK. He didn't hold out much hope, but a few seconds later he was greeted with a familiar British ringing tone. He hoped his parents were in. As far as he was aware they were always in these days. The familiar ringing tone rang a little longer and began to sound a lot less reassuring. Then his mother answered.

"Mum," Andy said.

"Andy, darling how are you?" his mother said.

Andy was about to explain that he wasn't very well at all, when his mother decided to unburden the thing that was mostly on her mind.

"Your father can be such a pig," she said.

"What?" Andy said.

His mother had never mentioned any marital difficulties to him before, but now that he was a self sufficient adult, she thought it was a good time to start.

"I mean," his mother said. "I have needs too."

"The thing is mum," Andy began to say, but the revelation that his mother had needs halted him in his tracks.

"It's not too much to ask at my time of life," his mother continued.

Now that Andy's mother had given herself some time to process what had happened with Andy's dad, she was feeling a mixture of anger, guilt and embarrassment.

"Isn't it?" Andy asked.

What Andy was attempting to tell her, aside from his predicament, was that he had no views on the subject and not that she should have her needs, whatever they were, and he really didn't want to speculate, met.

"This is the twenty-first century, Andy," his mother said.

Lydia had been quite specific about standing up for her rights. Most specifically the right to an orgasm. Andy's mum had been so happy she'd located her clitoris, as if it were Lord Lucan, that she hadn't thought how Andy's dad might react. Initially he hadn't said anything, but there seemed to be a rasping noise coming from his throat which might suggest he was suffocating. He certainly went pale as if a heart attack wasn't so far away.

"And your father's left me," she finally said.

Andy couldn't believe it. His parents had been a paragon of stability all his life. They operated as a pair. They even finished off each other's sentences. Now that he thought about that, it wasn't quite true. His mother sometimes finished his father's sentences, but not by saying what he had intended to say. But this was so shocking it made Andy forget the purpose of his call for a second.

"That's terrible, mum," Andy said.

"I know," his mother said and then, because she thought she was talking to an adult and not her son, she added. "An orgasm is not too much to ask."

It was Andy's turn to make noises which might suggest he was suffocating, as he'd just heard a word coming out of his mother's lips which had no place being there, in his view. If this was the twenty-first century, he was all for a return to the nineteenth.

"Where's he gone?" Andy asked reasonably.

"Who?" his mother said, as she was thinking about something else Lydia had said.

"Dad," Andy said. "Where's dad gone?"

Andy's mum couldn't help replaying the whole event in her mind and thinking about the collection of emotions which were gripping her. It was very distracting for her and, on balance, embarrassment was the most overwhelming.

"Oh, your father," his mother said. "He's gone down to the end of the garden."

This confused Andy even further and, given the things his mother had just said, he couldn't be certain that 'going down the end of the garden' wasn't a metaphor for something. Although, he thought, if it were and he *had* gone to the end of the garden, she probably wouldn't be complaining.

"I thought you said he'd left?" Andy said.

Andy's father was at the end of the garden with the rhubarb trying to get some 'fucking peace'. If the pursuit of the orgasm was new for Andy's mother, his father now took pleasure in regularly deploying the word 'fucking'. His mother's issue, and she'd pointed it out, was that he only ever used the word as an adjective and not, as she'd hoped, a verb.

"Shall I get him?" his mother said.

"Listen," Andy said. "I'm in a lot of trouble and I need your help. It's not my fault. I haven't done anything wrong, but I've been kidnapped and I'm in Africa. It's a country called Lobo. I don't have any money or a passport. I need you to come and get me," Andy pleaded.

But there was no response from his mother who had evidently gone down to the end of the garden to fetch Andy's father. She found him attempting to hack down the rhubarb.

"What are you doing?" she asked.

"I fucking never liked rhubarb," he said.

He wished, after he'd said it, that he'd put the 'fucking' before the rhubarb and not the 'never'. He'd have to work harder at this.

"But you love my crumble," Andy's mother said.

Andy's father turned round and stood tall.

"I've fucking never liked your crumble," he said and then a little red faced, and clearly angry with himself, he said, "damn, I've never liked your fucking crumble."

It was a much more satisfactory sentence and he turned back to hacking down the offending rhubarb. Andy's mother couldn't believe it. She'd been making it all these years, sometimes as a special treat.

"But I've made it for years," Andy's mother said.

The annoying thing was that she didn't much like rhubarb either. She'd only made it because she thought he liked it. If they hadn't been honest about that, what else was there? She'd have to speak to Lydia about the crumble. It might be relevant and Lydia was capable of finding relevance in nearly everything.

"My crumble," Andy's Mum said, a little distraught.

She knew the crumble must be a metaphor for something, but she couldn't figure it out, and there was something else tugging at her. What was it? Then she remembered.

"Andy's on the phone," she said.

Andy's Dad knew he was safe in the house if Andy was on the phone. He might even have to keep him on the line until his wife went off the boil, or whatever it was that was wrong with her. It was annoying to discover, once he'd finally made it to the phone, that Andy was no longer on the line.

Chapter Thirty-Nine

When Ali woke up her head was pounding. It was pounding with the alcohol and the beat of the music from the previous evening. Her feet were hurting too. But it had been a fun evening. She looked around for an indication of the time and eventually found it on her phone.

"Bloody hell," Ali muttered.

It was late. Andy hadn't called. She felt too tired to deal with that. She needed to get up. She believed that a self imposed health issue, such as a hangover, should not be an impediment for going to work. She pulled herself up. It was as if someone had slapped her on the forehead. Or the shots were shooting back. She staggered to the bathroom and began repair work. It took a while and eventually she made it to the coffee shop next to the hotel, which had become their meeting place. She had no idea whether anyone else would be there, but she was in dire, medical need of a coffee or two. Jess was already there.

"Hey," Ali greeted her.

"That was a messy evening," Jess said.

"Have you been here long?" Ali asked.

"No, just got here. It was a bit of a struggle," Jess admitted.

They ordered some large-volume coffees and sat in unusually peaceful silence. They looked a little shellshocked. They watched as cabs flew by.

"It was a good evening," Jess said eventually.

"Tony's quite the dancer," Ali said.

"Funny isn't it?" Jess said. "You think you know someone, but they have this other side to them."

"The disco diva," Ali said.

"The shots certainly got to Doris," Jess said.

"Daphne," Ali said.

"Who'd have known she was a big old bosomy thing who liked to let her hair down?" Jess said.

"I'm not sure she knew either," Ali said.

"Still, she's in safe hands with Tony," Jess said.

"Maybe she doesn't want to be in safe hands," Ali said.

Neither of them had given Daphne much thought before and it was hard to picture her involved in any kind of wildness.

"What are we supposed to be doing today?" Jess asked.

It was a measure of how seriously, or rather not seriously, they took Miles that neither could remember or care.

"No idea. Drink coffee until our hands shake. Go and see the sights," Ali said.

"We could phone Miles and ask him," Jess said.

"We could," Ali agreed.

They both knew they had no intention of calling Miles. If he needed them he'd call, and he'd talked about the trip being a bit of a holiday.

"Have you seen them yet?" Ali asked.

"Who?" Jess asked.

"Tony and thingy?"

"Daphne," Jess said.

"Yes," Ali said stirring her coffee.

"No," Jess said.

"I can't really remember how the evening ended," Ali admitted.

"Me neither," Jess said.

They looked out as the sun found a space through the clouds and the skyscrapers to strike their hungover faces.

"You do look rough," Jess said, laughing.

"I bloody feel it," Ali said.

They had somehow managed to pull through the bitchiness. It was as if drinking a dozen shots to pounding music was a more satisfactory way of getting to know someone, or establishing hierarchy, or whatever it was that had happened to them.

"Hold on," Jess said. "Look who's coming."

They watched as Tony and Daphne approached. There was something different. It was hard to say what but it looked like a new familiarity.

"Jesus Christ," Jess said. "You don't think..."

"No. Tony's gay. Isn't he?" Ali said.

Chapter Forty

Andy had often found the mindless tune that was inflicted on him, when he had to make a telephone enquiry, to be the most infuriating thing in the world. But silence was a bit unnerving. His only connection with the other side of the world, and the possibility of being saved from the hell that he found himself in, was the tenuous electronic line he was holding on to. It seemed suspiciously silent. After five minutes he knew something was wrong and it had nothing to do with his father at the end of the garden. He shook the phone. Robbie looked up at him.

"I think we've been cut off," Andy said.

Robbie leaned over and picked up another phone. He shook it.

"The exchange is down," he announced.

"How long will it be down for?" Andy asked.

Robbie shrugged his shoulders. In the few minutes since their interview the swear patches under his armpits had grown a few more inches.

"Not long," he said. "Three or four..."

Andy choked. Not again, he thought.

"Days?" Andy said.

"No. Hours," Robbie said. "What do you take us for?"

Andy went out into the sunshine. It was still early, but the temperature was ramping up already. He found some shade under a tree and sat there for a while. Three or four hours, he told himself, wasn't too bad. He could manage that. He watched the people walking by. There were a few men in suits and women in smart dresses, but most people wore jeans and tee-shirts, and it could almost be a street in Hackney. He was surprised how much he missed Hackney. He missed a level of normality. Here it was hard to figure how what was normal and what wasn't. A man walked up to him. He stood in front of him. Andy didn't know what to do.

"Hello," the man said.

"Hello," Andy said cautiously.

The man put his hand out.

"My name," he said, "is Hamish."

Andy looked at him doubtfully. He'd been to Scotland, the land of the fair complexion and red hair, and he'd met a few Hamishs. But none had ever looked like this man. He was a black man, as was everyone else around him, but the others were shades of brown. His skin was black. It didn't appear to reflect light. But his teeth were radiant in their whiteness. He was, Andy thought, a human lighthouse.

"Andy," Andy said, shaking his hand.

"You're not from round these parts," Hamish correctly observed.

Andy stopped thinking about Scotland and was reminded of a pub he'd once entered on the moors in Cornwall. He was lost and the pub was remote. He was fairly sure it had pagan symbols on the wall. And someone had said, "you're not from round these parts."

"No," Andy confirmed.

Andy had grabbed a quick pint in that Cornish pub and left. He had no idea that it was a game that the locals played for their amusement to scare tourists. They'd laughed like hyenas on gas and air when he'd left. If the landlord had heard he'd have given them a hard time.

"Were you in the job centre?" Hamish asked.

"I was," Andy said, his mind back in Lobo.

"How did it go?" Hamish asked.

"Not well," Andy confirmed.

"Robbie only has the one job," Hamish said. "Street sweeper."

"I'm on the list," Andy said.

Hamish laughed as if it were the funniest thing he'd ever heard. It was a proper belly laugh and quite infectious. He stopped in an instant.

"You want a job?" the man said.

He stepped even closer to Andy, as if he were telling him a secret. Andy wondered if social convention regarding personal space was different in Lobo. He noticed Hamish's tee-shirt which said 'shit happens'. Andy couldn't disagree.

"You've got a job?" Andy asked.

"I have," Hamish said. "I employ people."

It seemed unlikely, although Andy should have been used to the unlikely. He looked again at Hamish's teeshirt. He wasn't sure he found the message reassuring. Did he need a job or could he wait until he'd spoken to his parents?

“Yes, maybe,” Andy said. “I just need to make a call when the exchange is back on.”

Hamish nodded, digesting this information. Andy suspected he knew something he didn’t, but he didn’t want to get into any more trouble. He’d had a good year at work. He was only one step away from the chief creative and his salary was pretty good. He could pay his parents back and he was beginning not to care what it cost.

“Okay,” Hamish said. There is a basement bar at the end of the street called ‘Hell and High Water’. Ask for me there.”

Andy watched Hamish saunter off in the direction of the bar. He walked like everyone else. As if he didn’t have a care in the world. Half an hour later Robbie stuck his head out of the door and called him.

“Andy! It’s on.”

Chapter Forty-One

If something had happened between Tony and Daphne no one was saying, although neither looked quite as hungover as Ali and Jess. Jess was about to enquire when Miles turned up.

"Are you guys ready for lunch?" Miles asked.

They looked at each other, a little surprised that lunch had arrived so rapidly after breakfast.

"Hey, why not?" Jess said.

Miles nodded. He looked a little uncertain, which was unusual for him, but they didn't particularly notice.

"I know a place," Miles said.

Miles didn't really know a place, but he prided himself on being the kind of man who knew places and he'd found an Italian, which looked family owned, and not excessively expensive.

"This way," Miles said.

They followed him until they found themselves at a place which looked a little familiar to Ali.

"Isn't this a chain?" Ali said.

"I don't think so," Miles said.

"Yes, I think so," Jess said. "Isn't there one in Tooting?"

"I don't know," Ali said. "I live in Hackney."

"Well, whatever. It looks nice," Miles said.

They looked at each other and wondered if this was an admission that he didn't know a place at all.

"It doesn't matter," Jess whispered. "They sell wine."

Ali checked the time. It *was* lunch time.

"Hair of the dog," Jess muttered.

Miles made a bit of a performance finding a table, as if having a good table was compensation for eating in a chain outlet, which was only one step away from serving pizzas. He could be quite snobbish about these things and he was committed to the place now. He had a quick glance at the menu. At least it wasn't going to cost him an arm and a leg.

"We need to talk strategy," Miles said grandly.

The thought made Ali's head pound, but fortunately Jess had a solution.

"Shouldn't we order the wine first?" Jess said.

Miles agreed and allowed Jess to order some house wine, which he was pathologically incapable of doing. He took a glass of red and tasted it. It had that plebeian quality, which he didn't believe in, but which he frequently drank at home where no one could witness him, and which he found perfectly acceptable.

"Are you all enjoying New York?" Miles asked.

"Yes, it's great," Jess said and topped her glass up.

They waited for Miles to say something, sensing that he had something significant to say, but he mumbled a bit and looked at the menu. He paused every now and again to ask them if they were liking New York and they began to eat and, as he had no objection, order more bottles of wine.

"Jemima should be here soon," Miles said.

He said that a couple of times until eventually he went outside to call her.

"What's this about?" Jess asked.

Everyone shrugged apart from Daphne who went back to looking at the floor.

"I wouldn't mind working with Jemima," Ali said.

They looked at her.

"I wouldn't mind Jemima," Tony said.

"Yeah, right," Jess said. "As if she's your thing."

"He's not gay," Daphne said.

They looked up and Daphne turned a beetroot red.

"Well, well," Jess said, but Miles reappeared and stopped her from saying anymore.

"She's on her way," Miles said.

Chapter Forty-Two

"It turns out," Andy's mum said to Lydia, holding back tears, "he never liked my crumble."

They were in the new fashionable coffee shop in which Andy's mum had ordered a skinny latte, now fully aware of what to expect.

"Not liking your crumble. That's terrible," Lydia said, adding, "an orgasm is just a basic right. A fundamental right."

Andy's Mum looked a little confused. Lydia had a way of steering everything back to a basic right to an orgasm. While she didn't disagree, she clearly hadn't made herself clear.

"I was talking about my rhubarb crumble," she said.

They were sitting half inside and half outside in what had become their usual table. Andy's mother looked closely at Lydia. She had to be about the same age, but she was what Andy's mum called 'glamorous'. She wore her furiously dyed hair long and she displayed alarming amounts of cleavage. And she was confident.

"I think him not liking your crumble is where the problems lies," Lydia said wryly.

Lydia liked to refer to herself as a feminist and had very clear views about the empowerment of women. She had a small column in a woman's magazine and had made a habit over the years of using the words 'feminist' and 'empowered' in every article she wrote. She was also big on metaphors.

"No, I don't think so. I think he said he doesn't like rhubarb," Andy's Mum said, who wasn't big on metaphors.

Lydia had only hung out, which was a word she liked to use often, with Andy's Mum because she was doing an article on thoroughly unliberated women imprisoned by convention. The article had been cancelled, but she was continuing to see Andy's Mum as an anthropological exercise. There were moments when it could be a little painful and she had to explain everything.

"No, love," Lydia said. "You have to ask what makes your husband's cookie crumble."

As she had replaced one metaphor with another, Andy's Mum was none the wiser. Her face looked distressingly blank.

"Okay," Lydia said. "What *kind* of crumble does your husband like?"

This was completely baffling to Andy's Mum, but she felt she should hazard a guess as she wasn't making much of a contribution to the conversation.

"Apple?" Andy's Mum suggested.

Lydia would have looked to the sky in despair, but she knew that this conversation was likely to be the basis for something she was going to write and, for a second, she thought about the most erotic fruit. Then she said what she was thinking.

"Homo," Lydia muttered.

But Andy's Mum's thinking was so far away she remained confused and, at the same time, she felt a little patronised.

"Well, we're all Homo sapiens," Andy's Mum said.

The worst thing was that Andy's mum would have felt patronised all the time in the company of Lydia if she understood more of what she said. But Andy's mum knew she was very far past several flushes of youth, and some of the things that Lydia said struck a chord with her. Not least the business of orgasms. She remembered liking sex when she'd first encountered it, but recently it had dried up, while she felt she hadn't. Worse, she wasn't a hundred percent sure, particularly now she'd read a few articles from Lydia's magazine, whether she'd actually experienced one. She knew the light was going out on this one unless her husband got a bloody move on. It wasn't that much to ask.

"No," Lydia said. "I meant as in sexual."

It took a moment for Andy's Mum to connect the Homo of Lydia's previous comment with the sexual of this one. And she was horrified.

Chapter Forty-Three

Andy couldn't believe his parents. Where the hell were they? The phone had rung and rung and no one had answered. Every single time he had ever called them they were, absolutely without fail, at home. But not this time. Why hadn't he said something when she'd started talking about her needs? He felt embarrassed just thinking about it. He couldn't believe his mother had uttered the word 'orgasm'.

"They're not in," Andy said.

Robbie smiled. There was no reason to smile, but he was a nice man used to telling people that he didn't have the job they required, and keen to reassure them that everything will be alright.

"I'll try them later," Andy said and Robbie smiled again.

Andy went back to the same spot under the tree and wondered what he was going to do next. He knew his parents didn't have a holiday planned. His mother would have told him long before the scheduled trip, as she always did, and he would be given a breakdown. That was before the holiday. They'd once gone to Sardinia and his mother had described each fellow guest down to every minutiae of unnecessary detail. It included their appearance, their work, and the dynamics of their personal relationships. His parents weren't on holiday. They must have gone shopping.

His father hated shopping, but his mother didn't like driving. Fortunately their little town in Surrey had flourished and there were plenty of new places she could walk to, but the big supermarket was too far, and there were too many bags. He'd often thought that the supermarket shop was testing their relationship far enough without his mother's new-found 'needs'. It made him shudder despite the huge temperature. He tried to work out how long they'd be. It depended on which supermarket they went to. His mother would probably want to go to the posh one and his father to the cheap one. Either way they wouldn't be back for at least an hour, probably an hour and a half. He didn't want to use up all his calls. Andy decided to go for a walk.

Aside from the palm trees and heat, there were things that were very familiar and very alien about this little town. The similarities of human life were reassuring. He arrived at a fork. To one side the road widened and the shops were larger and more like those he'd seen in Dalston Lane in Hackney, to the other the road narrowed, like a Moroccan bazaar, and the shops were small and boutique-like. But, as there were no tourists, they contained food and clothes. Both were bright in colour and the place was alive with spicy smells. He could almost have been on holiday with Ali. It prompted a thought.

He had only the vaguest of ideas of where he was, but he knew it was in Africa and he knew it was hot.

Very hot. He also knew he'd arrived there by aeroplane. They had a runway. Perhaps he could be employed to bring in tourism. He'd have to get a cheap carrier to land there but, if they weren't too far south, it might not be so far from the south of Spain. He walked into a clothing shop trying to figure out how he could convince someone and get them to pay for his flight back.

"What are you doing here?" a voice said.

Andy looked up. It was Fullbush. Her arms were folded across her chest and she stood defiantly. He hadn't noticed that she was as tall as him, but then they'd been lying down.

"I was taking a look," Andy said innocently.

She turned away to suggest he wasn't welcome. Breakfast was beginning to feel quite a long time ago and Andy was feeling hungry again. Although hunger was never that far from his thoughts. Ali frequently commented on it. He was about to walk out when he decided he'd have one more go at talking to her. He had nothing to lose.

"I was given some sort of drug," Andy explained. "And someone kidnapped me."

Fullbush flinched. It was just a small tug at her shoulder. It wasn't quite acquiescence, but Andy felt it was a step in the right direction.

"And someone hit me in the stomach," he said.

She turned her head slightly. She focused her eyes on him.

"Then they hit me in the face," Andy said.

He pointed to the bruise. Fullbush hadn't noticed it before. She'd never actually seen a white man, in the flesh, before. She'd seen Tom Cruise and Brad Pitt, but only on a screen. Close up white people seemed to be a slightly strange colour. A colour, she couldn't help noticing, that didn't equip them for the sun. Andy had turned a strange pink hue.

"And then they put a bag over my head and threw me in a plane," Andy said.

Fullbush had turned her body round. She was beginning to feel sympathetic.

"And they hit me again," Andy said.

He pointed to a different part of his face, but his brief acquaintance with the sun on his walk along the road, had provided new colour which had disguised his injuries. He had more to say.

"I don't know where I am and I don't have any money or a passport."

Fullbush's demeanour had returned to when he'd first met her. Except he couldn't quite remember when he'd first met her. His mind had been walking in fields of gooseberries or something. It was something in the banana. He was going to be psychologically afflicted by bananas for the rest of his life.

"What are you going to do?" Fullbush asked.

"I've been trying to call my parents, but they seem to be out," he said.

As he said it he noticed the telephone that lay on the counter. It was next to the credit card machine. His eyes fell on the credit card machine first, dispelling his image of third world Africa. But an hour and a half had passed by since he'd phoned his parents last.

"Do you mind if I make a call?" Andy said pointing at the phone.

Chapter Forty-Four

Ali had slowed down her drinking and was hoping to curl up in bed early. The afternoon had stretched out and met the early evening and they'd moved from the restaurant to a piano bar which Miles said he knew, but had actually googled.

"Any sign of Jemima?" Ali asked.

"She can be difficult to pin down," Miles said.

"I've noticed," Jess said with some sarcasm.

It was a shame, as they were all looking forward to meeting her and seeing her at close quarters. Jemima was a woman who prompted crushes in everyone who met her. And Ali was balancing the excitement of really meeting her against the exhaustion, and need for an early night.

"I'll go and get her," Miles said finally and got up.

It left them on their own again and the dynamics had shifted.

"Will we be dancing later, Tony?" Jess asked.

The revelation that Tony may have had sex with Daphne was tormenting Jess. When she'd thought Tony was gay she wasn't remotely interested in him, but now that there was news to suggest otherwise, she'd changed her mind.

"Maybe," Tony said.

A little part of Jess was offended that Tony had chosen Daphne over her, even though she'd been very dismissive. This attitude and the obvious advances she was making to Tony were not being well received by Daphne.

"I think there's dancing at the back," Ali pointed.

She was winding them up. Ali was pleased she had no interest in chatting up, dancing or any part of the mating ritual. She was done with that. She just wished that Andy would call. She wondered if she was asking too much of him. If he wasn't ready for the business of marriage.

"Shouldn't we wait for Jemima?" Daphne said.

Daphne didn't want to admit it but the last time she'd had sex, prior to the previous evening, although it might have been morning, was around six years earlier. And it hadn't been that good.

"I think they may have something important to tell us," Daphne added.

But Tony had unleashed something in Daphne which had made her decide that she was going to do it again with Tony if she had to kidnap him and handcuff him to the bed.

"And we should wait," Daphne said.

It had a whiff of desperation about it and Jess was no stranger to that. She was going to exploit it as if Daphne was a vixen cornered by hounds.

"Oh, I don't think they'll have too much difficulty finding us," Jess said and got up.

As Tony had been derided for some while and his sexuality questioned, he was enjoying himself. He knew he was going to have sex with someone that evening and he wasn't often presented with a choice.

"Let's go," Jess said and grabbed Tony's hand.

She pulled him up and led him in the direction of the dance floor, although Tony wasn't an unwilling victim. It left Daphne glaring at the table.

"Aren't you going?" Ali asked.

Daphne scowled a little more. She didn't know what to say. The previous evening had made her feel so good and now she couldn't feel any worse.

"I don't want to compete with Jess," Daphne finally managed to say.

What she really meant to say was that she couldn't compete with Jess. Although she did have something further to say.

"She's a cow, that Jess."

Ali smiled. It seemed strange coming out of the lips of the ordinarily mild Daphne, but Jess was ruining her evening.

"She can be," Ali said. "You have to give it back to her. Don't take any shit."

This didn't really help Daphne. Ali sighed and got up.

"Come on," she said to Daphne. "Let's go and dance."

Ali led her to the dance floor and Daphne began to dance, a little haphazardly at first, and then she found her groove. Tony smiled and took her hand prompting black clouds on Jess's face, who'd forgotten she'd also been a bit of a cow to Tony. Tony moved between Jess and Daphne convincing Ali that he was protesting too much and unquestionably gay, whatever might have happened with Daphne. It wasn't long before it was generally agreed that the evening could only be improved by a round of shots, and Ali only agreed so that she could get through the next hour, and then go to bed. But that's not how her evening went.

Chapter Forty-Five

"I'm fucking going to the pub," Andy's Dad said and then, as an afterthought, "Damn. I'm going to the fucking pub."

Andy's Dad had worked in the bank almost all his life. He was of the generation that could start in the post room and make it to the boardroom. He didn't quite manage that, but he became branch manager and stayed there until the awkward talk that terminated his work life. What he didn't do, not once, was swear. He'd never heard his parents swear, nor anyone at the bank, and had been encouraged to believe that swearing was just a limitation of his vocabulary. Well, Andy's Dad thought, fuck that.

He'd watched Pulp Fiction and winced as they attacked his language with more foul words than simple verbs, nouns and adjectives. And it hadn't encouraged him to swear. Far from it. He'd believed in the purity of language, expressed with clarity and conveying a clear message. When the Labour MP got in and the local council was swayed to the left, something which was abhorrent to him, he didn't utter a single obscenity. But two things had changed.

The first was retirement. His ruminations at the end of the garden, and his impulsive attack of the rhubarb, had made him think. Rather than open the doors to all the things he could do, it had revealed all the things he didn't want to do. He'd wanted peace, and his life in the bank had been, he realised now, quite peaceful. It gave him a timetable to work to, which he liked. But that wasn't the main issue. Retirement involved spending a lot of his time with his wife and she was driving him crazy. And that was before she'd met Lydia. Andy's Dad hadn't even met Lydia, but he had strong views about what kind of a woman she was, and none of those views were charitable. Then there were the things that she'd put into his wife's head. The woman had become obsessed with sex and wouldn't even let him hide at the bottom of the garden. She'd even said something that Lydia had said about 'alfresco'. It took a few minutes for him to mine his vocabulary, as he often mistook the word with the thing about cooking pasta. Then he realised she meant outdoors. And then he realised she meant sex outdoors. That was the reason he was off to the pub. He was pretty sure that Lydia didn't have any ideas about sex in a pub.

The problem was that Andy's Dad had never really been a pub man before. He liked the occasional glass of wine and the odd half, but he'd never propped up a bar and chatted to people he didn't know. The idea sounded ghastly to him, but it was preferable to staying at home while his wife was in this mood.

Despite living in the same house for the last thirty-two years he got lost on the way to the pub, which wasn't where he'd expected it to be. When he got there he found other late middle aged men like himself, but none of them were drinking small glasses of white wine. They weren't drinking halves either and, as far as he could see they weren't drinking lager. He knew that in order to regularly hide from his wife in the pub he would have to fit in.

He looked around and found it was a more pleasant place than the slightly dour exterior had promised, as if he'd stepped into someone's front room. There was the remains of a fire burning in an old fireplace, which suggested the building was several hundred years old. It wasn't a bad place to escape.

"A pint of IPA," Andy's Dad said.

He'd seen people drink it before and it seemed the most innocuous. It arrived, and he paid for it, and took a few sips. It was hard to see what all the fuss was about. It was sort of watery and hoppy. He wished he'd ordered a glass of white wine. In the few times he had visited a pub he hadn't, as far as he could remember, sat at the bar. But there was a stool and it seemed right. He had a lot to think about. Not least what had fucking got into his wife? He rethought that: what had got into his fucking wife?

It was simple really. The 'fucking' was an adjective, and therefore should be describing the noun and not the verb. He had to remember that in the future, as he intended to swear a lot more in retirement. Then it occurred to him that 'fucking' could also be an adverb. Then he realised that none of this was helping him, and there was nothing simple about the problems he was having with his wife. Perhaps she was just going through a phase and she'd come out the other end. That was a reassuring thought which had made the IPA far more palatable.

"Are you alright mate? Why the long face?" someone next to him said.

Andy's Dad looked up. Remarkably, he'd nearly finished his pint, and ordered another without thinking as if it were the most natural thing in the world.

"Problems at home?" the man said.

Andy's Dad couldn't help noticing that the man spoke with an accent similar to his own. Despite his own modest origins he could be a bit of a snob. But that, and the effects of the first pint, gave him a little more ease than was normally his way.

"Exactly right," Andy's Dad said.

"Wife not giving out?" someone along the bar said and the others chuckled.

Andy's Dad didn't want to admit that the problem was the opposite of that.

Chapter Forty-Six

There was no reply. The phone rang the familiar British ringtone without interruption. Where the hell were his parents? What were they doing? Had they actually broken up? They'd bickered a bit, but not that much. For the first time Andy compared his own relationship with Ali to his parents. It seemed calmer. Was that right? Shouldn't it be the other way round?

"No answer?" Fullbush said.

Andy shook his head. He'd have to try later. He knew there was no possibility that his parents would go out in the evening. They'd be watching television. Or his mother would be watching Poldark and his father would be reading the paper pretending not to. His grasp of the plot was far too extensive to suggest he didn't follow it.

"No. I'll have to try later," Andy said.

He wondered what he'd do if he couldn't contact his parents. There was always a possibility that their phone line was broken. Would they notice? He didn't know. Then a thought occurred to him.

"Do you know a bar called 'Hell and High Water'?" he asked.

"Of course," she said. "Why?"

"I said I might meet someone there later," he said.

Fullbush thought about this. She was still slightly irritated that he had a girlfriend, but she felt sorry for him too.

"Someone?" she asked.

"A man," Andy said, adding brightly, "you could come too."

Fullbush gave this some thought when a customer came in. She turned and served the older woman, who looked at Andy suspiciously. Andy smiled back. It occurred to him that he'd just invited Fullbush for a drink with no means to pay for it. The woman left without buying anything.

"But I don't have any money," Andy said.

Fullbush sighed. She was a girl torn between doing the right thing and having a wild time. There weren't a huge number of opportunities to have a wild time in Lobo and she had attended every rave that Barry junior had put on. She was well known in Hell and High Water and she was thinking of going there anyway.

"Okay," she said finally. "I finish in an hour."

Andy looked at the clock on the wall. Most of the day had drifted by and somehow his parents had managed to spend it somewhere other than their home. He knew they'd be in by the evening. They had to be.

"I'll have a walk around," Andy said.

He walked through the bazaar and back onto the Main Street. Lobo was a friendly place. It didn't seem dangerous. It was just several thousand miles from Hackney. He wondered what Ali was up to. He imagined she was working late and preparing for the challenges of the following day. That was the way she'd always been, studious and focused. She wouldn't be up drinking and partying, he thought.

An hour later Andy returned to the shop to find Fullbush waiting outside. She'd changed her clothes and she looked, Andy couldn't help noticing, sensational. She had a good relationship with the owner of the shop and frequently borrowed clothes but, as she was a good advertisement for the shop, the owner didn't mind. She'd given it some thought and had clearly decided against the demure.

"Wow, you look great," Andy said.

Fullbush smiled and she took his hand and placed it in the crook of her elbow. It was possessive and chaste at the same time. She led him in the direction of Hell and High Water unsure where the evening would lead. She hoped it didn't get to the Jaeger bomb stage, as she tended to let go of the chaste when that happened.

Chapter Forty-Seven

There was something oddly dated about a strobe light in a club and it was just a further reminder that Ali had had enough. She was exhausted and ready to go to bed, although she'd felt that way for a couple of hours. She'd become separated from the others and was grateful for it. She could get back to her hotel room without feeling defeated by the evening. Another flash lit up the room and Ali focused on the exit. It was followed by darkness and she moved quickly through the flock of people gyrating to music she didn't find very musical. It was the next flash that diverted her attention. It wasn't the flash, but someone it lit up who seemed to be shining more brightly than the others. Jemima.

Ali froze. She wasn't a hundred per cent sure it was her. It was like a sighting of a rare bird with unusual plumage, but which could look like other birds from certain angles. She had to be certain. For some reason the frequency of the strobe light had been slowed down and she had to wait an age for the light. In the next flash she couldn't see her. She must have been imagining it. Ali resumed her stagger to the exit, but she stopped in her tracks on the next flash. It was Jemima. She was the other side of the room and Ali couldn't be certain whether she was looking at her, or concentrating on someone else. She steadied herself.

On the one hand she didn't want to interrupt her. Their initial 'you've got to be kidding' meeting hadn't exactly set them off on the right foot, and if Jemima was in the middle of something crucial, or intimate, that might make it awkward. But she didn't want to miss her either. Ali changed direction. She was beginning to find the lighting a little irritating and when she next got a clear view of the black-painted room she was disappointed not to see Jemima. Perhaps Jemima was avoiding her. She couldn't blame her. She altered her course again.

Ali knew how conflicted her feelings were. She wanted a domestic life with Andy, but she was also seduced by the alive nature of the New York work environment. She wondered if she had it in her to become one of those elite English editors on a glamorous magazine and leading an influential celebrity-laced lifestyle. Would walking away from Andy be the casualty of that ambition? The thought gave her an actual physical pain. And then - bang - there she was. Jemima was only ten feet away and now Ali was certain she was looking at her. And smiling. It was as if the sun had come out. Her heart jumped. If she'd thought about that she'd have known that it was, at the very least, strange. But she was in the middle of a heart jumping moment and all rational thought had found the exit and left the room. Then she was plunged into darkness. When the light came back Jemima wasn't there.

"Hey," Jemima said.

Jemima had brushed her body against Ali's and effortlessly taken her hand. Jemima's hand was oddly cold and, when she stood close to her and kissed her cheeks as if they were the oldest of friends, Ali felt it was the most normal thing in the world. And in a second her exhaustion vanished. Ali was ready to dance the night away and, it seemed, so was Jemima who pulled her into a crowd and twirled her and held her all at the same time. The lighting changed and they exchanged looks and Ali felt a real connection.

Chapter Forty-Eight

Andy's Dad was staggering back from the pub and it was bringing about a number of firsts. He had never publicly urinated and yet, despite not having required a piss while he was actually in the pub, he had now pissed on every crossroads on his return journey. He didn't have a choice. The stuff was most insistent that it leave his body. Public urination was better than a huge wet patch on his trousers, but it was a bit humiliating. He'd lost count of the number of pints, but it hadn't been that cheap. He was certainly pretty pissed. He stopped again and unzipped himself. A massive stream bounced off a street light until it occurred to him that it had electricity running through it, and he pointed it at a dustbin. It didn't seem to stop. Then a few of the things he'd said came back to him.

"Oh dear God," Andy's Dad muttered.

He couldn't believe he'd said it. But everyone seemed pretty free with their own revelations and he chipped in his own. It had brought about a bit of a pause. The flow of the conversation came to a halt like a nineteen seventies power cut.

"So your wife is desperate for it?" someone had said.

He was one of the less educated ones, but Andy's Dad could tell it had struck a chord with the others. The banter had run through various themes including areas he knew nothing about, but was more comfortable with, such as football and the motorbike

Grand Prix. He attempted to make a mental note, although his note taking abilities were severely impaired, to look into it. But then someone had mentioned 'getting his leg over'. He'd fled to the pub to get away from such chat, but this was different. This was light-hearted, easy-going banter and for a second it had drifted off in the direction of a joke about a prostitute with one tit. He hadn't entirely understood the punchline, but he'd laughed along with the others.

"I wouldn't say desperate," Andy's Dad had said.

If Andy's Dad hadn't been so pissed he would have seen everyone exchange glances. He'd attempted to say it with a laughing tone with the light inference that Andy's mum was getting plenty from him. It wasn't true and he sensed the others didn't believe him. He tried to change the focus onto Lydia, or rather the things that Lydia had said to his wife. That had been a mistake.

"A right to an orgasm, you say?" another had said.

He really wished he hadn't. Worse, he'd carried on digging determined to put himself in the deepest hole of embarrassment he could manage.

"A basic human right," Andy's Dad had muttered a little less convincingly.

It was his attempt at banter, which meant it should have been batted back and fourth and then moved rapidly on. But they became a bit fixated by it.

"Her name's Lydia?" one of them asked.

For a second he feared that someone might know her or, worse still, be married to her, but thankfully that wasn't the case. They were keen to find out how they could meet her. That was clear.

"I could give her her basic right," someone had said.

"Where did you say you live?" someone else asked.

Andy's Dad had lost control of the conversation. He would have left, but someone had bought him a beer. They did so without asking, as if he'd been a local for years, but Andy's Dad was unable to celebrate this as the talk had become more lurid. This was a disaster, Andy's Dad had thought. Why had he opened his mouth? There was an inference that one of them was going to go round and 'service' his wife. That was the word they'd used. And Andy's Dad had become pretty indignant.

"I'll be the one doing the servicing," he'd roared.

It prompted more exchanged glances and a long pause. And then someone had said quietly, "I don't think that's going to happen."

Andy's Dad's eyes had opened wide, and someone had sensed the tension and taken the conversation in a slightly different direction.

"Man has a basic right to an orgasm too," someone had said.

"You're on your own on that one," someone else had said.

Prior to that evening Andy's Dad had used the word 'orgasm' no more than five times in his entire life, and heard it uttered not so many more, but in the following twenty minutes it had littered every sentence. He was fucking going to have to find another pub, he'd thought. He had to rethink that – he was going to have to find another fucking pub. A few minutes after that a bell had rung.

"One for the road?" someone had proposed.

Andy's Dad wasn't very familiar with the bell, or the last orders it was calling, and he'd very nearly fallen off his stool.

"Best not," he'd said.

He sensed he may have made a faux pas, but couldn't figure out what it was. Then he remembered that drinks were frequently purchased in rounds and, as he hadn't purchased any recently it must have been his turn.

"My round," Andy's Dad had said.

Twenty minutes later he had attempted to negotiate his way to the door. There seemed to be a lot of obstacles in the way, despite what he hoped looked like his expert weaving. He'd nearly got to the door when he'd heard a noise.

"Psst," a voice had said.

It was one of the men at the bar. He was older and had been fairly silent on the subject of orgasms.

"Yes?" Andy's Dad had said.

"Try these," the man had said and thrust a little strip of pills into his hand.

Andy's Dad had accepted them, as it was easier than stopping and asking, as he had been desperate to get out of the pub. Now that he was pissing on the dustbin, lit up by the lamppost, he took them out of his pocket to get a better look. They were blue. That rang a bell, but quite a distant one. He thrust them back into his pocket and staggered on in the direction of his house. A few minutes later he could see it at the end of the road. It was an ordinary house built in the sixties, but it sat in a big plot with a large front garden with mature trees. Some of the houses nearby had been purchased and instantly demolished and replaced with sizeable affairs with big porticos.

"Not far now," Andy's Dad muttered.

It wasn't far, but it was too far. He had to take another piss. As he did so he wondered about the pills. He took them out again and noticed that they had a large 'V' stamped out on the side. That rang a further distant bell. He zipped up and continued his journey. A minute later he staggered into his drive. It was large enough to accommodate a handful of cars and the newly built houses were filled with expensive machinery. Some of these people felt that his trusty old Rover let the neighbourhood down. He fumbled for his key.

"Damn," Andy's Dad muttered.

He realised he wasn't going to make it. He turned, opened his flies, and fired off an impressive stream over the roses. He hadn't noticed the front door open behind him.

"What are you doing?" Andy's Mum asked.

Chapter Forty-Nine

Andy felt a little proud of his association with Fullbush. As they walked through the streets at a gentle amble, people looked at them. They looked at him because he was not just a white man, but a ginger one with a medieval beard. They looked at her because she looked sensational. And then he felt just a little bit guilty. He had no intention of sleeping with her should the opportunity arise, even though a friend of his had always said 'what goes on tour' about such overseas adventures. But he'd have the guilt written all over his face when he got back to Hackney. Ali would know instantly. No that he had the slightest idea what Ali was up to.

But Andy was in Lobo and Fullbush had taken him to the end of the road and to a pair of doors which seemed to descend into the ground. This was Hell and High Water. As they went down he could feel the rumble of the bass, the volume of the noise increasing with every step. He wasn't sure if he should be excited or frightened. Fullbush seemed to be gripping him tighter and, when they pushed threw the final pair of doors, it was a little quieter and calmer than he'd anticipated. He bumped into someone.

"Sorry," Andy muttered instinctively.

It was dark and his eyes were struggling to adjust after the sunshine outside. She steered him towards a bar and hopped onto a stool. There were crisps in bowls on the bar. Andy was starving.

"Can I have some of them?" he asked.

"Of course," Fullbush said and nodded to the barman.

The barman nodded back and pointed to the other people he had to serve first. Andy picked up the bowl and offered the crisps to Fullbush.

"No thanks," she said.

Andy took one and said, "they're nice."

"They're not my thing," Fullbush said.

"Oh? Why not?" Andy asked casually.

Fullbush peered at them.

"I've never liked fried insect shells," she said.

Andy stopped mid crunch. He had a mouthful of them.

"Insects?" he said through a mouthful of insects.

"Can't stand them," she said.

Andy wasn't sure whether to spit them out or chew them. He was hungry. He just wasn't sure how hungry. He crunched and swallowed in a second and put the bowl back on the bar.

"Insects," he muttered.

"Not those," Fullbush said. "They're potato chips."

He looked at her. A trace of a smile ran across her face. Andy realised he'd been had. He smiled.

"Drink?" she said.

The barman had arrived.

"Sure," Andy said.

Fullbush nodded and a drink arrived. He hadn't been consulted as to its contents and picked it up warily. It had a golden brown colour.

"Lager," Fullbush said.

"Cheers," Andy said.

The lager tasted exactly like lager, which was reassuring. It even seemed to be delivered in units which looked suspiciously like a pint. It seemed so normal.

"Tell me about your life," Fullbush said.

"I live in London in a place called Hackney and I work in an advertising company," Andy said.

"So how did you get here?"

"I was kidnapped by a man called Barry," Andy said.

As he said it the music seemed to stop and a silence descended on them.

"Barry?" Fullbush said.

"Tall guy," Andy said.

He almost said a tall black guy but, as everyone was black, it seemed a little redundant.

"And he threw me in his plane," Andy said.

"Plane?" Fullbush said.

"Oh shit," the barman said.

"Oh shit," Fullbush said.

"Shit?" Andy asked.

"What happened when you landed?" the barman asked.

Andy tried to remember. What had happened? He'd been a bit groggy as he'd been punched rather more times than he was used to. Then he remembered.

"There was a brass band," he said.

"Were they bad?" the barman asked.

"Terrible," Andy confirmed.

"Oh shit," Fullbush and the barman said.

Chapter Fifty

Ali slammed the hotel door behind her.

"Fuck me," she said to herself.

The evening had not gone the way she thought it would. She was undoubtedly pretty pissed. She could feel the room moving around her and she didn't think it was an earthquake. There had been a kind of earthquake. Jemima had appeared. The woman was a whirlwind of energy and sass and sex. Her energy filled the room. She was the most charismatic person Ali had ever met.

"I like the products here," Jemima shouted from the bathroom.

Ali staggered forward and lent down to the minibar. Despite all the booze she'd consumed more booze was required. They were celebrating something, but the narrative of Jemima's life moved at such a pace she couldn't be sure what. She felt some movement behind her and then Jemima slapped her arse. Ali hit her head on the top of the fridge.

"I've found some more gin," Ali said.

She grabbed it and pulled herself upright and turned. Jemima was lying on the bed. Although, as the hotel was boutique or bijou or whatever the hell they called it, Ali thought, that was the only place to sit. Jemima appeared to be lying back seductively but, Ali reasoned, Jemima did everything seductively. It was her default setting. Ali found some glasses and shakily put the gin and tonic together. She stood up.

"Here," Ali said, and handed Jemima a glass.

"Cheers," Jemima said, and knocked back an alarming amount.

"Cheers," Ali said and sat primly the other end of the bed.

"Hold on a minute," Jemima said and threw open her bag.

Ali watched her as she mined for something. Despite Jemima's perfection, her handbag was as chaotic as everyone else's. Ali found that reassuring.

"I know what the moment calls for," Jemima said, still mining in her bag.

Ali had no idea what the moment called for. She was a passenger on a train and she had no idea what the destination might be. She hoped someone would tell her.

"Found it," Jemima announced.

Jemima sat up on the bed, looked around and grabbed the hotel's menu, which had a hard cover. Ali looked on a little bemused until Jemima removed something which looked suspiciously like talcum powder but, she was fairly certain, wasn't talcum powder at all. Jemima removed a credit card. Ali would have looked at the card with a measure of awe. She'd read about the card and the significant reserves of cash that were required to acquire one, but it was more the cocaine Jemima was cutting up with it which was getting her full attention.

"Great coke," Jemima muttered, a little mesmerised by the process.

Ali was panicking. She'd never done coke before and really didn't want to start. But she didn't want to look uncool either. This was peer pressure. She knew if Andy was here he'd try some, so what harm could it do? She watched as Jemima rolled up a fifty dollar note. Little lines had been arranged and all that was left was the business of inhalation.

"After you," Jemima said, offering it to Ali.

Ali didn't know what to do. She knew she had to come clean.

"I've never done cocaine before," Ali admitted. "You go first."

Jemima chuckled at Ali's naivety. This was New York, the Big Apple, who hadn't done coke? Jemima snorted it down like an industrial vacuum with clean filters and a fresh bag.

"Bang," Jemima muttered.

Bang was not a word that reassured Ali. She would have preferred something more along the lines of 'that's nice', as if she'd made a fresh cup of tea and she was, as the English say, gasping for a cuppa. Bang felt a lot more dangerous. Jemima passed the hotel menu and the fifty dollar note to Ali.

"Alright pet?" Jemima said.

The phrase, and the accent in which it was delivered, was a little jarring for Ali, and she had to get her head around it.

"Pet?" Ali said.

This was not the accent of the Roedean-educated, daddy's got an estate, kind. Jemima laughed.

"You're from Newcastle?" Ali asked.

"That's me," Jemima said, now in full Geordie.

"Oh," Ali said.

She wasn't sure if she was disappointed that Jemima wasn't the real thing or impressed that she could carry it off. It might have been a mixture of the two, as Ali's facilities were feeling distinctly impaired, and she'd yet to embark on the talcum powder that wasn't talcum powder.

"Go for it, girl," Jemima said.

Now that she'd reverted to her true Geordie, she looked a little different, as if the sheen had been taken off. Although three mojitos, four gin and tonics and a substantial line of coke was enough to remove the polish from the shiniest of jewels.

"Okay," Ali said.

She looked at the innocuous line of powder and wondered what would happen if she liked it too much. Could she become an addict? Would she spend all her money on this curious white substance? Worse, was this what was required to elevate her to Jemima status? Which, to clarify, was a little goddess like. Ali knew she couldn't dither any longer.

"Here we go," Ali managed to say.

Ali copied the same snorting noises, but more in the style of a ten year old domestic Hoover with clogged filters and a full bag. Quite a bit splattered across her face, but she managed to inhale enough of it to feel as if someone had gently lifted her up and put her down again. It was quite pleasant. Not so pleasant that she would need to sell the fridge, kitchen sink and hairdryer to get her hands on some, but pleasant enough.

"You got some on your face, pet," Jemima said moving forward.

And Jemima kissed her. Ali had kissed many women. She kissed most of her friends when she saw them. It was the modern way of greeting and she liked it. But this wasn't the same. It was the rather positive insertion of the tongue that made the difference. Ali pulled away. She was attracted to Jemima, but this wasn't what she had in mind.

"Fuck me," Ali said in shock.

"Yes please," Jemima said.

Chapter Fifty-One

"Well, if you're sure," Lydia said, letting out what felt like to Andy's mum a derisory plume of cigarette smoke.

Andy's mum couldn't believe it. They were discussing her husband's sexuality and, as far as she could see, Lydia was determined to find him wanting.

"There's nothing wrong with being gay," Lydia said.

Andy's mum couldn't quite bring herself to say 'gay'. She'd only just stopped thinking the word 'queer'. She also couldn't remember ever having had a conversation on the subject with her husband, which seemed a little odd, now that she thought about it. In a lifetime together it was likely that the matter would be broached at least once. Unless he was deliberately avoiding it.

"You heard about Ray, didn't you?" Lydia said.

Andy's mum hadn't heard about Ray, but she knew Lydia was going to tell her, and it wouldn't be good.

"Married thirty-two years, two kids and, when he was Sixty-one, he tells her he's gay. I saw him the other day. He has three different partners, one is only twenty-six and he's having the time of his life. He was wearing a nice flowery shirt, now I think about it," Lydia said.

Andy's mum froze. Had she mentioned that her husband quite liked flowery shirts? It's his only concession to flamboyance. In all other regards he's the most conservative man she knows. But that just means he's reserved. Apart from the shirts.

"Ray says it's the best thing he ever did. Now he can lead the life he's always wanted and he's packing it in," Lydia added.

Andy's mum tried to remember the first time she'd sex with her husband. It had been a little perfunctory, as they'd both been nervous. He seemed to want it quite a bit. That shows he's normal, doesn't it?

"Now Ray's at it like a bag of rattlesnakes. Like a stabbed rat. Like rabbits on viagra," Lydia said.

She would have carried on – the subject was amusing her, as was the evident discomfort – but a young man had walked past and caught her eye. There was a time when the eye catching would have been the other way round. A time when she could see eyes following her in her peripheral vision. When she knew all eyes in the room were on her. Lydia sighed and got back to it.

"It's not *will he* have sex today. It's with whom," Lydia said.

Andy's mum could never remember her husband being that rampant. People who worked in banks weren't, in her view. They just got on and provided for their families. But she couldn't help wondering whether he *should* be that rampant. What was normal? Did normal exist anymore?

"It's up to him to find his true nature," Lydia said.

Andy's mum was feeling very uncomfortable. Her journey with Lydia had been filled with embarrassing moments, the worst of which was the trip to the sex shop. She had no idea what she was required to do with the plastic battery-powered devices she came back with. That wasn't quite true. She had *some* idea, it just seemed a little sordid to her. She'd obviously shocked her husband.

"Of course you could always apply the ultimate implacable test," Lydia said.

Andy's mum had not the slightest idea what the ultimate implacable test was but, as she was with Lydia, she didn't have to ask. She'd tell her anyway.

"Dress up in the works. Stockings, suspenders, basque and high heels. No man can resist that," Lydia said and then added, "No heterosexual man."

Andy's mum didn't know what to say. Her husband had thought she'd gone a little mad when she'd highlighted her clitoris, and she had no idea what he might do if she suddenly appeared dressed up like a prostitute. He'd probably run down the road screaming.

"If he can't get a mighty boner, then that will settle it," Lydia said.

Andy's mum blushed. They'd gone from talking about her husband's sexuality to his erection. This was mortifying. She didn't know where to look. Fortunately she noticed that her skinny latte was getting cold – it hadn't been cheap – and she gulped it down.

“Anyway,” Lydia said. “Got to go, babe.”

Lydia got up, air kissed Andy’s mum, and crossed the street forcing cars to come to a halt and leaving Andy’s mum a little flabbergasted. She wondered if Lydia even knew her name. She thought through what they’d said, and the advice Lydia had provided, and what she should do with it. She was fairly sure she hadn’t uttered a single word in the whole conversation.

Chapter Fifty-Two

Andy turned round and for some reason Fullbush had disappeared. The barman was at the other end of the bar and he was alone with his lager. He turned round and found Hamish.

"Are you still looking for a job?" Hamish asked.

Andy had hoped he could contact his parents, but if that failed, he needed a fallback plan.

"Yes," Andy said.

"Good," Hamish said and pointed at his beer.

"Yes, please," Andy said.

Hamish nodded to the barman. Andy didn't notice the barman's uncomfortable look as he dumped the beer and scurried back to the other end of the bar as quickly as possible. He was a barman who was accustomed to recognising trouble.

"So what brought you to Lobo," Hamish asked.

Andy was reluctant to tell him about the plane and the brass band, as the last time it had cleared the bar.

"It's a complicated story," Andy said.

Hamish nodded, waiting for him to tell it.

"But I need to get back," Andy said, unsure if that would affect his job prospects.

"I might be able to help," Hamish said.

"Good," Andy said.

"Can you drive?" Hamish asked.

"Sure," Andy said.

It was a skill he'd forgotten to mention to Robbie. The was a reason for this. Although he'd passed his test over three years ago, he hadn't driven since. He reckoned he could bluff it. Although he'd have trouble navigating as he was perpetually lost.

"When can you start?" Hamish asked.

"Now," Andy said looking at the second pint.

Andy felt he ought to ask more questions, as he might in a normal interview.

"What are the hours?"

"The hours?" Hamish repeated. "Irregular."

"And the route?"

"That's irregular too," Hamish confirmed.

"Where to?" Andy asked, hoping for a little more information.

"Out of Lobo, and north," Hamish said.

That was a good deal more specific and it sounded like a long way. The furthest Andy had driven was to his parents in Surrey. He'd only been in top gear twice.

"How much?" Andy asked.

"Two thousand," Hamish said.

Two thousand sounded like a lot, but he had no idea whether inflation had been an issue for Lobo, and if it was a fiver or the price of a car.

"Where to?" Andy asked.

The man shrugged. It seemed like a fair question.

"Benin," he finally said.

Andy was pretty sure he'd heard of Benin, which meant it might have a British embassy. But how was he going to get into anther country without a passport?

"Benin?" Andy said. "But I don't have a passport."

The man considered this and, as it happened, shifting people without passports was one of his specialities. He just needed a white man to drive.

"I can get you a passport," Hamish said.

"You can?" Andy asked.

"No problem," he said.

Things, Andy thought, were looking up. If he could get to somewhere with an embassy and an airport he could get back. He might even be able to talk to his bank and get some money for a flight. He wouldn't have to call his parents. He wondered how much the passport was going to cost.

"How much?" Andy asked.

"Two thousand," Hamish said.

Chapter Fifty-Three

Jemima was used to getting what she wanted and was not taking Ali's rejection well. In this regard she was becoming quite man-like and Jemima wasn't ready to give up.

"You could get some new tee-shirts," Jemima insisted.

Ali had no idea what she was talking about and made the mistake of asking.

"What?" Ali said.

"I went to New York and I had my first line of cocaine," Jemima explained.

The talk of cocaine put them back on a firmer footing, which was an incredible revelation to Ali.

"I went to New York," Jemima continued. "And ate my first pussy."

They were back. However hard Ali tried to steer her off the subject, she kept coming back. The idea of eating pussy was repugnant to Ali and she'd rather eat a live cat if she had the choice.

"I went to New York and sucked my first nipple," Jemima continued.

Jemima had a tendency to get a little fixated, particularly when her bloodstream was heavily infiltrated.

"No," Ali said. "It's not going to happen."

Ali would have left, but it was her hotel room, and she had nowhere to go.

"Okay, okay, I've got a solution," Jemima said.

Ali wasn't sure she wanted to hear it.

"I went to New York and someone ate my pussy," Jemima said.

Jemima had concocted a whole wardrobe full of tee-shirts, and she just hoped that if she could get Ali to wear one, then the others might follow.

"No," Ali said.

"Oh please let me eat your pussy," Jemima pleaded.

"No," Ali insisted.

"Please, please, pretty please," Jemima said.

"No," Ali said.

Ali had moved as far as she was able from Jemima while still remaining on the bed. Her legs were clamped shut. There was an exercise machine at the gym which involved opening and closing her legs while they were attached to weights. She wished she'd spent more time on it.

"But I'm horny," Jemima said in what was becoming quite a whiny tone.

"Shall we go out?" Ali suggested.

Ali did not want to go out, but if they both left the room then that would be a step in the right direction.

"You go out, I'll stay here and wait for you," Jemima said deliberately pouting her lips.

Jemima was delving in her bag again. She really needed to take something that didn't make her horny, but everything was making her horny. She had another folded packet of cocaine and she really didn't care, at this point, what effect it had.

"I need to get high," Jemima said to herself.

Ali sighed. She didn't want to hurl her out of the room, as she was the senior New York editor, and Ali had to think of her career. She feared that if she waited until she crashed she'd wake up in the middle of the night with an unwanted hand in her knickers. The other alternative was crashing out in one of the rooms of her London colleagues. That would be either Jess, or Tony, or the mousy one from accounts whose name she could never remember. The evening had convinced her that Tony was gay. Ali got up.

"I'm young and free and I'm in New York," Ali said.

She grabbed her jacket and marched to the door. It wasn't a very long march as the room was small, but she was hoping it was a stirring speech, and she'd gathered a follower. She hadn't.

"Good for you girl," Jemima said, patting the space by her in the bed ready for Ali's return.

Ali felt committed. She opened the door and walked into the corridor. Once the door had closed behind her she sagged a little. She was feeling really tired. Jemima was an exhausting woman. And Ali didn't want to sit in a bar on her own. She looked at the doors along the corridor and tried to remember which ones her colleagues had walked through. It was only a day or so ago, but it seemed like forever. New York might be too racy for her, she decided. The lighting was a little minimal and was mostly ankle height and between the doors. She decided that Tony would be the safest bet and she tapped lightly on a door. It was late, and she was unsure of the time, and she realised she was probably going to be waking him up. There was no answer. She thought it unlikely he'd slept somewhere else and wondered if she'd got the right room. Perhaps she hadn't. It must be the the next one. She tapped on the door. It took a moment before she heard some rustling. The door opened and a face appeared.

"Hi," Ali said. "I need somewhere to crash."

"Sure," the voice said.

It wasn't until she was in the room that it occurred to her that the voice was familiar to her, but did not sound like Tony. A light went on. It was Miles.

"Fuck me," Ali muttered.

"Certainly," Miles said.

Chapter Fifty-Four

One of the advantages of drinking in moderation was that Andy's Dad was rarely exposed to the monumental hangover which was now torturing him. He'd slept in the spare bedroom, although the spare bedroom was becoming his bedroom. It had a comfortable bed and occasionally his wife snored. He still had most of his clothes on. He'd got up at quarter to seven and gone to work for the last thirty years and he knew, without looking at his watch, that that was the time. He couldn't help himself. But today he was going to need some more time in bed. He turned round and slept for a few more hours. When he woke he had no idea what time it was, but he was pretty sure he was the only person in the house. Andy's mum was probably at her yoga classes with that dreadful Lydia woman, Andy's dad thought.

He took the remainder of his clothes off, except for his underpants, which only came off when absolutely necessary. It was then that he noticed a strange shape in his trouser pocket. It was the pills. He ran through the events of the previous evening. Inwardly he cringed and vowed never to step foot in the pub again, and he arrived at the moment he'd left. And the blue pills.

He now knew with certainty what they were. But he wasn't going to take them. Who knew what the side effects might be? He thought about that for a second and realised the answer. Google would know. There was an iPad on the bedside table. It was a present from Andy, and he had begun to use it more often recently for the news and the *Mail Online*. It was a bit of a guilty pleasure – not because he objected to the politics of the paper, he rather agreed with them – but because it was full of articles on women's issues. He'd got to know more than he wanted to on the subject. He opened Google and typed in 'effects of viagra'.

There were a considerable number of entries. What he didn't know, but would discover, is that these three words were being registered in various data banks and he would now be assailed, for the rest of his life, with emails from companies claiming to be in the pharmaceutical industry. But that didn't concern him at that moment. He read. It seemed that the principal side effect was an erection. Andy's dad puffed his chest out. He didn't need a pill to get an erection. Or did he? He hadn't really noticed that they weren't arriving as regularly, or persistently, as they once did. The decline had been too gentle for him to be aware of it. He'd assumed that it was just that he found his wife less attractive than he used to.

Andy's dad thought about that. She clearly *was* less attractive than she used to be, but she was also kind of the same too. At least she had been until she met Lydia. They'd once joked about what life would be like once Andy had left home, and here they were with him in the spare bedroom. He thought back to the previous evening. There seemed to be no shortage of men who wanted to 'give his wife one'. He realised what this implied. The fault lay with him. There were other side effects to viagra, including headaches, but nothing that suggested he was likely to have a heart attack. But he didn't want to tell his wife either. It made him feel like less of a man. He also didn't want to try it and then discover it didn't work for him. That would be frustrating and embarrassing and he wasn't sure which was worse. He needed to test it first.

There was a jug of water by the bed, most of which he'd drunk, and his head had cleared quite a bit. He had been thinking about cutting the lawn. As a mission statement for the day it didn't amount to much, but that was the essence of retirement. But he didn't want to push the lawnmower with an erection. That would be awkward. And he didn't want to take it at night, either. If he was back in the marital bed that might be awkward too. On the other hand, it shouldn't be awkward. His wife was right. They hadn't had sex in some time.

"Damn," Andy's dad said to himself.

Something that used to be so simple had become quite complicated. He'd used snoring as an excuse, as he knew his wife wouldn't know, as she would be asleep. He'd been hiding from her in the spare bedroom. That was why the iPad was there. He'd moved more stuff in and, if he wasn't there, he was at the end of the garden. He suddenly felt guilty about the things he'd said about his wife's rhubarb crumble. It wasn't entirely true. He didn't mind rhubarb. He'd just got so fed up with hearing about the things Lydia had said. When he'd said rhubarb, was he actually talking about rhubarb? He couldn't be sure.

"Bugger," Andy's dad said to himself.

He was getting in quite a mess. He looked at the pills. The lawn didn't actually need cutting. It could wait. He took one of the pills out of the packet and looked at it. It looked innocuous enough. He wasn't, by nature, an impetuous man. Far from it. Going to the pub was him being impetuous. This was something else. But a little part of him knew it was his fault and he ought to, at the very least, do something about it. He chucked the pill in his mouth and drank a few mouthfuls of water before he talked himself out of it.

He felt an instant tingling of excitement. But that wasn't because of the effects of the pill. That was because he'd just done something a little daring. Now seemed like one of those rare times when it was appropriate to remove his underpants. This was an experiment and he'd need sight of the barometer of that experiment. He looked down at his penis. It looked much the same as it ever did. It was certainly flaccid. He had a quick look at the *Mail Online*. There was a piece about swimsuits flattering different kinds of figures. *Figure* was definitely a word used by women, he thought. Men say *body*. He looked at the pear and the hourglass. He was an hourglass man. He supposed, if he had to assign a figure to his wife, it would be hourglass. She was slimmer when they first met, but her breasts had got larger as she'd got older which, when he thought about it, was not a bad thing. He looked down. Nothing.

Andy's father had never accessed pornography on the internet and wasn't about to start now. In his view there was enough stimulating material in the *Mail Online*. He expanded the pictures of the women in swim suits, but they all seemed too young. Then he hit the jackpot. It was an article entitled '*Fit and Fun at Fifty –middle aged women and their bodies*'. They were displaying quite a bit of flesh, but they were standing coyly and the important parts were covered. That suited Andy's dad fine. He found them most pleasing. He was sure he could feel a stirring. But he looked down and it lay there like a beached fish deprived of oxygen.

"Damn," Andy's dad muttered.

It was him. He was broken and he hadn't noticed it. It had crept up on him when he was looking the other way. A sense of his own mortality rolled over him and he closed his eyes. He thought he'd heard a noise and opened his eyes. He had. It was a tapping at the door. He grabbed the sheets and covered himself up.

"Can I come in?" Andy's mum said.

Chapter Fifty-Five

Andy couldn't find Fullbush. She'd completely disappeared. He'd agreed to meet Hamish the following day and, while he'd had a couple of pints, he hadn't eaten anything. He was starving. He wondered if he could find Fullbush's flat, and if she'd be okay if he knocked on her door. Better still if she'd let him in, and even better if she could feed him and he could use a phone. *Hell and High Water* had filled up and the music had been cranked to another level. It was hot and sweaty and he needed some air. When he finally made it to the street he was surprised to find it was dark. It was late.

Andy retraced his steps in the direction of the labour exchange. If all else fails, he thought, he might be able to use Robbie's phone in the morning. If he could at least get his parents to transfer some money to an account from which he could draw cash that would help hugely. He found the labour exchange and continued in the direction of Fullbush's place. It was further than he remembered and the streets were quieter, although the temperature hadn't dropped by much. It actually felt warmer. When he arrived at the flat he was pleased to see the lights on. He rang the door bell. It took a few minutes for her to come down to the door and when she did it was clear that she was not pleased to see him.

"What are you doing here?" she asked, looking up and down the street.

"Well," Andy said trying to think how to phrase it.

"Come in before anyone sees you," Fullbush said quickly.

She pulled Andy in who was, as ever, bewildered.

"What's the problem?" he asked.

"Describe the man that kidnapped you," Fullbush said.

Andy would have said he was a tall black man but this, he knew, was less than adequate.

"I think his name was Barry," Andy said, trying to think.

"And?" Fullbush asked.

"Well, he was tall," Andy said.

"And?" Fullbush asked.

"He had black hair," Andy said slowly.

"And?"

"He might have had some grey at the temples," Andy said.

"And?"

Andy racked his brains. He thought he was a little more observant than this but then he had been punched in the face.

"He wore a suit. Like a business suit," Andy said.

"And his voice," Fullbush said. "What was his voice like?"

"Oh yes," Andy said. "It was posh, like an Englishman."

Andy looked up and noticed for the first time a picture hanging on a door. It was a tall black man looking presidential.

"That's him," Andy pointed.

"Oh shit," Fullbush muttered.

A small panicked silence followed, which was broken by a disturbance outside. Fullbush got up and looked out of the window.

"Oh shit," she said again.

"Perhaps I can make a quick call?" Andy said pointing at the telephone.

Fullbush nodded, unsure what to do. Andy picked up the phone and dialled his parents. But no one answered.

"Damn," Andy muttered.

A second later there was a knock at her door. Fullbush looked around in panic. The lights were on: clearly someone was in, and there was no escaping. She ran around the flat quickly tidying up, and then she slowly opened the door, and looked out. There was no question who was the other side. She eased the door open and smiled, as if she was expecting a leading dignitary.

"Your highness, what an honour it is to have you in my abode," Fullbush said.

Although she attended Barry junior's raves and Lobo was a small country, she had never actually seen the supreme leader, the king, in the flesh.

"Look," she said pointing to the photo of him on the toilet door.

She hoped he didn't ask to use her facilities, as he might be less pleased to discover on which door she'd hung his portrait. She grabbed a quick look at him to see how closely he resembled his portrait. It seemed to her that there may have been an added soupçon of Photoshop, although it might have been closer to a generous helping. In the flesh Barry was just a tad disappointing.

"What is you name?" Barry asked.

"Fullbush," Fullbush said.

Barry sighed. His parents and those before him had taken the lead when they'd named him Barry and he'd hoped others would follow, but often they did not. He was going to have to put out a decree to prevent names like Fullbush. He turned and pointed at Andy.

"Where's the banana?" Barry asked.

"I've eaten it," Andy said nervously.

"And what happened?" Barry said slowly.

"The world went a little crazy," Andy said.

"Crazy good?" Barry asked.

"I guess," Andy admitted.

"I'm going to need your shit," Barry said.

Andy looked around for his stuff. He didn't have much stuff and would have packed a good deal more if he'd known he was going to be kidnapped.

"I don't have much stuff," Andy said.

"No," Barry said slowly, "your shit."

Chapter Fifty-Six

"There will be no fucking tonight," Ali said firmly.

She couldn't believe she'd walked into Miles's room. There were shades of frying pans and fires about the evening.

"Why not?" Miles asked.

Miles owned the business, he drove a Porsche, why wouldn't one of his employees want to sleep with him? This sort of thing used to happen to him all the time. Now it was just in his dreams. He hadn't quite fully woken up.

"Oh, for..." Ali began.

She was hesitant to use the 'f' word, as every time she did it was taken as a literal command.

"Are you sure?" Miles asked.

"Very," Ali said.

Miles grunted.

"And cover yourself up," Ali said.

Miles liked to sleep naked, and it might have been an indication of the other things on Ali's mind that she hadn't immediately noticed. Now that she had she could see that Miles possessed a rather unattractive aged scrawniness, and if there was something further down that might compensate for it, she wasn't going to look and find out.

"Okay," Miles said reluctantly and turned and put his trousers on.

He was the kind of man who wore trousers without underpants and, while he was turned, Ali couldn't help throwing a quick glance at his sagging buttocks. As he bent over his testicles hung like those on the boxer dog that used to live next door to her parents. The worse thing about this exercise was it making the prospect of Jemima's pussy seem positively appealing.

"So what are you doing in my room?" Miles asked finally.

"Jemima," Ali explained.

Miles laughed.

"Has she taken a shine to you?" he asked.

"Just a little," Ali said.

Miles and Jemima went back a long way and, at various points in his life, there was no human being he'd desired more. It had taken a while to realise it wasn't reciprocated.

"Is she offering you tee-shirts?" Miles said and sat down on the bed.

"How do you know that?" Ali asked.

"Oh, I know Jemima very well," Miles said putting on his monogrammed shirt.

"Really?" Ali asked.

"She was the girl of my dreams. The most beautiful and sexy thing I ever laid my eyes on. I couldn't stop looking at her," Miles said wistfully.

It was the first time Miles had said something which made him seem human to Ali. He seemed to be revealing the possibility he might have a soul.

"And a brilliant editor. She still is. The best in the business," Miles said.

Ali could see more hope, as Miles had actually managed to recognise Jemima's intellectual qualities.

"And so adventurous. I thought there was nothing she wouldn't try and when she suggested a threesome I thought I'd hit the jackpot," Miles said.

The possibility Miles might have a soul was disappearing.

"Me and a chick sandwich," Miles continued.

Ali was grateful she wasn't eating, as that sentence might have induced some vomit.

"But it turns out Jemima wasn't really interested in me," Miles said forlornly.

Miles relived the excitement and the disappointment in his mind. He'd have preferred it if Jemima had been a little more conventional. He looked around for his handmade moccasins. He wore them without socks. Miles didn't invest much in underwear.

"And that was kind of that," Miles reminisced. "It was a shame. It was a great wedding."

"Wedding?" Ali asked. "You were married?"

"Oh yes," Miles said. "But as I said she wasn't really interested in me."

"Well, she's definitely interested in me," Ali said.

"You should give it a go. I'm told she's sensational," Miles said.

He remembered watching Jemima launch herself between the legs of their third party. At first it was with great excitement but eventually, when he saw how much she evidently enjoyed it, with dismay. That was the turning point.

“No thanks,” Ali said primly.

Her views on the matter hadn’t changed despite Miles’s five star review of Jemima’s talents.

“You want me to get her out of your room?” Miles asked.

“If you would,” Ali said.

Chapter Fifty-Seven

"It makes you horny, doesn't it?" Lydia had said earlier that day.

They were at the yoga class. Their usual teacher was away on a retreat and a replacement had been drafted in. While Suzanna was slim and sensuous, Bruno was tall, calm and hideously masculine. Lydia winked at Andy's mum.

"Down facing dog," Bruno said, in his calm measured voice.

Lydia liked making comments like that to Andy's mum, as she knew it would embarrass her. Andy's mum would have responded, but she was too entranced by Bruno. She hated to admit it. But he *was* making her horny. Although most things were these days. She saw a picture of a man's hand on the side of a bus and it gave her a dull ache. It probably wasn't normal, and some of her old friends would have agreed with her, but not Lydia.

"And relax into the child position," Bruno purred.

Andy's mum studied his calm and content demeanour with envy. Why was she constantly distressed? But she didn't know that Bruno was forty-nine, living in rented accommodation, and so far behind the rent that soon he was going to be forced to live at home with his mother. He was three months behind on the maintenance for his three children, from his three wives, and he was a handful of hours away from having his car repossessed, which was his only possession.

"And time to go in peace," Bruno said.

It had almost a religious ring to it, although he hated the whole hippy yoga thing and had only taken up yoga to get laid. Who'd have known that women who did yoga were so fertile?

"Coffee?" Lydia suggested.

Lydia went off to have a quick chat with Bruno and ten minutes later they were in the coffee shop holding their yoga mats with pride. Andy's mum grabbed her skinny latte and their usual table, which was just outside.

"Well?" Lydia asked.

Andy's mum didn't know what she was on about, although she was certain that Bruno wouldn't pass through their lives without some comment.

"He is something," Andy's mum said.

She hoped she'd pitched it about right, not too prurient, and showing the kind of interest that would satisfy Lydia.

"I didn't mean Bruno," Lydia said.

"Oh," Andy's mum said. "What did you mean?"

"Have you done the test?" Lydia asked.

Lydia had written nearly a thousand words on the subject and her editor told her it needed a more satisfying conclusion, which was also what Andy's mum was hoping for. Lydia didn't care whether Andy's mum's husband was gay or not. Although it would make for a more interesting article if he was, and would spawn an avalanche of more material.

"No," Andy's mum said coyly.

"You're in the house together all day long. Just bung the gear on and creep up on him. If he doesn't respond then we might have to consider the possibility that he's batting for the other side," Lydia said.

For a second Andy's mum thought she meant that her husband had turned Labour, but it was worse than that. The problem was she felt foolish dressing up and Lydia didn't know her husband.

"Where is he today?" Lydia asked.

"He got back late," Andy's mum admitted.

"Really?" Lydia said.

She was hoping to hear that he'd gone to Brighton to join the gay parade, or he'd visited a club in London.

"He went to the pub," Andy's mum said.

"Oh," Lydia said, a little disappointed.

Andy's mum didn't want to tell her that her husband never went to pubs and, as it sounded normal, she didn't press it.

"He's in the spare bedroom," Andy's mum added.

Lydia's eyes rose high in her head. A text had arrived at her phone.

"Gosh, is that the time?" Lydia suddenly said and rushed off.

Andy's mum walked slowly home. She was thinking about lots of things. If she could have been ravished by Bruno that afternoon she would have, but that wasn't the life she led. That wasn't her destiny. When she got home she checked the end of the garden, but Andy's dad wasn't there. It took her a moment to realise he was still in the spare bedroom. She couldn't believe she'd caught him urinating in the front garden. She put on the kettle. She could take up a tea for him. She watched it boil. It was a bit like how she felt. She pictured throwing open the door dressed as Lydia had suggested. The stockings, suspenders, high heels. The full performance. She just didn't have the nerve. She made the tea and went upstairs.

Andy's mum was about to knock on the spare room door when she decided to make a small detour to her bedroom. It was becoming her bedroom and the spare bedroom was becoming his. She opened her underwear drawer. She ran her hands through the lacy underwear Lydia had also insisted she buy when they'd been at the sex shop. She decided she'd try it on. That didn't mean she was going to burst through the spare bedroom door. It took a while to get it all on and, when she was finished, Andy's mum was reluctant to look at herself in the mirror. She felt embarrassed. But this, Lydia had kept reminding her, was the test. She stole a quick glance, as if she was looking at somebody else. It might have been somebody else. She was unrecognisable. She flushed red with further embarrassment. She was too English for this exercise. They both were. She sat down and began to unroll the stockings. She felt nervous like the time they'd first had sex which was, she often thought, approximately a hundred years ago. But the nerves were exciting. Before she had the opportunity of giving it any more thought, she got up and walked to the spare room. It was now or never, as Elvis once said. She knocked on the door.

"Can I come in?" Andy's mum said.

Chapter Fifty-Eight

Andy was led out of Fullbush's flat and into the street. He'd expected a police force, possibly television cameras, and to be bundled into a van. But the president appeared to be on his own.

"Put your hands out," Barry said.

Andy did as he was told and Barry wrapped his wrists in gaffer tape.

"Get in," Barry said, pointing to the car.

Andy grabbed the door handle. It wasn't easy with his hands bound. It was a large silver car, which in 1993 was considered to be the pinnacle of motoring achievement. It was an S class Mercedes. But Andy couldn't open the door.

"It's locked," Andy pointed out.

"No, it just gets stuck," Barry said and gave it a yank.

It opened with a reluctant creak. Andy got in and tried to close the door.

"You need to slam it," Barry said.

Andy tried to slam it, but it was a bit difficult with his hands bound. Barry had to get out of the car and close it for him. He got back in and turned the key and the engine turned slowly and reluctantly. It didn't sound like it was going to start, but bit by bit, and one at a time, the cylinders began to fire until eventually the vast majority of the considerable collection were firing and forward motion was a possibility. Barry put the gear lever into drive. He pressed the accelerator and the revs rose, but the car remained resolutely stationary.

"Shit," Barry said.

This just wasn't appropriate for the king. He wanted a new Mercedes, but they were a hundred thousand dollars, and he owed that on the aeroplane. He would have paid it out of the state coffers, but he also owed that in electricity to a neighbouring country. Lobo was close to be being switched off. He wiggled the gear stick and the car made a little jolt. They were off.

"Have you been to the toilet?" Barry asked.

Andy was not sure what the king of Lobo was going to ask him, but this wasn't it.

"Toilet?" Andy asked.

Barry rolled his eyes. Now wasn't the time to be coy.

"Yes," Barry said angrily.

Again, Andy wasn't sure what he was being asked and how appropriately he should phrase his answer.

"As in number ones or number twos?" Andy asked.

"For fuck sake," Barry said a little exasperated. "Have you taken a shit?"

There had been many things that had happened to Andy but taking a shit wasn't one of them.

"Not recently," Andy admitted.

Barry floored the throttle. The front of the car rose gently. Barry sighed.

"So if you're not the biochemist, where did you get that banana?" Barry asked.

Andy knew he'd ask him about the banana. And, after eating it, he had a pretty good idea why. It was, as his mother might say, drugs. His mother could be a little damning about drugs. It was a view that came from reading the Daily Mail.

"Someone gave it to me at King's Cross station," Andy said.

He knew it wasn't very convincing and he wondered if he should fabricate a more convincing reason. He looked at Barry. Barry sighed again. He was finding his attempt at criminal activity very exhausting. But he had a plan. Gary had been very clear about where the banana seeds would be and their potential value. It was a rather unappetising thought.

"Why would they give you a banana?" Barry asked.

"I don't know," Andy admitted.

"Why would you take a banana?" Barry asked.

"I don't know," Andy said quietly.

Why had he taken the bloody banana? The answer was simple. He was hungry. He thought it better to keep that to himself.

"What happened when you ate the banana?" Barry asked.

"Well, nothing at first," Andy said.

Barry listened, although it was becoming increasingly difficult as the engine was making new rumbling noises, which was suggesting that the number of firing cylinders no longer out numbered those that weren't, and that total engine failure was not so far away. He remembered when he'd first picked up the car. He'd gone to Stuttgart and driven it thorough Europe. It was a mechanical Germanic masterpiece with an engine of silk. Now it sounded more like hessian.

"It was the following day, when you dumped me in a ditch," Andy said.

Andy had hoped that this might prompt some guilt in the king, but he seemed to be in a dream. Andy's experience with the banana had been quite dream like although, like most hallucinogenic experiences, it was unique to him.

"Then it went a little crazy," Andy said. "All the colours changed."

"Was it a good experience?" Barry asked.

"Amazing," Andy muttered.

The car was shaking now. Barry had ordered the top of the range twelve cylinder model and he wished he'd ordered the eight or the six, or something less complicated. Servicing had been a nightmare and now he reckoned only two of the cylinders were attempting to carry the idle ten. And then they weren't. The car rolled to a halt.

"Shit," Barry said again.

Andy wondered what was going to happen next and whether he should make a run for it. If he could find Hamish he might be able to get a passport and get out of Lobo.

"Do you know anything about cars?" Barry asked.

The honest answer was no. Andy looked at Barry. Barry could recite acceleration times and was *au fait* with top speeds of almost every performance car. His knowledge of how they ran was minimal and Andy's wasn't much more. But Andy had nothing to lose.

"A bit," he said.

Barry eyed him carefully. He had nothing to lose either. He pulled the release cable and the bonnet popped open. They got out of the car. Barry lifted the bonnet and they looked at the spaghetti of pipes and hoses and cables. This, Andy thought, might as well be a nuclear reactor. But Andy had an idea. If he got Barry back in the car, he could make a run for it.

"You'll need to untie me," Andy said.

Barry looked at him cautiously. He took out a penknife and cut the gaffer tape.

"Can you turn it over?" Andy asked.

Barry got in the car and turned the key and the engine chugged reluctantly. Andy could see that Barry had one leg out of the car. He needed to wait until he was more relaxed. He looked at the rocking mess as the engine shook. He had not the slightest, vaguest idea what to do, but confidently ran his hand through the mass of cables and leads. It was an exercise in optimism. He was looking for the detached lead which would resolve the issue. He could still see Barry's leg on the ground. He wasn't certain he could outrun him.

"Stop," he said to Barry.

It sounded pretty commanding, as if he actually knew what he was doing. But, he reminded himself, in the land of the blind the one eyed man is king. Although he was giving himself too much credit. And Barry *was* the king.

"Try again," Andy said.

The car chugged and Andy continued to uselessly fondle the various cables.

"Fuck!" Andy shouted, falling back.

A massive spark had just shot up his arm. Barry got out of the car. Andy looked up. There was a distant thought in the back of Andy's mind which was moving gently to the surface. It was about sparks and leads. It took a moment to refine the thought.

"I think your spark leads have perished," he said.

Andy got up and followed the spark plug leads. A number of them were caught on the metal of the chassis.

"Do you have any insulating tape?" Andy's asked.

"I've got gaffer tape," Barry said.

"Of course you have," Andy said.

Barry retrieved the tape and Andy carefully wound it round the leads at the point where they'd been breached.

"Try it now," Andy said.

This, Andy thought later, had been a mistake. He was so pleased that he'd resolved the issue, against all odds, that he didn't use the opportunity to make his escape. Barry turned the key and the engine purred into life and Andy got into the car feeling rather pleased with himself.

"Where are we going?" Andy asked.

Barry knew a restaurant which would loosen Andy's bowels.

Chapter Fifty-Nine

Jemima loved the buzz. She loved the buzz of the office, of a handful of gin and tonics, and of a nose-full of coke. What she didn't like was the opposite of the buzz. Her carefully constructed life, when viewed from the right angle, looked magnificent. But when viewed from the other angle it looked like a house on the edge of a cliff supported by sticks. She'd learned, when circumstances had tipped her towards the precipice view of her life, to self-medicate. But she'd already done quite a bit of that in quite a few creative ways. And she was horny. She'd have given anything for Ali to have planted her face in her sensitive regions, but it was clear she wasn't going to play ball. She looked around the room.

Jemima had a pretty smart apartment, which she actually owned, and was a result of a part sell out a few years ago which happily coincided with a moment when real estate had taken a little slump. It was worth a fortune now and it made her feel good. She also had a very extensive collection of the very highest priced vibrators including Bertha, who was her current favourite, and who knew precisely how to hit the spot. She wasn't called Bertha – Jemima tended to genderise her vibrators and, despite their obvious phallus shape, they were invariably female – because she was large. It was more the orgasms she provoked. Her actually name was rabbit related, but that didn't matter now.

Jemima wasn't moving from the bed as she was, at heart, a very optimistic girl. She felt that any second now Ali would burst through the door and throw herself at Jemima's feet. Perhaps not her feet, although that would be a good start. Jemima was staying put.

Instead Jemima decided to make herself more comfortable and removed some clothes. As with her narcotics, Jemima never knew when to stop, but she had no choice once there was nothing left to remove. She lay on the bed naked and played with herself. But she wasn't hitting any spots at all. It was as if she didn't know her own body. She looked around the room for something that might assist her. It was an astonishingly phallus-free room. She wondered if they included that in the mission statement of the boutique hotel.

"Shit," she muttered.

She got up and had a look in the bathroom. The shampoo bottles were squat and unsuited to the purpose which he hoped to put them to, which she found very annoying.

"Designed by bloody lesbians," Jemima muttered.

If there was an irony in this observation she didn't see it. She thought about getting into the bath and using the shower, but if she got wet she'd have to dry herself, and she couldn't rely on her balance. And then she froze. If this was a metaphor for her life she didn't like it. She couldn't even find something with which to fuck herself. Then she thought about the fridge.

"Excellent," Jemima said.

Some of the bottles were also a little too squat for her purpose, but there was a vodka bottle with which, she decided, she could make do. It still had quite a bit of vodka in it and she opened the top and poured some down her throat without looking for something to mix it with. It burned a little, but it gave her a satisfactory hit. She lay on the bed with the vodka bottle.

"Ouch," she said.

The vodka bottle was cold, almost painfully so. But Jemima took some comfort in that pain. It wasn't Bertha, but it was doing okay. She pushed her handbag aside and its contents tumbled out. There was another neatly folded packet of coke. And a few pills. What were they? She wasn't sure. She thought they might be MDMA and she liked the idea of that. The only question was whether to take one or the other. The one things that stood out with Jemima was her decisiveness. She hated people who dithered. She operated the philosophy that you took what you wanted. And she'd decided what she wanted.

"I'll have both," she said.

She grabbed the hotel menu and poured the contents of the neatly folded packet onto it. There was quite a lot. She cut a monster line and she went for it like a beagle in pursuit of a fox.

"Nice," she muttered.

She shook the vodka bottle. It was still quite full. She set about changing that. She threw the pills in her mouth and washed them down with vodka. She breathed in. She felt good. It wasn't easy feeling good these days. She lay back on the bed and proceeded to vigorously roger herself with the vodka bottle. That felt pretty good too. She closed her eyes. It was at this point that the collection of pills collided with the alcohol that was already in her system and the coke that had been more recently introduced. It prompted a full system shutdown.

Chapter Sixty

"Yes?" Andy's dad said weakly.

He didn't expect his wife to actually open the door. He swiped the little pack of pills with the back of his hand. They bounced off the wall and landed under the bed. This was embarrassing. He realised they needed to talk about this. Hacking down the rhubarb had not been a good solution to a problem he knew was brewing. At least it had begun to brew after his wife met Lydia. That woman had a lot to answer for.

"Can I come in?" Andy's mum said.

It wasn't easy adapting to retirement. He had so much spare time. How do people fill it? He suddenly remembered when he was young and had first worked for the bank. He'd been required to administer a retirement fund for a local factory. He'd asked the retirees what they planned to do. Some had loads of plans, others none. The shocking part was that those with none had died within six months.

"Come in?" Andy's dad asked.

He could see now which category he fell into. Of course the actuaries relied on those with no plans to ensure the others could be paid handsomely. There was a lot more money coming into his account than leaving it. He was richer than he'd ever been, yet he'd spent the last few afternoons at the end of the garden. He was at the end of the garden hiding from his wife, who wanted to live like a teenager.

“Yes,” Andy’s mum said, her resolve weakening.

He’d never had a gap year or travelled much. They’d had neither the money, nor the time, and then they had a mortgage and children. This was the way life should be lived. The cycle. It wasn’t a cycle that Andy was entirely wedded to, but he was getting there. He had Ali now. Soon they might have children. Although when that happens they’ll be a lot older than he was when he became a father.

“Of course,” Andy’s dad said with a croak.

He pulled the sheets even higher. He didn’t want to have to explain why he wasn’t wearing underpants. Then he noticed the underpants on the floor. She’d think that was odd. She might even think he was masturbating. There was nothing on the planet, in Andy’s dad’s view, that was more embarrassing than being caught masturbating. He made a lunge for his underpants.

“Ta-dar,” Andy’s mum said.

She’d been agonising over what to say. What does one say? She should have asked Lydia. Lydia would have known. Her mind had gone blank. She looked down at herself. Her breasts were pointing out. Then she knew what Lydia might say. Let the breasts do the talking. Although ‘ta-dar’ wasn’t bad.

“Sweet fucking mother of god,” Andy’s dad said.

He would have corrected himself and placed the ‘fucking’ before the god, which sounded sacrilegious but, under the slightly shocking circumstances, was appropriate. He was naked and half way to collecting his underpants. He had never given the processes of the mind much thought. But everything happened in milliseconds. He looked up and saw his wife and a millisecond later he had one of the biggest erections of his life. His eyes had sent a signal to his brain and his brain had demanded that blood be instantly pumped. He may have had further chemical assistance, but a second later she was in his arms, and a moment after that they would have made rabbits feel inadequate. The phone was ringing, but neither of them could hear it, and wouldn't have abandoned the exercise if they had. Or if the house had been on fire.

Chapter Sixty-One

Ali fumbled around for her room key, desperately wishing that the evening would end and she could get some sleep.

"Put it in there," Miles said.

Ali looked at him. She may not have stayed in that many hotel rooms, but she knew where to put the key. Or she thought she did.

"Not there, there," Miles instructed.

It took a while to open the door and Miles grew impatient. He knocked loudly on the door. It was loud enough to wake everyone in the surrounding rooms but not Jemima. There was no response. Ali fidgeted a bit more and eventually the key card peeped, a green light appeared, and they tumbled into the room.

"Oh shit," Ali said, knowing it was best not to say 'fuck me' again.

Jemima was lying on the bed, apparently unconscious. But it was evident that prior to that she'd decided to remove all her clothes.

"Sensational body," Miles said.

Ali looked sternly at Miles suggesting that now was not an appropriate time to make such an observation. Although she could see there was some truth in it.

"Jemima," Ali said.

It was also evident that Jemima had looked around the room for an object which might resolve her horniness issue. Even that had been frustrating as the latest, and most fashionable designers, did not favour phallus shaped bottles. There was a selection scattered between her legs which she'd rejected, before she'd arrived at something that was approximately suitable. It was still where she'd left it.

"Oh shit," Miles said, shaking her.

Jemima's life was a bit of a mess. Her shit-kicking force field was held together at great expense, both financial and emotional, and the realisation that she couldn't even locate a bottle with which to fuck herself had sent her over the edge. That and the collision of narcotics and alcohol.

"Oh bloody hell," Miles said.

Ali could feel the panic rising.

"I'm not sure she's breathing," Miles said.

Miles looked pleadingly at Ali. Six months ago Miles had received some Health and Safety instruction which, along with his insurance, demanded that there was a qualified first aider on site. It sounded like it might be a fun day out and Ali had volunteered.

"Oh shit," Ali said.

She had covered CPR, but it was on a plastic doll. When she'd finished the course it was with the knowledge that in a crisis situation she would call the emergency services. Not actually administer CPR. That would be crazy.

"Oh shit," Ali said again.

Jemima's body appeared to be entirely lifeless. She had to think.

"Okay, okay," Ali said, which was more panic than thought.

She continued to shake Jemima, but it wasn't prompting a miraculous recovery.

"ABC," Ali said.

"Eh?" Miles said.

"Airway. Is her airway blocked?" Ali asked.

They checked. Miles shoved his fingers in Jemima's mouth.

"No," he said.

"Breathing. Is she breathing?" Ali asked.

They put their ears close to Jemima's mouth, crashing their heads.

"I don't think so," Miles said. "What's C?"

He was hoping that the answer to this question would resolve the issue.

"Circulation," Ali said. "Does she have a pulse?"

Miles fumbled around, first with her wrist and then with her neck.

"I think so," Miles said.

"Call the emergency services," Ali said.

There was no getting away from it. Ali sat over Jemima, pinched her nose, and took a deep breath. Miles had been wrestling with the social etiquette of what to do with the bottle which was lodged between Jemima's legs. There was a little part of him which wanted to leave it there as if this was an installation in the style of Tracey Emin's bed. It might be entitled

'Jemima's Vodka Bottle' and would be riddled with nuance and irony.

"I think I better do something about this," Miles said dutifully.

He grabbed the bottle. It was at this point that Ali's London colleagues appeared at the door. Miles kicked it shut leaving them with an image they were able to misinterpret. There had been some debate as to how far someone might go in pursuit of promotion and there was a general irritation that Ali had gone off with Jemima, as they would have liked equal time with her. They all assumed there were limits.

"Unbelievable," one of them muttered in disgust.

They'd seen the naked Jemima, with Miles at one end apparently doing something with a bottle, and Ali at the other end snogging her. It appeared as if there was no end to what certain people would do to get ahead. But this was the least of Ali's concerns, as she feared she was blowing her remaining breath into a dead body. It was for this reason that she didn't see it coming and a significant pellet of vomit flew into her mouth, Jemima choked, took in a massive breath and came back to life.

Chapter Sixty-Two

"I beg your pardon?" Lydia said.

This hadn't gone the way she'd anticipated. She'd sort of revelled in her new friend's stagnant sex life. And deep down she'd hoped that the husband was gay. That could prompt a pile of new material.

"Over the work surface," Andy's mum said in almost a whisper.

Andy's mum now looked at the kitchen in a new light. It was full of work surfaces, which was normal for a kitchen. The thing was she couldn't tell what might happen should she lean on one. That used to be a perfectly innocent activity. But now there was always the possibility that Andy's dad might 'give her one' from the rear. Talking dirty was another new thing.

"And do you know what he said?" Andy's mum whispered.

Lydia didn't and didn't want to know. Andy's mum said it so quietly she couldn't hear it. Lydia had met up with Bruno and his all-consuming masculinity hadn't extended to his penis, which had hardly extended at all. It had the consistency of boiled spaghetti and, while Lydia was a yoga regular and frequent exerciser of her pelvic floor muscles, she wasn't that young and she'd had a few children. Getting one into the other had proved troublesome.

"And then he opened the fridge door," Andy's mum said.

It was remarkable that the opening of the fridge door could be sexual, but Andy's dad had made it so. He wasn't even sure what he was looking for and then his eyes had landed on something.

"The fridge?" Lydia said, attempting to retain the plot.

Eventually Bruno had got the little bendy fella into Lydia and then, with three puffs and a grunt, it was all over. She didn't know he was going to attempt to get it in, as it didn't appear ready for the act. She assumed he was going to do something skilful with her clitoris, but he had as much chance of finding the missing panels of the Bayeux tapestry as locating that.

"Whipped cream," Andy's mum said.

Lydia choked on her skinny latte. A little ball of froth flew across the table. That was the other thing. She would have demanded Bruno wore a condom, but he was in and out quicker than a lit firework. Worse, she'd examined herself that morning and seen something which wasn't a million miles away from whipped cream, and didn't normally reside there. This had happened to her in the past and it had been nothing. Was it possible, she wondered, to suffer a psychosomatic sexually transmitted disease?

"And then," Andy's mum said conspiratorially, "he grabbed a cucumber."

This was giving Lydia a headache. The worse thing, even worse than the possibility of a sexually transmitted disease, was she worried that the flaccid cock was her fault.

"A cold cucumber," Andy's mum continued, not entirely aware of her audience.

Lydia's self esteem could be a little fragile at times. As a sexual encounter it had failed on so many levels it had given her a kind of post coital depression. And Bruno's penis could be likened to many things, but a cucumber was not one of them.

"And do you know what it's like with the contrast?" Andy's mum asked.

Lydia didn't, and had no idea what was contrasting with what, and rather feared she'd be forced to find out. There had been a huge contrast between the idea of Bruno and the floppy reality.

"The cold of the cucumber," Andy's mum said quietly with just a quiver in her voice.

Lydia had been trying to give up random sexual encounters, she was married, but the pull of the unknown and the subsequent boost to her self esteem had made it a little drug-like. Except this time she'd scored some bad stuff.

"And the heat of..." Andy's mum said with a pant. "Him."

It took a second for Lydia to piece together what Andy's mum was choosing to tell her and she wasn't sure she'd got it right.

"Hold on," Lydia said. "He put the cucumber..."

She really wished she hadn't. It seemed as if it was never going to end. Andy's dad seemed like quite a stud.

"Yes," Andy's mum said quickly. "And then..."

Lydia wanted to close her eyes and cry. Bruno barely had the imagination to use his penis let alone a cucumber. Although, now she thought about it, a cucumber would have been an altogether more satisfying proposition.

"Yes," Andy's mum said, but she was just smiling to herself.

Andy's Dad had been digging the garden. There had been a moment when he'd been digging the garden and he'd been traumatised by Andy's mum's attempts to show him her clitoris. Sex had been very far from his mind. But now a door had opened in his mind and *all* he could think about was sex. There were an awful lot of ways they hadn't done it and Andy's dad wanted to change that. Consequently his mind was very much elsewhere and neither he, nor Andy's mum, were aware that the telephone was ringing, and had been for a while, and that their son was marooned in a foreign land and in need of their help.

Chapter Sixty-Three

Barry was delighted with the way the car was now running. So much so he took it on a detour to clear it out a little, and a rapid trip through the countryside could only serve to loosen bowels. He twirled the wheel around a series of bends, which he'd had built specifically for his entertainment back in the days when the country was richer. It wound up a hill at the top of which was a restaurant which overlooked the capital of Lobo and most of his empire.

"Where are we going?" Andy asked.

"We're going," Barry said, "to The End."

The restaurant also marked the boundary of Lobo and the neighbouring country and it was for that reason that it was called 'The End'.

"Oh shit," Andy said.

He should have run when he could have, what was he thinking?

"No, don't listen to the reviews," Barry said.

There had been a bout of food poisoning and the local press, which was very local and entirely unaware of the rest of the world, had slated the place. Barry liked it because it overlooked his empire. It was that and the fact that he didn't have to pay.

"Reviews?" Andy said confused.

"Yes, it was only a few isolated cases of food poisoning," Barry explained.

This didn't help Andy at all, not least because Barry had decided to go through the bends a second time. Barry wondered what it would be like in a supercar. He found the need to make some money to be so intrusive. It was such an inconvenience.

"Food poisoning?" Andy asked.

"Yes," Barry said. "It's a restaurant."

"Oh," Andy said.

The prospect of food was good. He knew now to grab any food that was available to him.

"Here we are," Barry said a few minutes later.

Andy looked out of the car. The other thing about his recent experiences was that he was unable to predict what might happen next. Two people came out and opened the doors of the car. They were clearly used to the yank required to gain entry.

"Your Excellency," one of the men said to Barry.

He was the owner, Pierre, and, as the supreme leader had cost him a fortune over the years, he wouldn't normally be so welcoming. But the food poisoning had rather killed trade and he welcomed Barry's support.

"Your usual table?" Pierre said.

Pierre's real name was Kevin, but he'd checked the world's lists of chefs and restaurant owners, and none of them were called Kevin. He didn't want to dig roads like his father had and for which, he felt, Kevin would be a perfect name. He'd never been to France either.

"Excellent," Barry boomed.

He found, when he was in the role of king, he couldn't help booming. It was what people expected. It made Andy's ears ring. They followed the two men into the restaurant. The roof appeared to be made of palms and the far side had a balustrade a metre high which was open to the air. A gentle breeze blew through the restaurant and was pleasantly cooling. They sat at the table.

"This," Barry declared with just a touch of a boom, "Is Lobo."

Andy looked out. It was quite a long way up and he could see a few twinkling lights as night had fallen. It tended to fall pretty quickly, but the heat hadn't abated.

"Lovely," Andy said.

He felt a need to further the conversation, maybe even advance it a little.

"How long have you been king?" he asked Barry.

"Twenty years, since my father died," Barry said.

It had been twenty years of decline, which did not make him the most popular Barry. It was a decline which initially had been bought about by Barry's spending habits. The menus had arrived.

"Oh," Andy said. "That's cool."

They both looked at the menus. Normally Andy would have asked whether they were having starters, but he realised now that he shouldn't waste the opportunity to eat. He was having a starter and a pudding and anything else they'd feed him.

"The foie gras looks good," Andy said.

It was good, excellent even, but it wasn't actually foie gras. When Pierre created the menu he took it from some of the greatest chefs of the world, none of whom were called Kevin, and it didn't always include the usual ingredients to make up the classic dishes.

"It is," Barry said with pride.

He was proud of his country and, while he knew it wouldn't be quite what it claimed, it would still be good.

"Any thoughts on the wine?" Barry asked.

One of Barry's earlier enterprises was the manufacture of wine. He'd invested quite a bit of the country's resources, having imported the grape from South Africa, which had been imported there three hundred years earlier from France. He'd spoken to experts, but he'd struggled to get anyone to build vineyards in his country. He'd found someone eventually who boasted a massive winemaking CV. Unfortunately none of it was true, and it had prompted issues. Some say it was the *terroir*, others the acidity of the water, but most just said it tasted of piss. As some of the poorer inhabitants of his country frequently drank piss they were able to qualify it, and suggest that it tasted like the piss from an animal on a diet of shit.

"What would you recommend? Something local perhaps?" Andy said.

He wondered what Ali would say when he told her he'd eaten in a fine restaurant with the king of an African country. In Africa. He didn't think she'd believe him and he didn't have his phone to take photos and corroborate his story.

"No, I think the Stellenbosch," Barry said.

There had been others who'd just said the wine was shit, but not everyone agreed. They said it didn't taste shit. It actually tasted like shit. Some of the drainage in Lobo was still pretty crude and he suspected that the water table contained more effluent that it should.

"From South Africa," Barry added.

Pierre didn't like it when he ordered the South African wine, as it was the only decent stuff and it was expensive, which would have been great were he paying. He'd located a wine which was cheap and quite drinkable and he'd printed out the Stellenbosch labels.

"Great," Andy said.

Andy was salivating at the thought, and a bottle of red wine appeared, and was poured into his glass. He knew as much about wine as he did about the mechanics of cars, but he knew he should appreciate it. This might be his opportunity to forward his idea about becoming an ambassador for Lobo. He swished the wine in the glass, held it to the light, and took a sip.

"Excellent," Andy declared.

They touched glasses and Andy was about to launch into his plan when Barry got to his first.

"The thing is," Barry said cautiously. "We need those bananas. There is money in those bananas and we need money."

Barry pulled a large plastic bag out of his pocket. It was the kind sold in supermarkets and was branded. Andy looked at it uncertainty.

“I’m going to need you to shit into this,” Barry said.

Chapter Sixty-Four

"I don't think I'd ever really had an orgasm before," Andy's mum said.

Lydia had been in two minds about going to the yoga class. Bruno had gone and their usual instructor had returned, both of which she was very happy with. But Andy's mum was driving her crazy.

"I mean I've had that buzzy feeling, you know," Andy's mum said looking wistfully in the distance.

Lydia really didn't know. It had been such a long time since she'd had that buzzy feeling, let alone an orgasm. She'd forgotten what the experience was like. Despite that she did not want to be subjected to a blow by blow account from Andy's mum. But blow by blow was what was in Andy's mum's mind.

"I'd never really enjoyed, you know, the oral part," Andy's mum said.

Andy's mum felt pleased she could make such a contribution to the subject that Lydia spent much of her time talking about. It was almost like they'd learned to do it for the first time. She was even excited about getting home.

"The what?" Lydia spat.

She'd talked to her editor about Andy's mum and it had spawned a series of articles about late life sex which Lydia was finding too depressing to write. That her editor should ask her to write about something entitled 'late life' was bad enough. That she wasn't getting any was even worse. Her own husband was fifteen years older than her, which moved him into the territory she thought of as 'fucking old'. An articulated lorry full of viagra couldn't stir that thing.

"You know, blowjobs," Andy's mum said scarcely lowering her voice.

With her new found confidence she didn't see the need to whisper. But she wanted to discuss it more, not least the name which was a bit baffling to her, as it plainly didn't involve any blowing.

"I mean there's something pretty commanding about having your bloke's cock in your mouth," Andy's mum said.

Lydia choked on her skinny latte. A couple of people may have looked round and Andy's mum seemed oblivious to it. There was no question what she was thinking about. It was the first time she'd said the word 'cock' out loud, although she might have said it once or twice when they'd been on holiday and a cock had crowed, but never in the context of the penis.

Chapter Sixty-Five

Ali didn't get to bed until late and, when she woke the following morning, she felt she'd earned the right not to do a great deal. She had been pretty heroic and she'd received a mouthful of vomit for her efforts. The taste hadn't quite left her. Thankfully Miles had sorted out the medics and Jemima was astonishingly unscathed by the experience. But Jemima, the woman she'd envied and admired, was not who she seemed. Ali wondered if we were all the same, paddling like mad under the water, but wearing a sheen of contrived calm. In Jemima's case it was more of a shield.

Ali lay in bed thinking about the evening's events getting up only to open the window so she could hear the beeps, shouts and squeals of New York life. And the next thing she wanted to do was to tell Andy. She wasn't going to waste time texting, she'd give him a call. She was about to press dial when it occurred to her that the circumstances of her heroic action might be considered a little questionable. But she was an editor and it just required some judicious editing.

She probably wouldn't mention how mesmerised she'd been on first laying eyes on Jemima. He didn't need to know her observations regarding her hands and legs or the dazzle in her hazel green eyes. There should be no mention of dazzle. She could tell him about her charisma and attitude, but she'd have to downplay it. She would have told him normally, but in light of what subsequently happened, it didn't seem like a good idea. She could mention the night out, but she couldn't remember much about it prior to Jemima's arrival. It had been rather forgettable. She had to mention Jemima, as she was the subject of her heroism. But she thought it best not to dwell too much on the teeshirt cunnilingus thing, particularly to the man she hoped might propose. She didn't want him to suffer the same anxieties Miles had, although Ali would never suggest a threesome, so it didn't matter. She decided to stick to a late night drink in her hotel room although, if asked about the time, she might knock an hour or two off.

Then there was the cocaine. She didn't want Andy thinking she was doing coke in New York, even if she had been doing coke in New York. But the coke was the probable reason that Jemima lost consciousness, so she'd have to keep that bit in. But she'd deny that she'd tried it, because in this version she was much less impressed with Jemima, and therefore not so prone to peer pressure. Then there was Miles. What was he doing in her room? She didn't want Andy thinking she'd invited Miles into her hotel room. Although she had done that, but not on purpose. She'd hoped to sleep in Tony's room. Ali was fairly convinced he was gay, but she could see that too, should be edited out, particularly as he might have slept with Daphne. And wasn't gay at all.

Then there was Jemima's nakedness. How did Jemima get naked? And what about the bottles? This was precisely the kind of salacious detail that Andy would enjoy, but then she'd have to tell him about Jemima's advances, and she didn't want to do that. Ali looked at her mobile phone and wondered what the hell she could tell him. The only bit that didn't sound too questionable was the vomit in the mouth and she could still taste that.

"Sod it," Ali said and pressed dial.

She'd tell him everything just as it happened. Why wouldn't he believe her? She'd yet to tell her colleagues, and it hadn't occurred to her that they wouldn't believe a single syllable. But Andy didn't answer.

Chapter Sixty-Six

While one part of Andy was concerned, donating his shit seemed like an odd request, the other part was enjoying the meal and the wine. He didn't have a very refined palate but the foie gras, although nice, had quite a unique taste. To him it tasted like something highly alcoholic and by the time he'd finished it he was feeling merrier, although he wasn't sure why. The steak that followed it had never hung on a cow and Pierre had been forced to beat it until it was almost tender.

"Very nice," Andy said.

Barry hadn't mentioned the banana again and Andy wasn't going to raise the subject either and, as the wine was flowing, it didn't seem to matter. But Barry had kept it flowing and was certain it would do its bowel loosening thing soon.

"It is, isn't it?" Barry said.

Andy saw his opportunity.

"It's such a beautiful country," Andy said. "You should do a deal with the cheap airlines and bring tourists in. I could set up a website and sort out the advertising – I do that sort of thing – and I could become an ambassador for Lobo."

Barry nodded. He was weighing up the virtues of tourists over narcotic bananas as a cash source. He wasn't averse to the idea of tourists, but there were issues.

“We would have to invest in the infrastructure and we would need hotels and swimming pools and restaurants,” Barry said.

“You’ve got restaurants,” Andy pointed out.

“But they’re not for tourists,” Barry said.

“Why not?” Andy asked.

Barry thought about this.

“That foie gras,” he said. “It’s platypus liver.”

“Oh,” Andy said. “It doesn’t matter. It could be part of the eccentricity of Lobo.”

“Do you know what the platypuses eat?” Barry asked.

“No,” Andy said.

“They eat the grapes for the local wine,” Barry said.

The taste of the grapes hinted at the taste of the local wine and it further fermented in the stomachs of the platypus which gave them very erratic behaviour. Pierre was forced to soak them in pure alcohol.

“That sounds great,” Andy said.

The brochure and website for Lobo was writing itself. This was precisely the kind of information which would bring the punters in.

“The grapes taste like shit,” Barry said.

“Oh,” Andy said. “But the local wine is great.”

“No,” Barry said. “That tastes like shit too.”

These would be details that would be omitted from the website, Andy thought.

“But the steak was great,” Andy said.

“It’s not cow,” Barry said, adding, “It’s not even horse.”

"What is it?" Andy asked.

Barry shrugged. He'd learned not to ask.

"Probably aged rhino," Barry said, adding, "Aged in the sense of old."

"It doesn't matter," Andy said. "You don't lie about it, you make it a feature. Where in the world can you get foie gras à la platypus?"

Andy waited for Barry's response, but it was slow in coming.

"Lobo," Andy said.

"Where in the world can you get steak à la rhino?" Andy asked.

"Lobo," Barry said.

"Where in the world can you get yellow salad?" Andy's asked.

"Lobo!' they both shouted.

It was the rallying cry celebrating Lobo's uniqueness. Andy could see the pictures in the back of his mind.

"I could make a video," Andy said.

Barry nodded again. He was torn. He could see the virtues of Andy's argument, but it all arrived at the same thing. In order to make money he needed money. It all came back to the bananas. He raised the plastic bag. It coincided with a rumble in Andy's stomach and the certain feeling that evacuation was imminent.

"Where are the toilets?" Andy asked.

Barry pointed to the sign and Andy took the plastic bag. It was better than being punched in the face. His bowels had been rigid with fear for some days and, when the evacuation came, it was fairly monumental. Andy was lucky to catch it all. Fifteen minutes later he returned to his seat with a bag full of shit.

"Let's go," Barry said and got up.

Chapter Sixty-Seven

Despite vowing to never enter the pub, Andy's Dad had slid in quietly and ordered a pint of IPA. He was even sitting in the same seat. He'd received a few nodded welcomes. He nodded back. He was there for a reason. Last night Andy's mum had proposed that they do it a second time. Proposed might have been too gentle a way of putting it, she'd sorted of insisted. And Andy's dad was up for it. The only problem was that he hadn't consulted a third party, who was to be involved, but was having a bit of a strop. So while there was full agreement that sex should happen a second time, his penis had gone on strike. There was a shop steward in charge who'd pointed out that not just had they exceeded all reasonable work hours, they were now moving, in light of his age, into issues of health and safety. Despite this, management was sent in to negotiate.

"Dear god," Andy's dad muttered and took a mouthful of IPA.

He had not the slightest idea that his wife could be so skilled and persuasive, and the strike was called off and they were back in business. But it had been touch and go, and it was for that reason he was sitting in the pub. Technically, although he hated to think of it that way, he was waiting for his dealer. The man with the viagra. Andy's dad had exhausted his supply and, as he had not the slightest idea what the stuff cost, he was sitting there with quite a bit of cash in his pocket, and every intention of spending it.

"Hey, how are you, mate?"

Someone had effortlessly slid by him, giving him a gentle greeting slap on the shoulder. He was one of the crowd, but it wasn't the man that had passed him the pills. Andy's dad hoped he'd be in and out there quicker than, he paused to think of an activity which involved going in and out quickly, but struggled to find one. But it didn't look like that would be the case. He might have to stay for the long haul.

"How's the wife? Still after some?"

Someone else had appeared. Andy's dad spluttered some of his beer onto the bar. He knew he couldn't cope with this kind of banter in any state of sobriety and knocked back the IPA and bought a round. He left a little pause.

"No, mate," Andy's dad said. "She's getting some."

Andy's dad didn't notice the exchange of glances. He was fairly sure he'd delivered the line well and it was actually true. She was. Twice a night, nearly. A couple of other people turned up and the conversation drifted to sport and with it a few more pints followed. But the older man with the pills was nowhere to be seen. Andy's dad knew his wife would be a bit disappointed when he got back, as the alcohol was likely to invoke another strike. Very probably a complete walk out. All tools would be downed. But Andy's dad had told his wife the purpose of his visit.

For some reason he couldn't fathom, the sex had opened lines of communication that had not been open before. They were telling each other things. And when he had explained about the viagra, Andy's mum just got more excited. Andy's dad's phone pinged. The mobile phones were new. Lydia had insisted. She couldn't believe they didn't have mobile phones and felt it was her duty to drag them into the twenty-first century. Andy's dad had only one name programmed into his and it was Andy's mum. The second 'absolutely vital' skill that Lydia had taught his wife was the facility to send texts. He peered at his phone.

"Has the eagle landed?"

Andy's dad put his hand round his phone so that the others couldn't see. He looked up. They were looking at him.

"Who's sending you texts?" one of them said.

For a reason Andy's dad couldn't explain, he blushed a little. This led his new crowd of friends to arrive at conclusions which were rather far from the truth.

"Playing away?" someone said.

"No," Andy's dad stuttered. "It's the wife."

It was clear that nobody believed him and he squirmed uncomfortably on the barstool.

"Be careful," one of them advised. "It cost me the house."

It was a statement that took out the jollity of the moment and could only be resolved by ordering more pints.

"No, honestly. It's the wife. She insisted, or her friend did," Andy's dad said.

"Is that Lydia?" someone interrupted.

"Well, yes it is," Andy's dad said. "Anyway she said we needed to get mobile phones. I don't know what for."

"She knows where you are," someone said.

"She does?" Andy's dad said, a little surprised.

"Yeah, there's an app that tracks you."

"Oh," Andy's dad said.

He'd meant it as an expression of surprise, but it had sounded like guilt again. He really wasn't good at this pub banter thing.

"Anyway, what did she say?" someone else asked.

Andy's dad stuttered. While he and his wife were enjoying newfound channels of communication he didn't want to extend them to the blokes in the pub. He didn't want to admit that he was only there to pick up some viagra.

"Oh nothing," he said.

Andy's dad might have said 'I've organised an orgy' as it was clear to everyone else that whatever the text said it was more than nothing. A few of the blokes were younger, many of the others had more precarious relationships, and consequently they were all aware of the modern form of flirtation that could be found in an exchange of texts.

"Are you going to answer her, then?" someone said.

Andy's dad stuttered again. He actually wanted to go to the toilet, but he knew that if he did, they'd suspect he was sending texts from there. He waved them away with the closest approximation to casualness Andy's dad was capable of. It wasn't very convincing and half a pint later he nipped off to the loo. Fortunately no one followed him and he got his phone out while letting a fairly generous stream of IPA fuelled urine hit the porcelain. He couldn't remember how to activate the keyboard from which he could make a reply. He stabbed buttons optimistically.

"You alright?" someone had appeared, a little silently in Andy's dad view, by his side.

His jet of urine missed the latrine and hit the wall and Andy's dad, who was not a man who generally left his penis unguided, brought it back on target.

"Fine," Andy's dad said.

He decided he'd wait until later to text. He would have switched the phone off, but he wasn't sure how. When he got back to the bar there was another pint waiting for him. He would have left, although he was thinking about hanging around outside, which might have been a worse plan. He steamed into it. A further pint might have followed and he was certain he heard a bell. There was no question it was time to go. Andy's dad staggered off the stool and waved goodbye. He was really quite pissed. He was so pissed he nearly missed it.

"Psst," a voice said.

Chapter Sixty-Eight

When Barry got in the Mercedes the level of alcohol in his blood was, by the standards of the rest of the world, over the legal limit. But, as the king, he had rarely been held back by such things, and he felt fine. The car fired up with turbine-like smoothness as if, he thought, it was asking for a thrash. He slid it into drive and Andy instinctively pulled his seatbelt on. Barry had carefully placed the bag of shit in the immaculately carpeted boot.

"Okay?" Barry asked.

"Sure," Andy said.

Barry floored the throttle. He couldn't help himself. The car gave a little wiggle, as if it were unsure as to how to proceed, and then it roared down the road.

"Bloody hell," Andy said.

He'd enjoyed the meal and he thought he'd presented a pretty decent pitch as ambassador for Lobo's tourist trade. He might not need to phone his parents. And he'd donated his shit. What more can be required of him?

"Am I done?" Andy asked.

Barry didn't answer. He was concentrating. He was driving the big saloon as if it were a supercar and a youthful one at that. He had plans to extend the road, it was more of a track than a road, and put in a longer straight. He'd only looked down for a second and the car was doing a hundred and twenty. He needed a straight where he could max it. It was this thought that absorbed him and when he arrived at a corner, which was a sharp left-hander. He was travelling at a speed which was rather more than the ageing tyres could cope with. He braked mid corner.

"Oh shit," Andy said.

It was dark and there were no street lights, and Andy could see solid-looking trees surrounding him. While things were going very fast, they appeared to slow down. The rear end of the car shot out as if it weren't attached to the front. It certainly had no intention of going in the same direction. They were off the road and heading for a tree. But there was a rock which deflected the car past the tree, removing the wing mirrors until they were heading for another tree. Barry yanked at the wheel and somehow they missed that tree too. There was no avoiding the third tree, which they hit head on. Although the Mercedes was a little elderly it was equipped with airbags, which fired in a second, and provided a soft landing for Andy. After the noise of the various collisions, there was an odd silence. The airbags deflated and Andy looked out. The tree had shortened the bonnet, but his arms and legs were fine.

"Hey," he said, to Barry.

Andy couldn't quite bring himself to say 'your excellency' and his experience so far was that Barry fell way short of excellent. But Barry was slumped motionless over the steering wheel. Andy shook him. He didn't respond. He shook him again.

"Oh for fuck's sake," Andy said.

This was a dilemma. If the king was dead it might look like he was to blame. It was hard to think how his bad situation could be made worse, but this would be it. If he called for help it might look like he was innocent. But he couldn't be certain of that. Andy got out the car. The door now operated with the slickness it had enjoyed when it had left the factory twenty odd years ago. It had stopped creaking. The rest of the car looked a wreck. Steam was quietly escaping from the radiator. Andy went round to the other side of the car. He opened the door.

"Your Excellency," he said.

They weren't words that tripped naturally off his lips, as they hadn't in the Ferrera Rocher advertisement. He shook him again. He heard something fall. It was Barry's mobile phone. Andy picked it up. He wondered what the number for the emergency services was and if Lobo had any. He tried 999. Nothing happened. He knew it was 911 in America and he tried that. Nothing happened.

"Bugger," Andy muttered and leant on the car.

He dialled the only other emergency service he knew. He phoned his parents. But it rang and rang as if they weren't in, which was really strange.

Chapter Sixty-Nine

Andy's dad was really quite pissed but, despite that, or maybe because of it, he rattled off a text like a teenager.

'The eagle has landed.'

He had the pills. They weren't even that expensive and, for good measure, he'd bought the entire stock and put in an order for more. He was weaving along the road, a straight line was a little demanding, and it occurred to him that he could take one now. It would be, given the amount of alcohol he'd consumed, a little optimistic. It might even prompt a further strike. But Andy's dad was oddly and unusually excited. He also knew that Andy's mum, who'd been waiting in anticipation, might also be a little excited. That thought was exciting too. He stopped to have a wee on a tree.

"There we go," he said.

He dampened the bark of the tree in a reassuring way, but his penis did not look likely to bring itself to its other function. But what did he have to lose? He shook himself and tucked it back in his trousers and took out one of the pills from the pack.

"Why not? he muttered.

He had not been much of a 'why not' kind of person, particularly in his role as bank manager, where he had been trained to look at everything with great caution. But this was retirement. This was the time to take up new hobbies. He swallowed a pill. He felt like he'd just done something very naughty indeed. He had a bank reunion to go to the following day and he wondered what he'd say if asked what his new hobbies were. He chuckled to himself and carried on. The pub was further away than he remembered and the night air was a little colder. It might have been that, or it might have been the things he was thinking about doing once he got home. Either way he could feel himself sobering up.

"Again," he muttered.

He hadn't particularly noticed the failings of the ageing human body, or at least he hadn't until his wife had pointed them out. But his bladder was clearly not as adept at storing urine as it used to be. He stopped and found another tree.

"Woo," he said.

But in his defence, he thought, he'd never had that much experience drinking large quantities of beer. For all he knew he might be no worse than he was when he was twenty. He didn't immediately notice that he was pissing higher up the tree. For some reason it reminded him of working in the bank. It was a sort of metaphor about becoming more senior, but he couldn't quite see how that translated into pissing on a tree. He wasn't *that* sober.

"Nearly home," he said.

He also wasn't a man who needed to express his thoughts out loud, but it seemed comforting. He only had a couple of streets left. He wasn't sure if he'd need another piss. He didn't feel like one, but he didn't want to arrive home, and either need to go in the front garden, or have to go as soon as he entered the house. He decided it might be wise to take a precautionary piss. Then he wondered if he should send another text. The problem was that if he did, his wife would expect sex, and he wasn't entirely sure he could deliver. He knew he wanted to, but the shop steward might point out that fair working practice does not include four pints of IPA. Or it might have been five. Then there was the problem of what he should say. He took his mobile out and looked at it.

He knew this was the modern form of flirtation, but he had not the slightest recollection of ever having flirted with his wife, even when they'd first met. They'd met at the bank. He was on a graduate training course and she was one of the tellers. He'd seen her, but not really noticed her. It was when they did the cashing up together at the end of the day. She'd laughed at things he'd said. Andy's dad stopped and steadied himself against a tree. Now that he thought about it he was aware that he'd never said anything in his life that was remotely funny, so the fact that she'd laughed was strange. Perhaps he'd been flirting and he didn't know it. Then he'd suggested they go for a drink.

"No," he said to himself.

Had she suggested the drink? She might have. No, now he thought about it, it was him. They'd gone for a drink, he was sure about that. What had they talked about? He was fairly sure they'd talked about the bank.

But it had opened the door for further drinks. Not that they'd drank much. His parents wouldn't have been pleased if he'd come home pissed. Then they'd gone to the cinema. It was at that time that his mother had said that they were courting, and if his mother had told him, it was probably the case. A few months later they had a meal together. They'd stopped talking about the bank and had started to talk about the future.

"Bugger," Andy's dad said to himself.

It was the realisation that they'd gone from workmates to a married couple without any flirtation in between. They'd just seemed like the right two people to get married and settle down, so why bother? Andy's dad knew in his heart this wasn't right. He took out his phone.

'The eagle is ready to fly again.'

He chuckled to himself, sent the text, and prepared himself for his precautionary piss on the last tree home. It was when the stream of urine ran close to his eye level that he realised that the eagle was flying already. He did his best to get it back in his trousers and a minute later let himself into his house. It was strangely quiet. There were a few leaves on the hall floor. They often blew in with the wind and he kneeled down to clear them up. Except they weren't leaves. They were petals. They ran the length of the hall. He followed them until he arrived at the neatly carpeted stairs. There were a couple of petals on each step. He followed them up to the first floor, unaware that he was on his hands and knees. When he got to the top he looked along the corridor. They led to the main bedroom. He could feel his heart pounding in his chest. He couldn't hear a squeak in the house. The silence was deafening. His ears were ringing with his raised blood pressure. He stood up. Andy's dad walked slowly to the end of the corridor, and to the door of the main bedroom, as if he were in a horror film expecting something to fly out at him. The door was ajar. He pushed it gently. He could hear the telephone ringing downstairs, but that didn't seem to matter. He wasn't about to go down and be told by someone in India that his computer had a virus. He didn't care if it did. He entered the bedroom.

"Mother of god," Andy's dad whispered hoarsely.

His wife was draped across the bed in a small sea of red petals which matched the lingerie which covered some, but not much, of her body. Andy's dad knew in his heart that it should have been him who had arranged the petals, but then it hadn't been him who'd suggested that first drink either.

Chapter Seventy

"Well, who would have thought it," Tony said.

Tony intended to extract as much entertainment from the event as he could, as his sexuality was no longer on trial. Jess, Tony and Daphne had met at the coffee shop by the hotel. Ali had not been invited.

"That Jemima has some body," Tony said wistfully.

The image of Jemima's nakedness hadn't left him and he was savouring it. As their view had been so fleeting they were assembling a picture from their combined memories.

"And that was a pretty deep snog," Tony pointed out.

They were all in agreement that Ali was not someone they would have guessed had lesbian tendencies.

"No question tongues were fully involved," Jess added.

"That was intense. Passionate even," Tony said.

They looked at him. He was enjoying the image a little more than they felt was necessary.

"She is gorgeous," Jess admitted.

"Very gorgeous," Tony said.

"Do you think Andy knows?" Daphne said.

They looked at Daphne. She hadn't volunteered much on the subject.

"Knows what?" Jess asked.

"That she's into women," Daphne said.

This landed like a new and fresh revelation, although there were few things more succulent than office gossip, particularly when it came to matters of who was sleeping with who.

"It would explain why he hasn't popped the question," Tony said.

"Or even called her," Daphne said.

"He's probably getting therapy," Jess said, realising she might have revealed something about herself.

But the others didn't notice. They were still trawling the contents of the picture that was trapped in their minds.

"Did you notice the hotel menu?" Tony said.

Everyone shrugged.

"It was covered in a white powder," Tony said.

It took a moment for the others to connect the dots.

"You mean they were doing coke?" Jess said.

They sipped their coffees chastely, as if they were a church gathering who had strong views regarding the ingesting of drugs.

"Would that have sent her a bit lezzie?" Daphne said and then regretted it.

"I don't think there's much evidence to suggest that taking cocaine alters your sexuality," Jess said.

"No," Tony said, "but it might have helped her abandon her inhibitions."

He'd said it rather knowingly and it might have revealed a more highly faceted sexuality than he wanted to admit to.

"That's true," Daphne said.

Daphne had very recent experience of abandoning her inhibitions and she'd loved every minute of it. This New York trip had been quite an eye opener for her. Jess's eyes flared a little, but she let it go.

"And then there was Miles," Tony said.

"What was he doing there?" Jess asked.

"What was he doing with that gin bottle?" Daphne said.

The bottle had perplexed them a little.

"I think it was vodka," Tony said.

"I think you're right," Jess said.

Jess wasn't very familiar with white powder, but she knew a thing or two about cheap vodka.

"No question," Jess said.

"What kind of vodka?" Daphne asked.

No one knew why she asked, although it might have been the attention to detail that was required of her job.

"Shagadov?" Jess suggested.

"Bonkadov?" Tony said.

They looked at Daphne who'd struggle to put dildo with dov and then given up. But there was another issue they had to attend to.

"What are we going to say?" Jess asked.

"Who to?" Tony asked.

"Ali," Jess said.

Chapter Seventy-One

Andy had to get help. He didn't understand any of the contacts on Barry's phone, and so he had to do it the old fashioned way, on foot. It was pitch black. This was a jungle. He could hear the rustle and squark of animals. He didn't want to stay in the car. He found the torch on Barry's phone and pointed in the direction they'd come. But he wasn't sure if he was lighting the way, or lighting a beacon for a predator. He turned the torch off and let his eyes adjust. There was some moonlight which cast eery shadows. He picked his way slowly back towards the road and then he saw something move.

Andy froze. It was large and low, like a crocodile. If he was eaten by a crocodile now no one would ever know. His parents and Ali would just think he disappeared mysteriously. They might even think he was running from commitment. He hadn't been. He would have give anything for commitment and domestic bliss in Hackney. The warm safety. The animal came closer. It moved with a stagger. Andy stepped back until his back hit a dense bush. He was trapped. This was it. He took the phone out and put on the torch in the hope that the blinding light might frighten the animal. And there it was. It was a duckbill platypus. He didn't seem much bothered by the light. His eyes were already a little bloodshot. The animal approached him and Andy moved back defensively, but there was no escaping. The platypus swayed from one side to another as it made its way forward. Andy was pretty sure they were vegetarian, but he couldn't be certain. There might be a rare flesh-eating platypus unique to Lobo. He probably wouldn't mention it on the website. The animal moved further forward, within a foot of Andy, and then it farted and vomited at his feet. A second later it was snoring. Andy stepped round it.

Andy looked around and found more platypuses. They seemed equally benign. He quickly followed the tracks of the car and realised they'd travelled over a hundred metres from the road, narrowly missing a number of trees. They'd been lucky. At least he'd been lucky. He got to the road. The road seemed safer, but he had no idea where he was, or which direction it was to the town. He fiddled with Barry's mobile until a map appeared. They were several miles from town. He started to walk. The road was oddly twisting, and he could have taken the occasional shortcut, but he was hesitant about walking through the jungle. This was Africa, he thought. There were likely to be all sorts of unpleasant predators lurking in there, as well as the platypuses.

An hour later Andy was no closer to town and there had been no passing traffic. If Barry was bleeding out it wouldn't look good for him. They would recognise him from the restaurant. He wasn't difficult to identify. He was doomed whatever he did. If he'd stayed with Barry and done nothing, it would have been just as bad. An hour later he could just make out the lights from the town. When he finally got there he had to find his bearings, as he'd entered the town from a different direction. But everything was closed up. People were in bed. It was almost silent. But not quite. He could hear a distant beat. A bass note. He followed it until he arrived at *Hell and High Water*. He descended the stairs. He had to raise the alarm otherwise the king might die. When he finally broke through the doors the music was louder than it had been the last time he'd been there. The bass note felt like it was rearranging his internal organs. He found the barman.

"The king has been involved in a car accident. He needs an ambulance," Andy shouted.

The barman, who was a little out of it, smiled, turned to the bar and made him a pina colada. It wasn't actually a pina colada, but it was as close as resources would allow. The bar owner operated a happy hour system, but they'd long passed that. This was the barman's happy hour in which he rarely remembered to collect money for the drinks, and was a time at which everything was set to eleven, particularly the music.

"The king," Andy shouted urgently.

But no one seemed to be listening. It didn't matter because even if they were listening they couldn't hear and, although they quite liked Barry, he wasn't as warmly loved as previous Barrys. They might have carried on partying. The barman delivered the pina colada and Andy leaned over, put his hand on the barman's shoulder, and bellowed.

"We need an ambulance!"

The barman laughed. He was *that* stoned he might need medical help. He turned to serve someone a mojito, which wasn't what they ordered, and was only an approximate mojito, but no one seemed to mind.

"Ambulance," Andy shouted again into the abyss.

He turned and a hand fell on his shoulder. It was Hamish. Hamish led him through the club into an office at the rear. It wasn't Hamish's office, but it was as approximate as everything else in the club.

"Where have you been?" Hamish asked anxiously.

"Well," Andy began unsure where to start.

"I have been looking for you," Hamish said.

"You have?" Andy asked.

"We're ready to go," Hamish said.

"The thing is," Andy said cautiously. "The king has been involved in a car accident. He needs help. He needs an ambulance."

Hamish nodded. There was always a period of time between Barrys which was a traditional part of the national mourning process. It was a time when tax was not collected. It was quite an appealing thought.

"Okay," Hamish said. "I'll deal with that but we must move now."

Chapter Seventy-Two

Lydia had prepared a fresh attack. Andy's mum had bored her, or more accurately tortured her, about her sexual antics and she needed to raise the bar. Her editor had told her that her recent pieces lacked 'sensuality and inspiration'. The more Andy's mum's sex life had developed the harder it had become for Lydia.

"Naturism, you say?" Andy's mum said.

Lydia nodded. She'd given up stirring her husband and gone back to Bruno. Bruno was like one of those big toys she used to give her kids. The packaging was the best bit.

"Is that like nudism?" Andy's mum asked.

She tried to picture herself wandering around in the altogether and it was a bit of a stretch. She'd felt self conscious enough putting on the lingerie. Although the lingerie was becoming her viagra.

"That's it," Lydia said, taking a sip from her skinny latte.

And, in a way, the lingerie had been another kind of viagra for Andy's dad. She'd never seen his pupils quite so dilated. There had been a general dilation, she thought with a smile.

"Yes, there's nothing like the freedom of feeling the fresh air on your body, particularly," Lydia said lowering her voice, "between your legs."

Lydia had plans for Bruno, but she worried that he was like a dachshund she once owned. He had been impossibly cute but the fucker, she often said, was impossible to train.

"Oh, I'm not sure my husband will go for that," Andy's mum said.

Andy's mum tried to picture it. She'd rarely seen her husband entirely naked. She'd seen little bits, but the whole was normally obscured by clothing, or a towel, or underpants. Or all three. He never took those underpants off. She'd bought ten pairs all the same colour from Marks and Spencer about ten years ago, and she knew he rotated them because they appeared in the laundry basket but, if it weren't for that, she might assume he continually wore the same pair.

"Wouldn't he?" Lydia said with some glee.

Lydia wondered how far she could push them. The thought made her excited about the potential articles that this approach might generate. That would be good for her and her editor. The inspiration might be back.

"Well, I could ask," Andy's mum said doubtfully.

Andy's mum had actually seen more of her husband's body recently than ever before and, given his age and attitude to exercise, it wasn't in too bad shape.

"The forecast for the next few days is terrific. A mini heatwave," Lydia said.

Andy's mum smiled. They'd always liked a bit of nice weather, but often they'd both been working. Now they had all the time in the world. It made sense to at least get him to the beach.

"And I know a nice beach, a naturist beach, in Hastings. It's not far," Lydia chipped in.

Now that Lydia thought about it she might grab Bruno and take him down there too. But before that she was going to have to sit him down and give him a tour of the female body, pointing out notable hotspots, and giving him specific instructions. She'd had sex with more skilled teenagers. Some had an instinctive grasp, like kids with computers. Others were not so gifted.

"We could certainly go there and see how it felt," Andy's mum said.

Andy's mum was getting that tingling feeling again. She wasn't much of an exhibitionist either, she didn't even possess a bikini, but maybe she'd reached the right time of life. Not the time of life when her body was at its best, but the time of life when she didn't give a damn what people thought.

"It's quite a long walk, through the woods, but naturist beaches always are. When you get there it will be beautiful and tranquil," Lydia said wistfully.

She couldn't believe she was jealous of Andy's mum's sex life. It made her determined to redouble her efforts and get Bruno acquainted with what's what.

"If you give me your phone," Lydia said. "I'll mark it and you can find it."

Andy's mum handed over her phone a little anxious that Lydia might look at the salacious texts she'd received from her husband.

"You can do that?" Andy's mum said.

Lydia fiddled expertly with Andy's mum's phone. They had described it as 'smart' in the shop, although Andy's mum wasn't sure what that meant.

"Here," Lydia said. "Just press that."

That was exactly the approach she was going to take with Bruno.

Chapter Seventy-Three

Barry woke up with a headache. It was a headache which suggested to him that Pierre had sold him the cheap wine again. Then he realised he hadn't made it home. A beat later he was awake enough to see he was in the car. There was a tree in front of him and it was closer than it should be. Barry pieced the rest of the evening together. He remembered the rear end of the car losing traction and the subsequent journey off road. He checked his limbs and, aside from a few cuts on his face, he was undamaged. He was also alone. Andy had gone.

He got out of his car and almost shed a tear. The panels of the car were crumpled. He remembered his trip to the factory in Germany and powering along on the unrestricted autobahn. This was the end of the car's life. He looked for his mobile phone.

"Platypus shit," he said.

He'd just stepped in some and it was runny and sticky. He tried to wipe it off, but it seemed determined to adhere to his shoes. He grunted and took a last look at his car and turned away. Andy had disappeared, along with his mobile phone, and he was a long walk from town. He followed the tracks of the car, stopping to kick the occasional drunken platypus. It helped him clear his anger and it just prompted the animals to fart. And then he remembered something. Barry walked back to the car and opened the boot.

"Shit," he said.

There was no denying it. The boot of his luxuriously carpeted car was covered in shit. Andy's shit.

"Shit," he said again.

He had no choice. Barry found a clean part of the ruptured plastic bag and used it to scrape up the scattered excrement. They'd come to a halt at some speed and Andy's crap was not the most solid, but he did a good job of getting into the bag. Barry walked back to the main road and it wasn't long before a pickup came along. He put up his hand and it screamed to a halt.

"Your Excellency," the driver said.

Barry got in the pickup silently and without being invited. This might be how he'd have to get around from now on. It was either that, or giving up his presidential jet, and the thought of that made him feel a little sick. That aeroplane made him feel good. It was the best thing in his life. He pointed in the direction of town and the driver stepped on it.

"Of course, your Excellency," he said unctuously.

Barry had a sudden revelation. The thing that was most important to him in life was his plane and then his car. And he couldn't make the payments on one and he'd wrecked the other. His son, Barry junior, was mostly just an irritation.

"A beautiful day, your Excellency," the driver said.

Barry could see the shallow nature of his life and it all hung around personal possessions. It wasn't clear to him if this was an epiphany, or if he was mourning the Mercedes. Either way, Barry couldn't stop himself. He began to cry.

"A truly beautiful day," the driver said.

The driver had never met the king. He hadn't even seen him from afar and this was a most awkward moment for him. Worse, it smelled as if the president had crapped himself.

"I think it will be beautiful all day," the driver added.

Barry could see no beauty in his life. He had to see his son and tell him he loved him. He wasn't sure if he did, but he knew he should, and that might be a good start. After that he would sell his aeroplane and run around in the gardener's pickup. He would become the people's king.

"Stop," Barry said.

They'd arrived at the town and the administrative building. He was going to sort out the plane. He was going to let it go, like a lover. He got out of the car without thanking the driver. There was more work involved in becoming the people's king than he thought. He entered the building and people around him bowed and muttered more unctuous greetings. His office was on the top floor, but the lift was broken again. He took the stairs. It was eight flights and Barry wasn't a man who believed in exercise.

"Your Excellency," someone said, as he passed him on the stairs.

There was a whiff of something that stopped him. It appeared to come from the bag that Barry was holding. Barry ignored him and pretended to look at his phone, but as he no longer had it, it just looked like he was examining his hand. But he needed to get his breath back. The problem was that each time someone addressed him as 'your excellency' he felt more and more entitled to that plane. As if he owed it to his people. It was more the other way round, but it didn't matter.

"I should have a plane," he muttered to himself and with that thought heaved himself up the remaining flight of stairs.

He got to his desk and prodded his computer. It took him instantly to his favourite website: eBay. He had sort of made a decision on the way up. He was going to become the people's king, but he was going to do it by downsizing his jet. It was a compromise. And then he'd go and see his son. But there remained one possibility. A possibility he'd dumped noisily on his desk. He picked up the phone and dialled a number.

"Gary," Barry said. "I've got a bag of shit for you."

Chapter Seventy-Four

"Okay," Jess said. "So what was Miles doing with that vodka bottle?"

They were in the same coffee bar, and although the air was crisp it was warm enough for them to sit outside. Yellow cabs were flying past and there was a noisy crossing with an army of people each side. It would have been unpleasant in London, but seemed fitting in New York. This time they'd invited Ali.

"Vodka bottle?" Ali said.

There had been a lot of things to see, and the kind of bottle which had become stranded between Jemima's legs had not, for Ali, been one of them. It was also clear that Jess did not believe a single sentence of Ali's explanation of the previous evening's events.

"Miles wasn't doing anything," Ali said.

That wasn't entirely correct. Miles was removing the bottle. He had done it for the greater good and the dignity of his ex wife. It was an action which would not normally be associated with such bold causes.

"No, I saw him with the bottle," Jess insisted.

"But he didn't put it there," Ali said.

It was the sort of exclamation which made her feel that the more she explained the worse it got.

"Hold on," Tony said. "I get it. You were..."

Tony paused as he struggled to find the correct verb for what he thought had taken place. There was no subtle way of putting it.

“Fucking her with the bottle!” Jess declared.

“No. No, of course, I wasn’t,” Ali said.

Jess looked at Tony and Tony raised his eyebrows. There was a general consensus that the lady was protesting too much and bottle fucking was precisely what she’d been doing.

“Well, whatever floats your boat,” Tony said.

They were still questioning whatever it was that floated Tony’s boat, but at the moment the focus was on Ali.

“No, I went to Miles’s room to get him to get rid of Jemima,” Ali said.

This was met with a pause as the event was digested. Jess decided to unpick it.

“You went to Miles’s room in the middle of the night?” Jess asked.

“Miles, the owner of the company?” Tony asked.

“Lecherous Miles?” Jess asked.

There was no possibility it could have been another Miles, but they both felt the event required some milking. Jess and Tony exchanged glances.

“Not exactly,” Ali explained. “I left Jemima in my room and I thought I could spend the night in Tony’s room.”

“My room?” Tony said.

“Yes,” Ali admitted.

“Why?” Tony asked slowly.

“Well, it’s safe. Isn’t it? You’re gay,” Ali said.

“He’s not gay!” Jess and Daphne shouted.

Ali attempted to exchange disbelieving glances with Jess, but she wasn't playing ball.

"So why were you in Miles's room?" Jess asked.

"I got the wrong room," Ali insisted.

"And why were you snogging Jemima?" Tony asked.

"I wasn't snogging her," Ali said. "It was CPR!"

"Was it now," Jess said, switching to sarcasm.

"Who was the actor who was caught with someone who wasn't his wife and said it's not my fault, I'm a sex addict?" Tony said.

"How is that relevant?" Ali asked.

"How, indeed," Jess replied.

Jess started tapping her fingers on the table. Despite the noise of the cars rumbling by, and the bleep from the crossing, it was quite loud and annoying. Ali looked down the street. She could see the Empire State Building. They had been allowed some time off and Ali didn't want to spend it being cross-examined.

"I'm going up the Empire State Building," Ali said and got up.

Neither of them moved as they still felt resentful of her transparent ambition which had led her to what a newspaper might refer to as a lewd act. Ali didn't care as she wanted to be on her own. Andy's complete lack of communication was annoying her to the point that she wondered if she should be concerned. It wasn't like him not to answer the phone and he usually sent her texts. And this was the longest they'd been apart.

"Okay," Jess shouted and got up to follow her.

Tony got up a second later, but Ali didn't slow down for them.

Chapter Seventy-Five

Andy found himself behind the steering wheel of a truck. It was quite a climb into the driver's seat and it was a sizeable truck, and he took a moment to familiarise himself with the controls. He hadn't driven for a long time, and when he had it was to pass his test in a Nissan Micra. There was nothing micra about this lorry, which looked like it had been converted into a coach and done so with minimal resources. The rear of it was filled with people who looked very much like illegal immigrants. This wasn't just an illegal activity: it might also be immoral. But if Barry was dead, and he was the last person seen with him, then he had to get the hell out of there.

"Here you are," Hamish said.

There were other changes. Hamish had suggested that he'd look less distinctive if he 'lose the beard.' It had taken a bit of hacking, but eventually Andy had lost the beard. He felt a small mourning for its passing, as if he was losing his youth. Hamish handed him the passport he'd forged half an hour earlier. Andy looked at the picture of himself. He looked older than he remembered. He doubted he could make it into Britain with the passport, but it would get him away from Lobo, and that would be a good start.

"Ready?" Hamish said.

"No problem," Andy said, feeling the sweat running down his back.

Andy turned the key. The engine turned and burst into life, shaking the seat and the dashboard. He checked the pedals.

"ABC," Andy said to himself and, for good measure, added, "Accelerator, brake, clutch."

He pressed the clutch to the floor and grabbed the long stick which he hoped would select the gears. It was vague and approximate but that, he now knew, was the spirit of Lobo. He sent it in the general direction of first and pressed the accelerator and lifted the clutch. The lorry moved forward. Hamish had given him instructions and a sat nav.

"You stop in two hundred miles," Hamish said.

Andy would have given him a wave, but his hands were already fully employed. The road was clear and he rose through the gears until eventually he got to top gear. The sun was coming up and it was light, but still cool. He drove with the window open and slowly enough for someone to bang on the window behind him, making him jump and nearly veer off the road. Half an hour later he was feeling a little more accustomed to driving a truck and had edged up to forty miles an hour. As a further hour passed he finally eased it up to fifty and his passengers stopped complaining. He could see them in the rear view mirror and most, it seemed, had fallen asleep. There must have been fifty people crammed into the rear.

Eventually Andy felt a little more relaxed. The roads, although dusty and occasionally not well surfaced, were straight and without interruption. He looked around the cab. It had a tatty makeshift quality about it, with wires hanging down and holes in the dashboard. There was even a radio which worked. He pressed buttons until eventually he was accompanied by Britney Spears. It was a radio station which clearly favoured Britney, as it played little else. It was while he was fiddling with the tuning that he noticed that one of the leads dangling from the dashboard looked very much like an iPhone charger lead. He fumbled around looking for Barry's phone, thinking for a second he'd thrown it away, but eventually he found it and attempted to plug it in. For a second the screams from his passengers distracted him as he'd veered onto a grass verge, but eventually he united the phone with the lead. It wasn't followed by a positive bing. It wasn't working. He'd have to moderate his use of the phone.

Three hours later Andy pulled in. This was the place Hamish had told him to stop, according to the sat-nav, and Andy was unsure whether he should let his passengers out for a break. He assumed they were passengers and not prisoners, but he couldn't be certain of anything. He got out of the truck. It was a large dusty carpark with a single storey building to one end. It looked like the truck stops he'd seen in France. There was a light wind, but it didn't disguise the heat of the day, and Andy felt tired. It occurred to him that there were three features of escape, not two. Eating, taking a dump and sleeping. He'd managed two out of three and perhaps that was the third rule, that you're only ever able to do two out of the three. But now he had a passport, albeit a dodgy one, and had a functioning mobile phone. He took it out and phoned his parents.

"Mr Andy?" a voice next to him said.

Andy hadn't noticed a small weaselly man appear next to him. A cigarette was perched on his lips and he was dressed in denim, despite the heat. He looked a little like a cowboy.

"Yes," Andy said nervously.

This was the next stage of the journey.

"Hamish?" Andy said.

Every person he was to meet was called Hamish, which suggested that Hamish was probably not called Hamish either, but it made it easier for Andy to remember his contacts.

"It is so," Hamish the cowboy said.

He'd been waiting for three days and had rehearsed his opening line and had finally arrived at 'it is so' which he felt had the right touch of mystery about it. Hamish the cowboy was an aspiring actor of the kind that pronounces 'act' and 'tor' as if they're two different words.

"What next?" Andy asked.

"Fuel," Hamish the cowboy said pointing at the Jerry cans in his pickup.

He said the word fuel as if it were multi-syllabled and with a gravelly delivery, which was influenced by

Al Pacino, with just a subtle hint of Clint Eastwood. His only regret was that he'd been given so little dialogue. He felt he had a duty to make the most of every word.

"And," Hamish the cowboy said, although now he sounded like a lord of the realm Shakespearean actor.

And there was also a touch of Frank Sinatra singing 'New York, New York' in which he ends one line with an 'and' and hangs onto it for dear life before getting to 'if I can make it there, I can make it anywhere'. It was hard to picture in a dusty carpark close to the Lobo border, but Hamish the cowboy felt he'd captured it. So much so he'd nearly forgotten the word that followed it.

"Food," Hamish the cowboy said, pointing to the single storey building.

That was nearly the conclusion of Hamish. He had one more thing to do. He lifted himself into the cab and took the little sat-nav that Hamish had given Andy and reprogrammed it.

"That is," Hamish the cowboy said with an embellished, but in his view multi-nuanced pause, "Your next destination."

This time Andy was fairly convinced it was Patrick Stewart in his capacity as Jean Luc Picard while captaining the second generation of the Star Ship Enterprise. Hamish went off to fetch the Jerry cans and Andy and his passengers made their way to the building at the far end of the carpark. Andy thought he'd use the time to phone his parents. He dialled the number and, bizarrely, it rang and rang and no one answered.

Chapter Seventy-Six

"How many fucking times do I have to tell you?" Lydia yelled.

Bruno looked up like a scolded lapdog. He was getting jaw ache and his tongue had gone numb. He'd always thought sex was supposed to be fun, but this wasn't fun at all. She grabbed the back of his head.

"Here!' she shouted.

Bruno attempted to do as he was told, but his eyesight wasn't that great and, even if he was wearing his glasses, it all looked the same to him. His mind tended to wander when he got bored and now he couldn't remember whether the thing he was in search of was at the top or the bottom.

"Not my arse!" Lydia screamed.

Bruno was becoming a little resigned. He'd had a one in two chance and he'd got it wrong. That was the story of his life.

"You're like bloody Freddy," Lydia said, pushing his head away.

"Who's Freddy?" Bruno asked reasonably.

"He was my bloody dog," Lydia said.

"Oh," Bruno said, a little dejectedly.

"A fucking dachshund. Fucking untrainable," Lydia said.

The worse thing was she'd paid for the room. She had to as Bruno was, in his own words, 'potless'. Her husband was away for a few nights and she wanted to get value for her money. And an orgasm. She feared that Andy's mum would tell her about her basic human right to have an orgasm.

"Stop playing with yourself," Lydia demanded.

Now Bruno looked like the guilty lapdog that had taken a shit on the carpet. He was just seeing to himself. He'd always seen to himself.

"You are not having an orgasm until I've had one," Lydia said.

Bruno had never been subjected to the orgasm police before and he was finding it a bit intimidating. She grabbed his head again and threw it into position as if she was locating a door on its hinge. She was quite precise. A few seconds later Bruno finally managed to hit the spot, but his slobbering wasn't quite triggering the desired response. She moved his head up and down, but she was beginning to think she was using him like a vibrator with worn batteries. Except her vibrator had been designed by someone with an understanding of female anatomy. Bruno continued to lap away, but the steam had gone out of both of them. Lydia sighed.

"Perhaps you can give me a massage," Lydia said.

Bruno had never been quite sharp enough to suffer issues of self esteem, but he was feeling something now and it wasn't good. He wasn't sure if it was used or abused but, as he felt a little scared of Lydia, he got out the massage oil. He'd actually trained as a masseur and, although he was nowhere near the top at massage school, he was pretty competent at it. And she was facing down which limited the opportunities for yelling at him. He applied the oil and ran his hands over her back and shoulders. He kneaded the muscles which were tight and more interested in other forms of release.

"Lower," Lydia muttered.

Bruno hadn't quite finished, but was just smart enough to realise that Lydia was after the kind of massage that would have got him thrown out of massage school. It involved sexual organs. He squirted some oil on her buttocks. When Lydia wasn't writing her salacious articles, she was either taking yoga lessons, or at the gym. Consequently she had a very toned body for someone who'd crossed the half century. But her buttocks were reassuringly fleshy, and only occasionally interrupted with the odd dimple.

"You have a nice bum," Bruno said.

He said it without thinking. If he had applied thought he would have said the wrong thing, but this pleased Lydia, as she was wondering whether she should visit a surgeon. The last time it had been her face, and she'd looked like she'd had a car accident for weeks afterwards. She'd been forced to hide in the country.

"Thank you," Lydia said.

It was the nicest thing she'd said to him, and he continued with the glee of the freshly rewarded puppy. It was even quite sensual, and he began to feel as if he'd returned to a pastime which was fun. Bruno was getting excited. She'd held him back and he was ready to go. Bruno flipped Lydia over with the intention of entering her.

"What?" Lydia said.

While she liked to be in control of things, she didn't want to dampen his ardour. A little bit of urgent passion might be the solution and the buttock kneading had been quite pleasing. She was naked, on her back, and her legs were open. She was ready. But she wasn't expecting a splash of something damp across her feet.

"Sorry," Bruno muttered.

"Oh dear god," Lydia said through clenched teeth.

She wondered if she should go home, pick up some fresh batteries and commune with her vibrator. Conversationally there wasn't much between them. She looked up at Bruno. His face was dejected, as if this time he wasn't the dog that had pooped on the carpet, but taken a dump on the bed. Probably the pillows. A little unexercised part of her brain felt a bit sorry for him. She had him for the day, she might as well make the most of it.

"I'll tell you what," Lydia said. "Let's go to the beach."

Chapter Seventy-Seven

Fingers Marvin was lost, and his car had suffered a catastrophic engine failure. It had run out of petrol. Marvin had become quite good at stealing cars, but was not so skilled at fuelling them. He found cars to be very needy. He was on the run. Although the British newspapers had generally agreed that finishing the business of PPI, and particularly the practice of cold calling, was a good thing, the authorities had frowned at the method he'd chosen to exact his revenge on the endless phone calls.

Marvin had acquired a number of nicknames in his life including 'Spoons Marvin' when he'd killed a Grub-For prison warden with a spoon. It was following the near full automation of the prison system, which was masterminded by a former CEO of a budget airline, who found his natural home running an organisation where not caring about the customers was a positive asset. And Marvin had escaped.

He might have got away with it, but Marvin discovered a predilection for severing and collecting fingers. He'd acquired quite a collection and when he was discovered, and the press learned that he had a sixth finger on his left hand, it was inevitable that he would be called 'Fingers Martin'. Although he subsequently lost his sixth finger it was a nickname that stuck, and Marvin escaped again, and lived quietly in a deserted cottage on Bodmin moor, until he found his true love. He tried to live a normal life and even owned a mobile phone. It was that and his lover's rejection which led to his downfall, and the endless PPI calls proved too much. He found the call centre and resumed his finger collection. It rid the country of PPI salesmen, but Marvin had been on the run ever since.

"Bother," Marvin said.

Although Marvin severed fingers, and had murdered a few people, he didn't swear much although, as he was often on his own, he did conduct lengthy dialogues with himself. He got out of the car. He'd been forced to leave the country and had hidden in a freight plane. Consequently he hadn't the faintest idea where he was, but these things didn't concern Marvin. There was something that was on his mind.

"Dinner," Marvin said.

When he'd lived on Bodmin Moor there had been a ready supply of rabbits, which he'd trapped and eaten for years, until he'd eaten them all and was forced to go to a supermarket. He'd developed a passion for duck, particularly accompanied with honey, and that might have been a further factor in his downfall. He walked into the woods, although it was more like a jungle, and looked for fresh meat. He thought it unlikely he'd find a rabbit or a duck, although it seemed rich in inebriated duckbill platypuses. They were slow and seemed to fart a lot, but they didn't look very appetising. An hour later Marvin changed his mind.

"Needs must," his mother had once said.

Not that he'd known his mother, but he imagined that it was the sort of thing mother's might say. He killed a platypus. It didn't put up much of a fight, as if it was grateful, and he built a fire.

"And what shall we accompany it with?" he asked.

In his brief time attempting to lead a normal life he'd discovered that it was hard to find a television show that didn't involve cooking. He imagined he was on one of those shows.

"Excellent question," he said.

It wasn't clear which side of the conversation he was, but it didn't matter. He looked around. It was then that he discovered the principal diet of the platypuses, which fermented in the sun, and might have been the reason they were inebriated and farted a lot.

"Grapes," he said.

"Excellent choice," he agreed.

He began to pick the grapes and then decided, for good measure, to try one.

"Oh," he said.

There was no question of it. The grapes tasted very much like shit and, as he'd stayed at a Grub-For prison which served short-haul aviation-inspired food, he knew precisely what shit tasted like.

"I know a solution," he said and thrust his hands into his bag.

It was a large battered shopping bag, and was as organised as a Brexit negotiation, but eventually he found what he was looking for.

"Honey," he said.

Fortunately he'd packed some, and he generously basted the platypus, and cooked it lightly. Marvin liked his meat rare. He tasted it.

"Oh shit," he said.

He meant it less as an expletive and more as a description of the taste. He cooked it some more and when it was growing quite dark in colour he tried tasting it again.

"Shit," Marvin said.

The 'oh' part wasn't required. He cooked it thoroughly until he'd damn near cremated it and reminded himself it wasn't duck.

"Excellent," he said.

It wasn't excellent. It was, by any measure, pretty horrible, but Marvin's palate had been blunted by his prison life, and it was better than nothing – which was the less attractive alternative. It was growing dark and he went back to his car to sleep the night. It was on his trip back that he noticed another car abandoned in the woods. It had obviously hit a tree at some speed. He peered in. It was empty and, as it was larger and more comfortable than his car, Marvin decided to stay the night in it.

When the sun rose the following day the jungle was alive with noises which woke Marvin. He had to decide what to do. He'd hoped to find a place that was rich with wildlife which he could live off and, after availing himself of the jungle's toilet facilities, he realised that this wasn't it. Hardy as his stomach was, he couldn't live on a diet of platypuses. He examined the car. Although it had obviously hit the tree at some speed, and the bodywork was very battered and the airbags had gone off, the engine – and crucially the radiator – did not appear to be too badly damaged. It helped that the key was still in the ignition and Marvin had nothing to lose by turning it.

"Excellent," Marvin said as the engine burst into life.

Marvin engaged reverse gear and ten minutes later he was back on the open road. He had no idea which direction he was going in and would have continued until he'd found a nice place to stop. It was a thumb that caused him to lift his foot from the accelerator. Fingers Marvin was more a fingers man but, as his mother might have said, 'needs must'.

Chapter Seventy-Eight

The food at the truck stop had been better than Andy had anticipated, and all his passengers ate cheerfully with him. There was even a flushing toilet and the only further thing he would have liked would have been three hours of sleep. But Hamish the cowboy was beckoning them to leave. It didn't take long for them to fill the truck and this time Hamish the cowboy got in the cab with him.

"To," Hamish the cowboy said, applying every known nuance and a few of his own, "the border."

This was the heart of Hamish the cowboy's role and, unknown to Andy, his too, although his part did not require any dialogue. He just needed to be white, although with the Lobo sunshine he was veering towards pink. Half an hour later they approached a barrier which was the only opening along a wire fence. There were two armed guards. Hamish the cowboy got out of the truck and approached them. He'd reworked his line a little for his own pleasure.

"I have a letter for you," Hamish the cowboy said.

It was more of an envelope, and it didn't contain a message. Or rather it contained a message they all understood. American dollars. They opened the barrier and Andy drove through. Hamish the cowboy turned to walk back to the truck stop. It would take him most of the day, particularly as he had chosen to do so in the style of John Wayne. It hurt his hips a little but,

Hamish the cowboy thought, one must suffer for one's art.

"Bye," Andy shouted.

He was out of Lobo. Andy drove more confidently and a little quicker, but he was tired. He knew that if he didn't get a rest soon he would be in danger of falling asleep. The sat-nav suggested he wasn't too far away from his next stop.

Twenty minutes later he saw it. It was, much like the previous stop, a dusty carpark. He brought the truck to a halt, turned off the ignition, and leant forward onto the steering wheel and fell instantly asleep.

"Mr Andy?" a voice said.

Someone was shaking him. His sleep was so instant and deep he couldn't say if he'd slept for five minutes or five hours, although he knew he needed more sleep. Andy managed to drag his head off the steering wheel.

"I need to sleep," he said sleepily.

"Okay," the man said, and Andy put his head back on the steering wheel, and fell asleep again.

He dreamt he was in Hackney, involved in the simple activity of playing the PlayStation and watching television. Ali was in the kitchen and he could smell cooking smells. He had a beer in his hand. And then someone was shaking him.

"Mr Andy," the voice said.

Andy dragged his head into the most upright position he could achieve.

"Hello?" Andy managed to say.

He looked at the man shaking him. He was short and fat with an almost spherical shape. His skin colour was lighter, as if he was Mediterranean, and he wore a running shirt. The hair from his chest, arms and back stood at least four inches high. He was completely covered in hair.

"Hamish?" Andy asked.

"Yes," Hamish the fur ball confirmed.

He was here to take Andy to the next part of his journey which, he hoped, would get him to a country with a British embassy.

"I take you next place," Hamish the fur ball said.

Hamish the fur ball was sweating heavily, although the temperature had dropped slightly. Hamish the fur ball sweated continually and obviously. Part of it was his body hair, but mostly it was his nervous disposition. Almost everything he did went wrong and, as this was illegal, it was unlikely to be an exception.

"Okay," Andy said. "When do we eat?"

Andy was feeling hungry again, as if he were getting used to three meals a day. Hamish the fur ball maintained his shape by eating continually and had just finished a huge bowl of pasta while he'd been waiting for the truck. Despite that, he was starving.

"Not till later," Hamish the fur ball said, looking nervously around him.

Hamish the fur ball had once inherited a sizeable sum and proceeded to make investments in steel, until the price crashed, and then oil, after which the price crashed. He followed that with further investments with a diminishing pool of money with only one consistent result: whatever market he entered crashed shortly afterwards. He'd assumed that human trafficking wouldn't be so market sensitive. He turned to his pickup. Hamish the fur ball also had Jerry cans full of fuel and he fumbled with the weight of them. Andy would have helped, but he could feel the call of nature beckoning him. He had to deal with that first.

"Are there any toilets?" he asked Hamish the fur ball.

"Not here," Hamish the fur ball said and pointed into the bushes.

Andy knew he had to go and that holding it in would be a mistake. He found some tissues in the cab and grabbed his mobile phone. It really didn't seem possible that his parents wouldn't be in.

"I'll be back," Andy said with more than a hint of Arnold Schwarzenegger.

The car park was surrounded by scrub land and the nearest cover was at least a hundred yards away, which was fine with Andy as he needed to stretch his legs. He dialled his parents number and waited for them to answer. He could hear the familiar British ringing tone, but no one answered. He waited and waited until something electronic between him and his parents in Surrey decided he'd waited long enough. They weren't in.

"Shit," Andy said.

He'd arrived at the bushes. When he was young his parents sent him to scout camp, and it was there that he discovered a dislike of camping, and partaking of activities outdoors that should really be carried out indoors. The alternative involved fumbling in the bushes and he hadn't been keen on that. But things were different now. He found a dense bush, hid behind it, and lowered his trousers and crouched down. His trousers appeared to be in the way. He grabbed them and pulled them away, but he couldn't be certain that there might not be an issue. He didn't have any other clothes and an accident would be a problem. He stood up and removed his shoes, and socks, and his trousers, and underpants and squatted. It was a wise move as his stomach was a little unsettled, but it all proceeded without incident. He stood up, now half naked, and thought that this was the only way to a take a shit in the forest. It wasn't the way people from Surrey did it, and he certainly couldn't imagine his parents parading around half naked, but it was the most effective. He put his clothes back on and wondered how he could wash his hands. He wouldn't feel comfortable until he did. He found a large leaf and wiped his hands on it, but it wasn't the same without water. Then he heard what sounded like a stream. He followed the noise to a small dribble, it wasn't much but it was enough to wash his hands. For a second he thought about washing a little more extensively, but he'd been away from the truck for a while.

Andy dialled his parents again. He wasn't hopeful and was beginning to assume the was a fault on the line. It rang and a second later someone answered.

"Shanghai takeaway," a voice said.

"Sorry, wrong number," Andy said and dialled again.

He let it ring as he walked back and it was almost distracting enough for him not to notice that the truck was surrounded by police, and Hamish the fur ball was in handcuffs.

"Shit," Andy said, disappearing back into the bushes.

Chapter Seventy-Nine

"Not far now," Andy's mum said.

Andy's dad, who was carrying the bags, was beginning to sweat. His legs were aching and his feet were hurting. They'd been walking for miles through a negligible path in a dense wood. He wasn't convinced she knew where they were going. She kept taking sneaky glances at her phone, which was odd. Suddenly she stopped.

"Listen," she said.

Andy's dad listened, but the blood was pumping too loudly in his ears to hear anything.

"What?" he said, trying to get his breath back and grateful they'd stopped.

"Can't you hear it?" she said.

Andy's dad tried. He didn't understand why a trip to the beach should be so complicated and demanding. His breath settled and he could hear it.

"The sea," he said.

"Yes, nearly there," Andy's mum said, and took off as if she was possessed.

She hadn't come clean with Andy's dad, although she wasn't quite sure if she could strip off in public either. She didn't know whether the thought was exciting or terrifying. She'd wait until she got there to decide. Finally she could see a clearing in the wood and beyond it blue sky and sea. They really were nearly there. Andy's mum hadn't told Andy's dad, but for half an hour they were walking in the wrong direction. She hadn't quite mastered the map facility on her apparently smart phone. To its credit it was smart enough to point out that they were going in the wrong direction.

"At last," Andy's dad said.

They'd finally hit the rather stony beach and found just a small smattering of people.

"That's why it's worth the walk," Andy's mum said, as if she were an expert at such things.

"I suppose," Andy's dad said.

He didn't like crowded beaches, and this one was pleasingly empty. They were enjoying what people called a 'warm snap' and the sky was clear and blue and the air warm. It was as if they'd gone on holiday to Spain. The thought relaxed Andy's dad, as he had an uncertain relationship with beaches. He'd built sand castles with Andy when he was young and felt better with a bit of sun and colour on his body, but he'd grown bored. He sometimes sat in the sun in the garden, and he occasionally removed his shirt when he cut the grass. The key, he knew, was a good book, and Andy had brought him one of those new fangled Kindle things on which he'd downloaded a small library.

"This way," Andy's mum said with certainty.

Andy's dad followed, a little concerned that the ordeal was not yet at an end. They walked past a few people, as they headed for the most deserted part of the beach. He looked at the rocky cliff face and looked at the stratas of soil, as if it contained the history of the earth, which it sort of did. Most of his reading had been to better himself, his parents weren't recreational readers, but he'd shifted to crime and was rather looking forward to a particularly lauded thriller he'd downloaded.

"What the..." Andy's dad said.

He'd lowered his gaze from the history of the earth and found something equally primal. It took a moment for him to fully digest. He certainly wasn't imagining it.

"Hold on," he hissed, grabbing Andy's mum's arm. "These people aren't wearing any clothes."

"I know," Andy's mum said.

She said it was the casual tone of a woman practiced in the art of naturism.

"You know?" Andy's dad said.

Andy's dad looked round at his wife, eyebrows raised, and recognising he'd been conned. This was a further part of the journey they were going on. He stopped looking at the naked people and fixed his eyes on the pebbles a few feet ahead of him. He didn't know what the protocol for nudist beaches was, but he guessed it didn't involve staring. He doubted they'd believe him if he said he was studying rock formations.

"But we don't have to be naked if we don't want to," Andy's mum said.

But Andy's mum was getting that little tingle again, and she knew she couldn't visit a naturist beach and leave never having removed her clothes. That would be like going to a beer festival and drinking wine.

"Okay," Andy's dad said and relaxed a little.

They walked a little further until the naked people were a distant dot. The beach was large enough, and only a minimal number of people had made the trek through the woods. It gave them quite a bit of privacy. He dumped his bags and slumped down.

"I'm starving," he said. "What's there to eat?"

Andy's mum took out the sandwiches, which were wrapped in aluminium foil, and arranged them on the towel. She'd already made her decision. The only question was whether to strip off before, or after, they'd eaten. She didn't want to drop sliced cucumber on her naked body. Or did she? The thought, the outrageous naughtiness, gave her another little tingle. As she'd never really tingled before she wondered if she should bring it up with Lydia the next time they shared a latte.

"Great," Andy's dad said.

She'd even packed a couple of small beers and he took one and twisted off the cap. He removed his shirt and grabbed a towel, which he wrapped carefully around himself, and he peered into the bag. Andy's mum had packed everything. Well, almost.

"Where are my trunks?" he asked.

As he asked the question, he realised he knew the answer.

"You didn't pack them, did you?" Andy's dad said, looking up at Andy's mum to discover she was entirely naked.

Chapter Eighty

Andy checked the battery symbol on Barry's phone to discover it didn't have much life left in it. He sat down. He was stranded again. But he had a fake passport and a dying phone. He tried calling his parents again, but he didn't think they'd answer. They didn't.

"Shit," Andy said.

Why, he wondered, had he taken that banana? It seemed like a month ago, but it was only five days. Ali would be home soon and he wondered what she'd do if he wasn't there. He tried to think of someone else he could call, but the problem was that he could only remember his parents' telephone number.

And then the answer came to him. He googled the nearest British embassy. It was only two hundred and fifty kilometres away, which didn't sound so far. And there was a telephone number. He pressed dial. The phone found a connection and then paused. He knew what it was going to do in that pause. And it did.

"Shit," Andy said again.

There was a swirly symbol on the phone, and it was the swirly symbol of battery death. He got up. The truck had disappeared, and with it his passengers, and Hamish the fur ball. There was one road and one direction. He started to walk. He put his thumb up. He had no idea who would stop but he had nothing to lose, or so he thought. An hour later no one had stopped and it was growing dark. He didn't want to sleep in the bush, but soon he'd have no choice. The falling sun was in his eyes when finally a car stopped. He walked up to it. It was quite badly dented and looked a little like Barry's car. He looked in, ready to run, and was surprised to see a white man at the wheel. There was a little pause, and for a second he wasn't sure if he should get in, but he didn't want to sleep in the bush. He got in. It looked even more like Barry's car on the inside, which was strange.

"Hello, I'm Andy," Andy said, offering his hand.

The driver looked at his hand. He studied the fingers. They were quite long and artistic. It was the hand, or rather the thumb, that had prompted him to stop. Not that thumbs were his thing, it was more fingers. It almost made him hungry.

"Marvin," Fingers Marvin said.

Andy shook his hand and noticed a strange nub where a six finger used to reside. He could tell that Marvin wasn't like other people, and it felt a little like he'd sat next to the weirdo on the bus. But most weirdos, he assured himself, weren't dangerous.

"Nice to meet you," Andy said.

But the psychiatrist who'd worked for Grub-For had drawn conclusions which suggested that Fingers Marvin was very dangerous indeed and should be kept incarcerated at all costs, and for the rest of his life. But the words 'at all costs' weren't in the vocabulary of the former short-haul aviation CEO and the newly automated prison had suffered a computer error, which resulted in half the inmates being poisoned, and the other half walking out the door.

"Yes," Marvin said.

His time in prison, and subsequent hiding in Bodmin moors, hadn't honed his social skills, which weren't the most refined in the first place. He was more accustomed to talking to himself. He found people very needy.

"Nice day," Andy heard himself say.

The press were much kinder to Fingers Marvin when it came to his campaign against PPI workers, as it made recruiting for call workers almost impossible, and it was generally agreed the country had had enough.

"Yes," Marvin said.

Marvin looked at him and put the car in Drive and pulled off. He'd never taken a driving lesson, or passed a test, but it didn't bother him. He'd never bought a car or insured one either.

"You're not local, then?" Andy asked.

Marvin had issues fuelling the car. He'd not attempted to put petrol in a car before and, for a first time, it had gone fine. The issue arose when a stubby fingered man insisted on payment. His fingers were rolling around in the boot of the car.

"No," Marvin said, adding, "Norfolk."

Despite the fact that Marvin was on the run, he rarely disguised himself, and frequently revealed details of his life that would easily identify him. His mind didn't operate in the same way as others and there were brief moments when he had a slight insight into this difference. When that happened he made greater efforts to assimilate himself and employ conversation that might, he thought, put people at their ease.

"Should be a full moon tonight," Marvin said.

Marvin's understanding of what might put someone at ease differed from conventional wisdom, and he tended to talk in non sequiturs, which confused people and led to conversational dead ends.

"Is there?" Andy asked.

Marvin generally blamed the person he was talking to, as he could think of a number of things to say should someone point out that there will be a full moon tonight. 'Is there' was about as big a response as any he got on the subject.

"Yes," Marvin confirmed.

He'd lived a long time living off rabbits and without electricity, and was more attuned than most to the cycles of the moon. He looked down at Andy's lap. Andy was fidgeting and Marvin could see his fingers moving over each other. This could have been a telltale sign to suggest that Andy was nervous, but Marvin wasn't sensitive to such things.

"Great," Andy said.

Marvin would have agreed, but he was thinking about fingers. That petrol pump man had whetted his appetite to gather a new collection. For Marvin the removal of another's fingers was a passion to which he was inevitably drawn. It bordered on an addiction and there were moments when it was the only thing that filled his mind. He couldn't help himself.

"You have nice fingers," Fingers Marvin said.

He hadn't meant to. It had just come out. Even Marvin knew it was an observation which was unlikely to make someone comfortable.

"Sorry?" Andy said, a little alarmed.

Andy had concluded that Marvin was gay and was hitting on him. It wasn't the first time this had happened to him and he knew he had to put him straight. But he didn't want to upset him either. He needed this lift.

"Nothing," Marvin said and looked straight ahead.

Chapter Eighty-One

At first Andy's dad found it difficult to concentrate on the plot of the book, which was set in America, and involved various government agencies charged with the responsibility of keeping the nation safe. Every now and again he'd realise that he was entirely naked, and then he couldn't remember whether the protagonist worked for the CIA, or the FBI, or whether it mattered. After he reread the opening chapter three times he decided it probably didn't matter and continued to the second. There was a double agent. By the end of the chapter he couldn't remember who was the protagonist and who was the double agent, as he was aware that anyone could walk by and see his genitals. He'd barely seen his genitals, and they'd been attached to him all his life. He read the second chapter again and identified who was who, although he wasn't convinced it mattered. It was while he was in the third chapter that a couple walked by. They were naked, just like him and Andy's mum. That was another issue. He'd avoided looking at Andy's mum's naked body, as he was rather frightened by what it might prompt. He wasn't finding it a very relaxing experience. The naked man looked up at the them and the naked woman followed his gaze.

"Afternoon," they said.

Andy's dad attempted to squeak a reply, but he was too horrified that these people had just looked at his penis, at least he assumed they had. He'd certainly looked at their nakedness. The strange thing was that they seemed so ordinary, just like him.

"Good afternoon," Andy's mum said.

She'd been lightly dozing, or it might have been discreetly feeling the light breeze on her naked body, but she lifted her head and smiled. Her breasts wobbled a little and Andy's dad thought that now these ordinary people had seen his wife naked. He hoped no one from the bank walked by. That would be mortifying.

"They look like us," Andy's dad observed.

"Oh, I think you can give him a run for his money," Andy's mum said.

Although there weren't *that* many layers to this comment, it took Andy's dad a couple of minutes to get what she was saying. He looked down at his fortunately very limp penis, possibly limp out of terror, and saw that it probably was just a shade larger than the naked man who'd walked by them. He wondered if he should take a look at his wife's naked body, or launch into the fourth chapter. He took the safe option. Someone had been shot. It was either the protagonist with the CIA, or it might have been the FBI, or it might have been the spy. Either way they'd shifted to Istanbul and while he knew there was a reason, he couldn't remember what it might be, or if it mattered. He put his kindle down.

"Beautiful day," he said, finishing off the small beer.

It occurred to him that if someone from the bank came by it might not be mortifying, it might actually be quite cool. On Monday they'd go back to the bank and tell everyone. He knew, if that was the case, he had to stand tall. He sneaked a glance at Andy's mum. She seemed fitter than he remembered, although he was more familiar with her clothed body, and wondered if it was the yoga, and whether he should take it up. Or start going to the gym. He looked at her white skin. It was lightly freckled and there were few traces of motherhood on her stomach, just a tiny mark which would have been hidden in what people call the bikini line. It was a fairly redundant word on a naturist beach. Right at that moment she looked no different to when they'd first met. Andy's mum moved her hand lazily onto Andy's dad's inner thigh. Andy's dad choked.

Who, he thought, would have known that the inner thigh could be such an erogenous zone. In his mind he put up a police barricade – the kind with those big plastic shields – it was holding back the tide of blood. That barricade was in danger of being breached. He had to get back to Istanbul. He was certain now. It was the spy who was actually the protagonist, and he worked for the CIA, and he was there to stem a potential terrorist attack against the USA. If that wasn't the plot it was near enough and he continued with as much focus as he could manage. By the end of the fourth chapter there were two problems. The first he could deal with. The spy actually worked for MI5. The second was Andy's mum's casually resting hand. It had moved further up. He would need reinforcements to keep that barricade in place, but chapter five wasn't helping. He was getting the distinct impression, however much he wished otherwise, that the MI5 agent was in a hotel room with a croupier and sex might be on the cards. Why now? Why couldn't he have mowed the terrorists down with a machine gun? Andy's dad continued and it wasn't long before the croupier was in her underwear and the author was supplying him with unnecessary detail and description. He flicked past to the end of the chapter, certain that it wasn't relevant to the story.

"Lovely," Andy's mum muttered.

It was a bit of a non sequitur, sat there all on its own, with no subject preceding it or, it seemed, likely to follow. It was just 'lovely'. Andy's mum was finding their beach adventure much more relaxing than Andy's dad and her casually draped hand was now describing small circles on Andy's dad's inner thigh. The barricade was coming down. He sneaked a peak at his penis. If it might have been marginally larger than the naked man's before. Now it was significantly larger. He dived into the next chapter to discover the croupier wasn't a croupier at all. It seemed as if the croupier, who may not be a croupier, had killed the bloke from MI5. He had no choice. He had to read the previous chapter. The MI5 agent had stripped her to her underwear then, and Andy's dad hated to read this, caressed her breasts.

"Oh God," Andy's dad muttered.

Andy's mum smiled to herself and moved her hand from his inner thigh. At the same time Andy's dad was reading that the MI5 agent had thrust his hand into the knickers of the croupier. Worse, the author was quite specific about what he was now doing with his fingers. This was unbearable not least because Andy's mum had wrapped her hand around Andy's dad's penis. The plastic police shields were on the floor, the mob was trampling over the shields. The tide couldn't be held back. It didn't help that the croupier, who was actually a KGB agent had just strangled the MI5 agent with her bra. It was, it seemed, a dual purpose bra.

"Would you like," Andy's mum said with aching slowness, "to join me in the bushes?"

Chapter Eighty-Two

"The thing is," Andy said cautiously, "I think she wants me to propose."

He'd finally managed to say it. He hadn't even said it out loud, let alone to another person, but there it was, laid bare. It was the next stage in a conventional life, like his parents. Find a girl, get a career, buy a home and get married.

"But the thing is," Andy said. "It's a little frightening."

Not that Andy was averse to commitment. He was genuinely committed to Ali. It was just the order of things.

"The next step, on the conventional path, is children and that's even more frightening," Andy said.

He couldn't quite picture himself in the park teaching his son to ride a bike. Or the bit before that when you have to change nappies. He wasn't very committed to handling another's shit.

"I mean the responsibility. The sheer grownup-ness of it. It wasn't *that* long ago I was at school," Andy said.

It was ten years, but ten years didn't seem that long ago, because so much stuff had happened. He didn't want all that to slow down.

"And the idea of suddenly becoming a father, at my age, seems pretty daunting. I know I'm not that far from thirty, I know that, and I guess my dad was young at the time. But that was a different time," Andy said.

He wondered, for a second, whether he was frightened about having a life like his parents. It seemed so sterile and dull.

"The thing is," Andy pondered. "When you're young you want to grow up and do adult things, you know, drinking and sex and that really is the best period. It's better than the period before it and I worry that it's better than what comes after. You get to an age when you finally have freedom, freedom to get up in the morning or not, if you don't want to. Or decide shall I go to the pub or not? Shall I have a couple of pints or five?"

It was ominously silent in the car, but Andy hadn't noticed as he had other things on his mind. He had more to say.

"And the next stage is children, which seems like such a big responsibility. Then you really have grown up. Maybe that's it. I like where I am and I don't want to grow up anymore. This amount of grown up-ness is enough."

Andy didn't think it odd that his thoughts on growing up hadn't prompted a discussion, or even a reply.

"And then when the kids get older, so do I. When you get to the next stage, the other stages follow leading inevitably to getting old. And then it's all over. It's gone in a flash and you didn't notice it happening," Andy said.

He'd begun talking about Ali to make his sexuality very clear. But it had prompted further thoughts and now, accidentally, he'd fallen into the philosophical veering towards the nihilistic.

"It's like my life is rushing past me at such speed I can't grab hold of it and slow it down. It's as if," Andy said hesitating, "it's one step closer to..."

Marvin's primary interest was in severing at least one of Andy's fingers for his new collection and he had not the slightest interest in his sexuality. But Andy had been going on about it for some time and Marvin had not been fully absorbed in the narrative of Andy's life journey.

"Death," Andy finally managed to say.

It was the process of growing up. Andy wasn't ready to grow up. He wanted to sit on the sofa and play PlayStation and eat a bag of chips with a few beers. He didn't want to become his parents. He wanted to stave that off. It wasn't as if he equated marrying Ali with death. It just felt like one step closer to it. It was then that he noticed that he was getting several steps closer rather rapidly. Marvin had quite possibly never heard anything quite so boring and had fallen into a very deep sleep and, as he was driving the car, this was something of an issue. The car was wandering across the road.

"Marvin!" Andy shouted, shaking him.

There was a huge truck coming the other way and the car was drifting into its path. Horns were blaring, but Andy couldn't make out from where. He grabbed the steering wheel and yanked it. The nose of the car shifted rapidly to the left, but it felt as if the rest of the car didn't have time to catch up with it, and the car kept turning until it was no longer turning. It was rolling. And then it felt as if the lights had been turned off.

Chapter Eighty-Three

Andy's dad might have thought about the embarrassment of being caught by the police and the subsequent arrest, and the small piece in the local paper which all his old colleagues at the bank would read. Would he become 'disgraced former bank manager?' Would it prompt debates about public decency and the decline of society? Would they have a mugshot of him against a height chart? Would the council be forced to hire protectors of public morality who would hide in the bushes?

"Lovely," Andy's dad muttered.

He might have been thinking those things, but he wasn't. It seemed a strange thing, that he might attempt to deconstruct later, that in the course of sexual congress the brain thinks about nothing else but the act itself. That he'd managed to mutter 'lovely' was an achievement in itself, peppered as it was by unconscious grunts of a distinct and unmistakeable nature. This was the furthest step he'd ever taken on the wild side and it suited him fine.

"Lovely," Andy's mum managed to say.

They both knew with an unusual connectedness that 'lovely' would become a catchphrase and a pre-emptor of activities of a carnal nature. It would be the most concise way of initiating sex and the word would be banned in any other context. She would never again say 'those roses look lovely'. The word would acquire protected status. And, if Andy's mum was leaning on the kitchen sink and looking out at the well-kept garden in which Andy used to play, and uttered the word 'lovely'. They'd both know. This was the first application and it was working very effectively for both of them.

"Really lovely," Andy's dad said, although he wasn't aware he'd said anything.

Andy's mum and dad were at it like rabbits in the bushes and 'really lovely', were he to remember saying it, would mark the final few thrusts, and the conclusion of the event. Andy's mum made a series of incoherent noises that confirmed that it had been more than satisfactory for both parties.

"We'd better get back," Andy's mum said.

A few minutes later they were lying on the beach, basking in the sun, as if nothing had happened. As if butter wouldn't melt in their mouths, as Andy's mum's mum used to say. But they'd acquired a kind of sheen and Andy's dad's penis had retreated to a more fulsome default setting.

"I think there's a second beer," Andy's mum said.

"Excellent," Andy's dad said and rummaged in the bag.

He took a sip and launched into the seventh chapter of the book, which now appeared to be about a femme fatale KGB agent called Anoushka. She battled her way through a few more agents until she met her lover and the author provided a very specific account of their sexual exploits, which Andy's dad quite enjoyed. He even wondered if he could provide the lover with a few tips of his own.

"Oh look," Andy's mum suddenly said.

Andy's dad looked up and saw a couple walking in their direction. They were naked and hand in hand and walking by the water's edge. They seemed no more interesting than the previous couple who'd passed by them, and he went back to his book. He found Anoushka in London. She was a double agent and actually worked for MI5, which was strange as he was fairly certain she'd killed an MI5 agent with her bra. Unless that agent was also a double agent. Andy's dad noticed Andy's mum was waving. He looked up.

"Do you know them?" Andy's dad asked.

"Oh yes," Andy's mum said.

The couple came closer. Andy's dad gave his own penis an unconscious glance, he couldn't help himself, and felt an inner piece, which was unusual for him.

"That," Andy's mum said, "is Bruno."

"Bruno?" Andy's dad said.

"He was a temporary yoga teacher," Andy's mum said.

Andy's mum looked at Bruno's broad shoulders and tanned and hairy torso. She remembered his extraordinary masculinity. But as her eyes dropped down his body it seemed to evaporate.

"And that is Lydia with him," Andy's mum said.

Andy's dad had never met Lydia, but he'd heard all about her. It was strange that their first meeting would be with both of them naked. He wasn't sure if he should get up and shake her hand. He decided he'd just lean over. As she approached he ran his eyes over her body. She was a little too bony for him.

"Lydia, hi," Andy's mum said. "This is my husband."

Chapter Eighty-Four

"If you could give me five hundred words on that," Jemima said.

The 'if' sounded like a request, but was more a command and the accent was back in place. Ali was spending her last day in the New York office and Jemima and her force field were back where they should be. They hadn't spoken about what had happened in that hotel room, there might have been a flicker behind the eyes, but Jemima was back in charge and proceeding as if it was nothing.

Ali was helping out on a gossip magazine and they'd received breaking news. A celebrity divorce had become a rapprochement. This wasn't a heart breaking story, or an insight into a conflict, and it wasn't a political scandal either. But it was fun and Ali found a way to give it a fresh angle. She tapped away at the keyboard with purpose. Tony was attempting to make his mark in the design section and Jess was helping with a shoot down town. It wasn't exactly Sex in the City, but it was a more satisfactory bonding exercise than the socialising had been. Forty-five minutes later Ali decided she was satisfied with the piece and she pressed send.

Ali looked up at the glass office at the end of the building. Jemima was on the phone and moving about in a feline fashion. When she finished the call she looked down at her computer and tapped the keyboard.

Ali watched her, hoping she was reading her piece, and hoping she liked it. For a second she thought she could see a flicker of a smile. She had a very sensual mouth. Ali stopped herself. She did not want to know what that mouth was capable of. Jemima stood up, turned and looked directly at Ali. She smiled and gave her a thumbs up. Ali smiled back.

Ali got up to get some air. There was a small roof terrace, which was used by the smokers, although most had given up by now, and Ali took the cast iron staircase up to it. She took her mobile with her. There was a gentle breeze and she breathed in the air of the city, which she found more reassuring than fetid. Andy had not called her. She dialled his number, but was not surprised when he didn't pick up. There must have be an issue with his phone, she thought again. She tried his parents. She wondered if they might have heard from him. But they didn't answer either. There was something oddly isolating about being in the middle of a city of millions and yet still feeling a little alone.

"Hey," a voice next to her said.

It was Jemima. She hadn't given up smoking, as it both steadied her nerves and kept her slim. She doubted she'd live long enough to have to worry about lung cancer.

"Good piece," Jemima said.

"Thanks," Ali said.

Ali wasn't quite sure what to say to the woman who'd begged to eat her pussy and whose life she'd saved.

They weren't repeatable circumstances. At least she hoped not.

"Thanks for doing that the other night," Jemima said.

Jemima wasn't good at praise, apologies, or thanks, and Ali wondered whether, if she'd eaten her pussy rather than save her life, she'd say the same thing.

"My pleasure," Ali said and smiled.

Of course had Ali done the former rather than the latter she doubted she'd have said that, and there hadn't been much pleasure in receiving a mouthful of cocaine-fuelled vomit.

"Are you going to come and work for me then?" Jemima said.

Ali hadn't anticipated that. She had ties to London. Ties to Andy. But there was a buzz to the place that made even drinking a cup of coffee exciting. That, she knew, could wear off.

"I already have a job," Ali said.

Despite her less than flattering view of Miles, she liked her job, and the way it fitted into her life. It was a part of her life, and she feared that if she moved to New York, her job would become all her life as it evidently had for Jemima.

"Has Miles not told you?" Jemima said.

"Told me what?" Ali asked.

Jemima left a little pause.

"I bought the company," Jemima said.

Ali had wondered about the purpose of the trip to New York. It hadn't been about acquiring an office, as Miles had implied, but selling one. Ali wondered how Jemima was able to buy the company. Perhaps there was family money, and the whole Geordie thing was just a cocaine fuelled fantasy. She wasn't sure she wanted to know.

"Does that mean you're closing the London office?" Ali asked.

Jemima puffed a little on her cigarette. She actually felt very calm when she was working and had no problem making big decisions. It was outside her work where the problems lay.

"That depends," Jemima said.

"On what?" Ali asked.

"On finding the right person to run it," Jemima said.

Ali wasn't keen on losing her job or gaining a new boss. Miles was the devil she knew and he didn't interfere with her.

"Is Miles not staying?" Ali asked.

"No, Miles will be out the door as quickly as his saggy buttocks will allow," Jemima said.

"Do you have anyone in mind?" Ali asked.

Ali understood why people smoked, as now would have been the prefect time to occupy her hands with the distraction of smoking. But it made her cough just thinking about it.

"Yes, I do," Jemima said.

Ali wasn't too concerned, as she had a friend who worked in an employment agency and she often called her with interesting propositions.

"Who?" Ali asked.

The traffic lights had just changed many floors below them and two cars and a motorbike had decided to conduct a drag race. The noise of the engines echoed around the tall buildings as if they were enclosed in a courtyard.

"You," Jemima said.

Chapter Eighty-Five

"Well," Lydia said. "If you've not tried it."

They were having their post yoga skinny latte. Lydia felt like she was losing it. When she'd seen Andy's mum on the beach she'd hoped it would be a little awkward and it was. For her. The key to Bruno, she knew, was not to unwrap him. He was not remotely like an onion, and sadly he wasn't like a single-layered banana either. She'd carried on walking along the beach with Bruno until they were far away from Andy's mum and dad.

"No, I've not," Andy's mum said.

That morning Andy's mum had been to the dentist for an annual check up and she'd picked up a couple of the women's magazines. She'd idly read a few articles without really engaging. She was surprised how explicit they were and then she'd come across a piece by Lydia.

"Do you think I should try?" Andy's mum asked.

"If you're in pursuit of the most intense orgasms," Lydia said.

Andy's mum watched her. Lydia had puffed out a big plume of smoke. Andy's mum had read that article and then she'd found a few more. She didn't recognise herself at first, not least because she'd changed so much, or her sex life had. But there were a few salacious details which were unmistakable.

"I'll text my husband and see what he says," Andy's mum said.

Lydia's eyes opened in a rather alarmed fashion. She hadn't expected that. She watched as Andy's mum expertly texted her husband.

"You never know," Andy's mum said.

The worse thing, Andy's mum thought, was the tone of the articles. She was being laughed at. Lydia had made much of the rhubarb crumble and the inference that her husband was gay, which he plainly wasn't. The worse thing about the pieces Lydia had written was the lack of affection.

"There," Andy's mum said brightly. "So do you know how we can get involved in this swinging scene?"

Lydia had just pressed her skinny latte to her lips and she spluttered, and a little ball of foam zinged across the table. This wasn't how she'd anticipated this going. A ding from Andy's mum's phone announced a return text. Andy's mum read it out.

"I'm up for it!"

"Really?" Lydia said.

Andy's mum showed her the text.

"You really have opened our eyes," Andy's mum said, adding, "Did Bruno give you one in the bushes?"

This was the first time Andy's mum had used the phrase 'give you one' and she was pleased she could direct it to Lydia. Lydia hadn't anticipated this either. Although they had ventured into the bushes and Lydia had, and there's no other way to put this, sat on his face, to discover he'd learned precisely nothing from the very specific lessons she'd attempted to give him.

Unfortunately for her it had worked for Bruno who'd made a mess all over his stomach. She'd driven back, dropped him off, gone to the little corner shop, and bought fresh batteries.

"Of course, it was great," Lydia said.

She followed it with an inhalation of her little rollup and a puff of smoke, as she'd insisted they sit half in, and half out, of the cafe at their usual table. Andy's mum was beginning to recognise this as an indication that Lydia might not necessarily be telling the truth.

"He looked at little disappointing to me," Andy's mum muttered, turning her head away.

It was how Lydia frequently delivered many of her remarks which seemed, on the surface to be harmless, but were a little mean in tone. To Lydia it was if she'd been slapped in the face. The most galling part was that it was true. There was a further ding from Andy's mum's phone. She read out the text.

"When can we start?" Andy's mum read. "It looks like he's really embracing this swinging idea of yours."

Lydia groaned inside. She'd never tried swinging because she didn't want to. The whole thing seemed a little unsavoury to her. She struggled to find something to say and then failed.

"You've not tried it either, have you?" Andy's mum suddenly said.

Lydia reached for her rollup, but Andy's mum put her hand on hers, and looked her in the eyes. Lydia sighed.

“No,” Lydia said. “It sounds awful.”

They laughed for a moment and then Lydia realised something.

“You’re having me on too, aren’t you?” she asked.

“Yes,” Andy’s mum said. “I don’t think we’d be up for all that swapping nonsense.”

They laughed a little more and Andy’s mum added, “I quite like what I’ve got.”

Lydia stubbed out her cigarette. She took the last mouthful of her skinny latte and she decided to come clean.

“And I don’t much like what I’ve got,” Lydia admitted.

“That’s a shame,” Andy’s mum said.

“You’re right about Bruno, but disappointing doesn’t cover it. He couldn’t find a clitoris if it had a flashing light and if he did, by accident, he hasn’t the slightest idea how to operate it. The man is hopeless and untrainable.”

“Shall I get some more lattes?” Andy’s mum said.

“Fuck it,” Lydia said. “Shall we go to the pub? I’ve got some apologising to do.”

Chapter Eighty-Six

Andy could hear whispering. His eyes were closed, but he could sense the light. It did seem unnecessarily bright. He tried to think about what had happened. They'd travelled a long way and made it through a few borders. But it wasn't that. Then it came to him. He was telling Marvin about the pressure to take his relationship to the next level.

"You're sure it's the president of Lobo's car?" someone said.

"No question," someone else said.

"And he's called Barry?" another asked.

"They're all called Barry," the first person said.

"Has anybody been to Lobo?" the second person asked.

"No," the third person said said.

"Never heard of it," the first person said

"I don't know, he could be," the second person said.

"But he's white," the third person pointed out.

"Almost ginger," the first person said.

"Could be a bruise," the second person said.

"Nah, he's ginger," the third person said.

"He does have a lot of bruises," the first person said.

"Lobo used to be under British rule, didn't it?" the second person whispered.

Someone fiddled with the computer. They were relatively new to the internet and there had been a plague of monkeys eating through the phone lines. It wasn't very reliable.

"It's gone again," the first person said.

"I'm sure it was under British rule," the second person said.

"Their seed got everywhere," the third person said.

"But ginger?" they all said.

They looked down at the patient. This was politically awkward. The leader, the king, of a nation found in a crashed car in another sovereign state. It was very complicated. It would raise issues of road safety. Not that the roads were remotely safe, but it didn't need to be pointed out.

"He's coming to," the first person said.

They watched as Andy's face flickered. He still had a bruise from where Barry had hit him in the face. He had further bruises from when Barry had lost control of the car and he'd acquired a few more when Marvin had been at the wheel. Or rather when Marvin had succumbed to a deep sleep when Andy had attempted to explain his fears of marriage.

"We need to get him out of here," the first person said.

"No messing about," the second person said.

"We've got a plane waiting," the third reminded them.

Andy felt as if he was suspended. He opened his eyes and he saw whiteness. The ceiling was white. The walls were white. The starched uniform of the woman speaking to him was whiter than white. It was like a television commercial for washing powder in which they had actually achieved a whiter than white whiteness. Did this mean he was in heaven?

“Your Excellency,” the first person said.

There had been a lengthy diplomatic conversation and the conclusion was it didn’t matter who the hell he was, they had to get him the hell out of there. There was no question that there was only one person who drove that Mercedes. The registration was Lobo1. It had to be Barry, and Andy had been the only person found in the car.

“Where am I?” Andy said.

“You’re in hospital,” the first person said.

It didn’t sound much like a heavenly voice to Andy. He was in hospital. That explained it all. He was in Hackney. It must be Homerton hospital. The whole trip had been a trip, a hallucination. Not that he had any memory of taking anything that might prompt a hallucination. He’d had a couple of beers, he remembered that, then he went to get a bag of chips. He had a vague memory of a banana.

“How are you feeling, Your Excellency?” the second person asked.

It took a moment for Andy to realise that the ‘excellency’ in the sentence was him. That seemed strange, even for Hackney.

“Is this the Homerton?” Andy asked.

The three men looked at each other. They moved away.

"Is the Homerton some sort of death ritual?" the first person whispered.

"It could be, they're pretty strange up there," the second person pointed out.

"If we point it out, it sort of shifts the blame," the third person said.

"But it might be a bad thing too," the first person said.

"Let's humour him," the other two said.

They returned to Andy, who was fairly convinced it wasn't the Homerton, but couldn't be sure of anything.

"If you like, Your Excellency," the first person said.

"If it pleases you, Your Excellency," the second person said.

"Your Excellency," the third person said, running out of inspiration.

"What happened?" Andy asked.

They looked at each other. They'd been given strict instructions as to how to deal with this.

"Your Excellency, you were in a car accident," the first person said.

"But the roads here are very safe," the second person pointed out.

"We never have road accidents here," the third person said.

The others looked up at him. They were all in agreement that he might have overstated the situation.

“But accidents happen,” the first person said.

“Just not very often,” the second person said.

“Hardly at all,” the third person said and then regretted it.

The others frowned.

“But we have a plane ready for you,” the first person said.

“To take you back,” the second person said.

“To Lobo,” the third person said.

Andy panicked. He’d spent the last two days trying to get away from Lobo. It was enough to make him feel faint. He could feel himself drifting but, at the same time, an idea was emerging in his head.

“I have a personal physician,” Andy managed to say.

His mind was drifting, but he managed to get it out.

“In London.”

Chapter Eighty-Seven

Andy's mum was not accustomed to drinking in the afternoon, or very much in the evening, but Lydia had insisted on gin and tonics and she couldn't think of a reason why she shouldn't. They were on their third and Andy's mum felt a little tipsy. Now that they'd waded into the reality of Lydia's sex life, it was tragically barren.

"I'm so sorry," Lydia said.

She'd promised to do some apologising and she hadn't disappointed. Andy's mum was quite enjoying it, but made a mental note to tell her that the next time was enough. Or maybe the time after that. Lydia was not someone who apologised by nature so Andy's mum knew to make the most of it.

"Bruno's winky," Andy's mum said, "Was a little on the little side."

"And the worse thing," Lydia relied, 'is that winky is exactly the right word to describe it. Bruno definitely has a winky. And a winky winky one at that."

Lydia raised her glass and they glanced them together in celebration, or recognition, or something, of the winkiness of Bruno's winky winky.

"And it wouldn't matter if he knew what to do with it," Lydia said.

"Well," Andy's mum said.

It didn't mean very much, although it might have been the recognition that Andy's dad was not winky, and he was capable of knowing what to do with it.

"He probably doesn't even know how to urinate out of it," Lydia said, waving her hand for another round of gin and tonics.

Andy's mum looked at the gin being poured into the glasses, a little alarmed. She might have to phone Andy's dad to get a lift home. She wondered if she should send him a text. The only problem was that they'd yet to use the texts for anything other than a kind of flirtation. If she sent him a text he'd assume it was a prelude to sex.

"And the man was untrainable," Lydia said, not having exhausted the subject of Bruno.

"Do you want to leave your husband?" Andy's mum suddenly asked.

In all the banter, mostly at Bruno's expense, there had been little said of real depth. This was a big question.

"I'm not sure I do," Lydia admitted. "But he's seventy-two and not interested in sex. And I'm ready for an Indian summer of sex."

Andy's mum sighed at that. It seemed so final, as if it was the summer that took them to the end of their lives. She'd not thought that with Andy's dad although, in a number of ways, they were having a kind of Indian summer.

"Sometimes," Andy's mum said cautiously, "we analyse too much. Sometimes it is better not to think of the future, but to live and enjoy the present. Don't think too hard. Find another Bruno."

"One with a proper winky," Lydia interrupted.

"And the ability to use it. And enjoy it for a day, or a week, or a summer."

They clicked glasses again and Lydia looked down. She was feeling emotional.

"I'm so sorry," Lydia said again, placing her hand on Andy's mum hand.

"That's okay," Andy's mum said.

She now felt that Lydia had apologised enough.

"The thing is," Lydia began.

Lydia had not had a very satisfying week, aside from her liaison with Bruno, and it had brought about a small revelation.

"I realise now that most of my friends are younger," Lydia said.

"Younger than who?" Andy's mum asked.

"Than me," Lydia said and then, by way of admission, "Than us."

She'd met a couple of her young fashionable friends at a wine bar in town with mirrors on every surface and, aside from avoiding her reflection, she realised three things. The first was that she no longer had much in common with them, and the second was that their bond was not strong. They weren't good friends. Not the sort that would help her when she was feeling down. They were the kind that knew their Louboutins from their Provocateurs, but it didn't go much beyond that. It was the third thing that she was going to struggle to say.

"And," Lydia continued unsteadily, "I have more in common with you."

Lydia knew she hadn't quite expressed what she'd hoped to, because it involved revealing more of herself than she was comfortable with. But she didn't want to mess this up.

"I'm trying to say that I enjoy your company more than theirs and I don't want to lose you as a friend. And I'm sorry for being such a bitch."

Andy's mum was touched although, as she'd finished the third large gin and tonic, she was more than a little touched by the alcohol.

Chapter Eighty-Eight

Ali had wanted to tell Andy about her heroic moment and she'd called his mobile, but there was no reply. She was finding it rather frustrating. She'd absorbed the news that she was going to lose Miles as a boss with great ease. Acquiring a new one in the form of teeshirt-issuing Jemima was not quite as bad as it seemed, as she thought she was quite an impressive operator, and she'd never thought that of Miles. It was the further news that she was to become the new London boss that was a little harder to absorb. Not that she'd accepted the job. At least not yet. She was meeting Jess, Tony and the accounts girl whose name she'd forgotten again. She thought it was Doris. She was running late.

This was their last evening and although their collective energy was running low, there was a feeling that should make it a big one. They opted for the hotel bar, which didn't involve travelling too far, and was in the basement. Like the rest of the boutique hotel it was kitted out with a black and white Art Deco theme, and a lot of mirrors. It had the feel of a pick up joint about it, although that seemed to apply to most of the bars they'd visited in New York, Ali thought. Or it might have been a reflection on the kind of places that Miles and Jemima frequented. They would have been perfectly suited to each other were their sexuality more closely aligned. Ali got herself ready and took the lift, or the elevator, to the basement. When the doors pinged open she was greeted with the tinkle of a piano. It had a sophisticated feel to it which was good, as she was growing tired of her London colleagues. She wondered if she should tell them about Miles and the job offer. She decided it was best not to. They were in a line sitting on tall bar stools.

"Hi," Ali said.

Jess turned to her.

"Do you know what..." there was a small pause as she searched for a name. She found it. "...Daphne has just told me?"

"No, I don't," Ali said, making a mental note that the accounts girl is Daphne, and not Doris.

"Miles has sold the company. Did you know that?" Jess said angrily.

Ali made the mistake of not immediately answering.

"You did," Jess said. "Why was I the only one who didn't fucking know?" Jess shouted.

"I didn't know," Tony said.

Jess looked at Tony in a way that suggested that he wasn't importantly enough to know. Tony huffed a little indignantly.

"I've won awards you know," Tony said.

Ali and Jess raised their eyes. Tony's design award was some time ago and the general consensus was that he had extracted as much mileage as was possible from the event. Daphne looked at her drink and then the floor.

"Is that why you're here?" Ali asked Daphne.

Daphne wished she'd kept her mouth shut. It was the first time she was privy to some information that others weren't and she couldn't help herself. She might have got herself in trouble.

"I think so. Yes," Daphne mumbled.

They all looked down at their drinks. Miles had yet to receive their collective bar bill, and now was the last opportunity to exploit it. It was a thought which made them all thirsty.

"Another?" Tony said.

They nodded in agreement.

"So who's buying the company?" Tony asked Daphne.

Daphne had said too much already. She wasn't going to say anymore.

"I can't say," Daphne said quickly and looked down at her drink.

"Hold on," Jess said brightly, turning to Ali. "I bet you know."

Ali paused again.

"You bloody do know," Jess said.

Ali looked down. She wasn't going to admit to it. Or the job offer.

"I believe Miles is going to make an announcement later," Daphne said.

"Is he now," Jess said.

Jess was, Ali had always noticed, big on sarcasm. Almost every sentence was peppered with it. Not that she'd get rid of her if she was in charge, or make an issue of it, but she could be a bit if a cow. Although that wasn't a firing offence. If it was they'd all be in trouble.

"Oh look," Daphne said.

It was Miles. This was, Ali thought, good timing.

"Have you got something to tell us?" Ali asked.

Miles smiled. There was very little which made him feel awkward. He'd made some money out of this and he didn't give a shit.

"Have you all heard?" Miles asked.

"No," Jess said pointedly.

Miles smiled, not remotely concerned by Jess's attitude, as it wasn't going to be his problem any longer.

"I've sold the business," Miles said.

They didn't know how this would affect them individually, but they all agreed, while the bar was still open, that they should celebrate it.

Chapter Eighty-Nine

Andy's dad had gone down the pub. It was the same pub, along the same meandering route, with a small group of men who'd become his chums. He couldn't quite bring himself to use the word 'mates', but it was pretty close. He wasn't there to buy pills, although if they were available he probably would, just in case. He was there because there was nothing on the telly and Andy's mum was out with mad Lydia, as Andy's dad thought of her, and he fancied going to the pub. He doubted he'd drink only a couple and come home, and suspected he'd be weaving his way back after five beers and urinating on trees, but he didn't mind.

"Hey guys," Andy's dad announced himself and plonked himself down on what had become his barstool.

There was a general muttering of welcome and, unbid, a pint arrived in front of him. Andy's dad realised something for the first time in years. He was a contented man. He couldn't have said that while he was working, even though he mostly enjoyed it and he'd feared retiring, as he didn't know what he was retiring to.

"What have you been up to?" someone asked.

The first few weeks of retirement were spent in the garden and it was only now, that he'd discovered other things, that he realised he didn't much care for gardening. He didn't mind it, but it wasn't a passion.

“You’ve picked up a sun tan,” another said.

And he now knew that survival was to do with passion, even if, god forbid, that passion was train spotting. But it could be many things and Andy’s dad was convinced there was much more he could find to be passionate about.

“I went to the beach,” Andy’s dad said.

It received nods of approval, but there was a general feeling that more information was required. Andy’s dad was more than happy to provide it, but he didn’t want to blow the impact of the story, although he hadn’t decided how much he was going to reveal. He’d only drunk one pint.

“Whereabouts?” someone asked.

Andy’s dad explained the difficulties of getting there and the long, rambling route through the woods. The others looked on, a little confused as to why he would choose to take such a lengthy journey just to arrive at a beach, but one of them was getting an inkling.

“Were you with the wife?” he asked.

Andy’s dad nodded. He didn’t point out that it was the wife who had led him there, as he wished to cast himself in the role of sexual adventurer, and all round slightly wild man.

“It’s one of those nuddy beaches, isn’t it?” someone said.

Andy’s dad delivered a world-weary nod. It was a masterclass of nonchalance, perhaps helped by the further pint that had landed in front of him. Andy's dad was enjoying the reinvention of himself.

"Were there a lot of people there?" someone asked.

"A few," Andy's dad said.

He said it as if he cast his eyes over naked bodies every day of the week. He'd seen as many naked bodies that day as he'd seen all his life. But he had more to say.

"And we were lying there," Andy's dad said, "when suddenly Lydia appeared with the yoga teacher."

"Lydia!" someone said.

No one had met Lydia, but they collectively liked her, or stories about her.

"The right to an orgasm woman," someone explained to a newcomer.

"With the yoga teacher?" someone else said.

Andy's dad hadn't intended to mention it, but the third pint was sliding down nicely, and he saw no reason not to. He lifted his hand holding his forefinger barely an inch from his thumb. Everyone laughed. Andy's dad had extracted some shadenfreude pleasure from Bruno's minimal dimensions.

"And Lydia?" someone asked.

Andy's dad was tempted to put his hand up and make a middling gesture, but the power of Lydia in his stories came from her apparent hotness, and it would have been a shame to lose that. So he settled on a detail which made his audience aware of the extent of his view of her.

"Not a pube in sight," Andy's dad said.

This prompted general merriment and Andy's dad got his round in. The conversation drifted off, and it was around the fifth pint that Andy's dad let something slip out.

"You gave the wife one in the bushes?" someone said, clearly impressed.

Andy's dad's face flickered an acknowledgement and there was more laughter. He knew he had to look for new passions, as this passion, the passion for wild sex, wouldn't last forever. It was as he thought this that his eyes met that of an older man. It was the man with the pills.

"Not Lydia then," someone said.

"No bush there," another pointed out.

"Hi," Andy's dad waved to the older man with the pills, no longer concerned about discretion.

It may not last forever, Andy's dad thought, but it had a lot more mileage left.

Chapter Ninety

Andy's mind was in a haze. It was as if he was travelling in an aeroplane, but he couldn't be certain of anything. People seemed to be attending to him as if he was royalty, which was a surreal enough concept. They were giving him pain killers and he was drifting in and out of sleep. Maybe life, he thought, was just a dream. And he'd wandered off course and landed in someone else's bad dream. But, now he'd dissected the noises around him, he was certain. It felt like the plane was falling, preparing to land, and suddenly the wheels chirped. They were on the ground. He could feel the aircraft vibrating as it taxied to its bay. Finally it came to a halt. Nothing seemed to happen. Andy assumed they were waiting for the stairs. Eventually with a squeak the door opened. And then he was carried out of the plane.

"What's that noise?" Andy asked.

Sir Bernard had been woken in the middle of the night, which had been awkward, as he was very definitely not conducting diplomatic business, and another divorce would cost him the country house. Despite that, and because he'd paid for the services he was receiving and they hadn't been cheap, he'd said, "I'm not getting out of bed for that tinpot leader." Instead he'd done the next best thing and sent a brass band to greet him. In his experience African leaders love a brass band.

"Don't you recognise the Lobo national anthem?" someone said.

Andy could see the sky and it made him smile. Droplets of rain spattered across his face. The sky was cloudy and broody and the wind was cold. The hot snap had snapped and the weather had reverted to a colourless misery. And it felt good.

"England," Andy muttered.

He was home. He held his head up to be reassuringly lashed by the rain and the wind. He'd made it back.

"Of course I recognise the Lobo national anthem," Andy said.

Chapter Ninety-One

Andy's mum had taken up Spanish lessons and Andy's dad had thought for a moment about joining her, but he didn't feel passionate about it, and he knew he needed that. It was a Tuesday night and he was in the pub. He'd decided to limit himself to once a week as he feared that he could have too much of a good thing. His body limited his facility for sex, but there was very little to limit more regular trips to the pub, except a feeling that he might become an alcoholic. The conversation had turned uncharacteristically serious.

"Have you got any kids?" someone asked.

Andy's dad realised he hadn't thought about Andy in a while. He felt Andy had shifted into adulthood and he no longer required him.

"Yes," Andy's dad said. "A son, Andy. He's nearly thirty."

Most of the other bar-propers were parents and they discussed their children with affection. Now that Andy's dad had settled into becoming a regular, he was frequently surprised by the range of topics discussed, and the opinions expressed.

"Is he married yet?" someone asked.

There had been a brief conversation about one of his new chum's daughter's wedding. He'd growled a little about the cost, but hadn't dwelled on it, and it was mostly said with pride.

"No, not yet. But he's living with a nice girl and they seem solid," Andy's dad said.

Again, he felt guilty that he hadn't spoken to his son, as he was only guessing that their relationship was solid. They certainly seemed okay together. Andy's mum spoke to Ali fairly often and he was reminded of something she'd said.

"I think he's close to popping the question, though. They've bought a place together so, I guess, that's next," Andy's dad.

"Or babies," someone pointed out.

Andy's dad didn't feel too concerned about his son having a child out of wedlock, it was not unusual these days, but he suspected that it wouldn't happen like that. He thought of his son as quite proper and he was certain that Ali would insist on marriage first.

"Have you met her parents yet?" someone asked.

It was a good question. They'd nearly met them on a few occasions, but it had not actually happened. Ali's parents came from Cornwall and didn't visit the capital, or the Home Counties, if they could avoid it.

"No, not yet," Andy's dad admitted.

He wondered if he should organise a trip to Cornwall. He'd only been there once, but he'd heard the beaches were nice. He suspected they had naturist beaches there. He wasn't sure if he had a passion for naturism, or if it was just having sex in the bushes. He assumed it was possible to do one without the other.

“I guess it will happen soon. I must give him a call,” Andy’s dad said.

“But you don’t want to put pressure on him,” someone said.

“It’s up to him to decide when he’s ready,” another said.

“That’s true,” Andy’s dad admitted.

But he still felt he should speak to him. He didn’t want to parent him, or even guide him. He just wanted to hear his voice. A pint later the pub had thinned out and Andy’s dad realised it was the working week, which still applied to a few of his new chums. It wasn’t too late and he wasn’t too pissed. He took his usual route home and stopped at a tree, only this time he took out his mobile phone. He’d programmed three numbers into it. One was the home phone, the other his wife, and the last was Andy. He understood that young people carried their phones at all times and constantly played with them, accessing all sorts of things. He wasn’t that technologically averse, but he didn’t see the need for constant communication. He pressed the dial button. Andy’s dad held his mobile to his ear, but was surprised when the call was instantly directed to voicemail. He hadn’t anticipated having to leave a message.

“Andy,” Andy’s dad said. “It’s dad. I just thought I’d give you a ring on my new mobile phone.”

There was a pause while he decided whether he should say anything further, but he couldn’t think of anything, and hung up. Since he was standing by the tree, he had a quick pee. By the time he got home he could see the lights were on and Andy's mum was back from her Spanish lesson. He unlocked the front door.

"Soy una mujer," Andy's mum said, as he entered the house.

"Lovely," Andy's dad said, without giving it much thought.

They both froze. He'd uttered the code word to initiate sex without thinking, which was careless. It was like the president tweeting the nuclear codes, he thought. Then he thought that was probably overstating it. But Andy's mum had worn her new clothes, she'd been guided a little by Lydia, and two hours of Latin language might have got her a little frisky. It was hard to tell these days, as she was far quicker to friskiness than she used to be. He had meant to ask her whether she'd heard from Andy or Ali, but she'd stopped in her tracks, and now he'd grabbed her hand. He decided to ask her later.

Chapter Ninety-Two

Ali was on the plane. It had been a very long week and she was grateful that she was seated a long way from her colleagues. She felt tired and she would have slept, but she had other things on her mind. She'd accepted the job. She'd have been crazy not to. She'd read that lucky people always made use of the opportunities that life presented for them. It was going to be hard work, and she'd decided she was not going to work like Jemima at the exclusion of everything else. And she wouldn't put pressure on Andy either. There would be no more sledgehammer hints. She'd wait for it to happen organically. With that thought in mind she drifted off and didn't wake until the plane hit the tarmac in London.

There was a stiff wintry breeze as she got off the plane and she optimistically checked her phone for messages from Andy. There weren't any. She tried calling him. Nothing again. She'd hoped for a second that it was her phone refusing to cooperate with the American system. She picked up her bag and jumped on the train. Much as she liked New York, London was home. An hour later she was outside her front door. She was about to knock when she decided not to. She didn't want that to go unanswered like all her telephone calls. For a second she panicked. Perhaps she'd got everything wrong. Maybe Andy had left her. She felt a moment's bereavement, but she couldn't quite believe it. She took a deep breath and opened the door. She could hear noises from the television. She walked into the sitting room.

"Andy?" she said.

The television was on and Andy was asleep in front of it. She sighed a little sigh of relief. Although it wasn't the perfect picture he was, at least, still there. She was about to shake him when she noticed something. There were flowers on the table. They were in a vase and the table was covered in petals at the centre of which was something that looked like a small box. She looked at Andy. He looked different. She was pleased to see he'd lost his awful hipster beard. That was a great improvement. But it was more than that. His face was bruised. She looked back at the small box.

"Blimey," she said.

Ali wasn't the kind of girl who said things like 'blimey', but the small box looked unmistakably like the kind in which rings were housed. Andy had never bought her any jewellery and, when asked, he'd said he had no views on the subject. So the ring was likely to be symbolic of something. Something like marriage. She shook him.

"Hey," Ali said.

Andy opened his eyes and smiled and with it the bruises became more apparent. His eyes looked a little older too, as if he'd quietly matured when she'd been away. He'd had plans for the evening which involved a bended knee, but 'Battlestar Galactica' came on the television, and it would have been criminal not to have watched that for the seventeenth time. He hadn't quite managed, as he'd fallen asleep. It had been a very tiring week.

"What the hell happened to you?" Ali asked.

Chapter Ninety-Three

Andy's bruises had almost healed, but the experience had changed him. He didn't think so, but it was obvious to Ali. He seemed more settled. They'd walked from the train station – the same commute Andy's dad had made for thirty years – and Andy hadn't seen the family home for a while. He'd rung the doorbell, but it seemed to take a while for his parents to answer.

"That's strange," Andy said.

He was surprised to find the front garden looking a little untidy. He seemed to remember his father saying something about doing more gardening in his retirement. For a second it occurred to him that retirement may not suit his father. Then the door opened.

"Andy," Andy's dad said, tucking his shirt in.

Despite Andy's adulthood they'd not arrived at a way of greeting each other and neither were sure if they should shake hands. It was Andy who took the initiative and he hugged his dad. It was their innate Englishness that made these exchanges so awkward. Had they been from continental Europe they would have been kissing and embracing for years. Andy was similar to his dad in many ways, but he'd been on a strange adventure. He had a story to tell them.

"Alison," Andy's dad said, and he gave her a hug.

Alison's family were far more tactile and she'd always taken the initiative. But with Andy she frequently needed to take the initiative. Andy's mum appeared.

"Darling," she said and kissed her son.

Andy was more skilled at greeting his mother than his father. Social convention was less demanding.

"Alison," Andy's mum said.

Andy's mum kissed Ali, and stepped back to look at her as if she were the daughter she'd never had.

"You look well," Andy's mum said.

"Actually," Ali said, also stepping back. "You look terrific. What have you been doing?"

Andy and Ali were surprised that such an innocent remark should prompt such immediate redness.

"Are you blushing?" Andy said.

"Me? No. I don't think so," Andy mum said, getting redder still.

They moved into the sitting room, which overlooked the garden. There was a set of patio doors which overlooked the sizeable garden. The garden looked wilder than Andy remembered.

"I thought you were going to do more gardening," Andy said.

"No," Andy's dad said firmly. "I've decided I don't much care for gardening."

Andy was surprised to hear it. The garden was long and widened at the end. He remembered playing on the lawn as a child.

"Oh," Andy said.

His childhood memory was of a well kept lawn and garden and it was correct. Andy's dad had felt it was his duty as a father and husband. He'd reassessed his duties.

"I'm going to get a gardener," Andy's dad said.

"Or we might move," Andy's mum said.

Andy was surprised to hear it, and realised he still had a childlike attachment to the house. He'd moved on, but he didn't expect his parents to change. Ali nudged him.

"Move? Where to?" Andy asked.

"We were thinking near the sea," Andy's dad said.

"Near our favourite beach," Andy's mum said.

"You have a favourite beach?" Andy asked, astonished.

It was a further mystery to Andy why the word 'beach' should make his mother blush. He wondered if he knew his parents at all. Ali nudged him again.

"So what have you been up to?" Andy asked.

He was fairly certain this was an innocent question, but it seemed to prompt the same confusion and embarrassment in his parents.

"Your dad goes down to the pub now," Andy's mum said.

"Hey, way to go dad," Andy said.

"He has his collection of chums," Andy's mum said.

"And your mother goes to Spanish lessons," Andy's dad said.

Andy's mum giggled. Andy had heard his mother laugh before, but he had not the slightest recollection of her ever giggling. It was a little strange. Ali gave him another nudge. Andy was finding the nudges harder to ignore.

"And yoga classes," Andy's dad added.

Andy was about to say something when Ali delivered a nudge which was close to winding him. She knew she had to take control.

"Stuart and Wendy," Ali said. "Andy has something to tell you."

Now there was no escaping it. Andy took in a breath of air, but his eyes momentarily landed on the fruit bowl and a banana which lay on top. He's eaten his last banana. He had no intention of ever eating another banana. The thought made him feel queasy.

"Well?" Andy's mum, said.

"Well?" Andy's dad, said.

There was no more stalling. Andy took in another deep breath, and moved his eyes away from the fruit bowl, and looked at Ali.

"I've asked Alison to marry me."

Nearly the end.

Encore

Marvin had been lucky. Andy's tale of relationship agony had been so crushingly boring that it had rendered him entirely unconscious. It had been quite a severe crash and there were no more airbags to go off in the car but, despite that, when he came to he was only mildly bruised. But he had to get away as quickly as possible. He'd found a suit in the boot of the car. It was a little too large for him, but it changed his appearance. It had a rather unsavoury smell but he didn't dwell on it. He knew he had to learn chameleon-like skills to integrate into normal society. Marvin wasn't normal.

He'd listened to Andy's hideously tedious diatribe about his relationship problems and all he'd wanted to do was cut his fingers off. Marvin had walked away from the wrecked car with an appetite to do some harm. He was almost self aware enough to know this wasn't how most other people felt, but he wasn't going to let that bother him. He didn't want to change. But Marvin didn't want to go back to prison either.

It hadn't taken long to steal another car and with it Marvin made his way across the continent, stopping only occasionally to trap, kill and eat something. It calmed his nerves and eventually he found a place in which there was a ready supply of rabbits and ducks. Marvin managed to push his passion for collecting fingers to the back of his mind, as he settled into a new and calmer existence. He found a deserted shelter and made it his home. He would have been fine, but he was forced to take a trip into town. He needed more honey to go with his duck dinner.

Marvin had managed to change some currency and was able to purchase the honey in the conventional way. It was while he was leaving the supermarket that the delicate balance of his temperament was challenged. It was a group of smiling people blocking his path. He tried to move round them, but they were insistent he engage with them.

“Would you like a Watchtower?” one of them said.

Marvin thought about this. He’d once shared a cell with a music fanatic and Marvin had tolerated it for a while. Watchtower rang a bell and then Marvin remembered. He knew he had to lay low and appear normal.

“Would that be Bob Dylan or Jimi Hendrix?” Marvin asked.

The smiling people continued to smile, but they didn’t register his response. Their eyes appeared to be glazed as if they were brainwashed, but Marvin hadn’t noticed as he hadn’t looked into their eyes, and he made a further attempt to walk round them. Another of the smiling people blocked his way.

“What do you think of Armageddon?” the smiling man asked.

Marvin thought hard. He knew this one. Wasn’t their lead singer Ozzie Osbourne? No, he thought, that was

Black Sabbath. Had Def Leopard changed their name? Marvin couldn't remember, but he was certain it was a heavy metal band.

"Great band?" Marvin suggested.

Marvin made another attempt to get to his car but a smiling man blocked his path. He put his hand up. The smiling man had long slim fingers, which would have been more than welcome in any finger collection, Marvin thought. He could feel his tenuous hold slipping away. He could feel the black veil appearing and then it came to him.

"Fucking Jehovah's Witnesses," he said and pushed his way through the crowd.

He needed his cutters from the boot of the car.

Very nearly the end...

A year later

"Isn't it beautiful?" Barry asked his son.

Barry junior admired the small banana tree. As they were surrounded by banana trees it wasn't immediately obvious what made this one more beautiful than the others. But Barry was using it as a metaphor in an attempt to instil the work ethic in his son.

"I mined that shit," Barry said earnestly.

It might have been the combination of platypus related foods, and the fact that Andy had not defecated for some while, but that shopping bag was full to the point of overflowing.

"There was a lot of shit," Barry said.

It had been an exercise in hope and optimism, and a determination to resolve the issues of a small nation, and it had come down to finding banana seeds in a pile of shit. But Barry hadn't given up. Gary, on the other hand, had taken one look at it and said, "you're on your own."

"They're very, very small," Barry said.

Barry junior had smoked a joint just before the arrival of his father, as he anticipated some sort of lecture, and knew from experience that it was easier to tolerate if he was just a little bit stoned. But, as Barry junior wasn't good at moderation, he was more than a little stoned. The air was filled with it.

"What are?" Barry junior said.

A huge gap had grown between them and he frequently hadn't the faintest idea what his father was banging on about, particularly as he didn't share his father's passion for supercars.

"The seeds," Barry said.

They looked at the tree. It was the product of those seeds which Barry had so patiently harvested. His civil service had begun to question the sanity of their king and then they'd caught him with a pile of shit on his desk. Questions had been asked, but the general consensus was that mad kings fared no worse than sane ones.

"Particularly when they're stained brown," Barry said adding, "in a sea of brown."

They looked at a single banana which they'd plucked three days earlier and which was turning dark. They had been waiting and neither of them knew that this kind of conversation would become commonplace once they'd consumed the banana.

"You have to feel them with your fingers," Barry said.

Barry junior had heard enough of Barry's shit-mining stories. He just wanted to try the banana. It didn't look that appetising, but Barry had taken a number of unappetising narcotics in the past. There were few things that held him back in the pursuit of getting comprehensively stoned.

"And each seed felt like a victory," Barry said.

He wondered if his search for the seeds would develop into a story that parents would tell their children. It would be an inspiring lesson in perseverance and hope. A Shawshank Redemption of the narcotic banana. Barry was unaware that his thoughts were being heavily influenced by the fetid air of Barry's junior's house.

"And finally there were enough," Barry said.

He was elevating the experience to religious levels. But now they both knew they were ready.

"Shall we?" Barry said.

"Yes please," Barry junior said.

Barry junior was rather skeptical of the alleged effects of the banana grown from shit-caked seeds, but he hoped it would stop his father talking. It was giving him a headache. Barry picked up the banana and quietly unwrapped it. He took a bite and offered it to Barry junior who took a further bite. They chewed. They swallowed. And for a moment nothing happened.

"Okay," Barry junior said.

As Lobo's expert on the effects of narcotics Barry junior was a little underwhelmed. There was no soothing high or soporific calmness. His eyes were just seeing what was in front of him. But Barry was one mouthful ahead of his son. When it arrived it was as unexpected as a Ryanair pilot landing an aircraft and hitting the ground. Twenty minutes later nothing was ever going to be the same again. Louis Armstrong had arrived.

"Hey man," Barry managed to say.

Lou Reed had joined Louis Armstrong. Barry and Barry junior's missing bond was found in an instant and Barry's desire to own a supercar collection disappeared as swiftly as black-stained seeds in a sea of black.

The End

gilescurtis.com
Email me (if you like) at
gilescurtis@mail.com

As ever, many thanks to my friend Steve Caplin for his ongoing support and calm nature, and to an unsuspecting reader who unknowingly lent his name. Also to another friend of mine who, in the hope of securing a meeting, hitched a lift in the jet of an African leader and was welcomed in Paris with a brass band.

If you enjoyed this book you can find more Giles Curtis comedies on Amazon –

‘Hell, Hull and Epiphanies’

Gerry doesn’t get out much, but when he does he encounters Mandy – free, a little wild, and half his age. But by day Gerry is Gerrard, who is not only married, he’s a vicar. A vicar with doubts. Although Lucinda, his wife, has very few doubts when a trip to Birmingham goes startlingly right. And ageing gigolo Nelson never sees himself as a messiah until Albert convinces him he can walk on water – or is that just revenge for Nelson having put his head down the toilet at school?
Does Gerrard really witness the Second Coming? Will Lucinda’s American prove himself in Hong Kong? And will the Late Contessa ever retrieve her Bentley?
Find out in Giles Curtis’s twelfth rip-roaring, hilarious romp through the intricacies of fidelity, faith and epiphanies.

‘Five Minute Warning, Harry’

Harry feels downtrodden. Downtrodden by senior management, who have decided to retire him, and by his meddling, sex-obsessed father in law. But mostly by his wife, Hilda. And she tells him they must retire to Cornwall.
There is talk of reconnection, but neither can remember being connected in the first place. Harry takes up a creative writing course, through which he

can live out his fantasies – fantasies of murdering his wife. But Hilda reads his story and, lost on Bodmin Moor, is confronted with devil worshippers, a convicted call centre worker with a habit of cutting off fingers, and a birdwatching hitman. In her absence, and befuddled by his writing tutor's hallucinogenic muffins, Harry looks very guilty. indeed.

'Faecal Money: A Very Lucrative Crap'

Sam's trousers were round his ankles. The microwaved chicken – long past its sell-by date – had made a hasty exit. He was down a ditch in the middle of nowhere, and there weren't any tissues. Suzy had dumped him. Things weren't going well. He was only one wipe away from his life changing forever when he found a blue IKEA bag packed with banknotes. Gary wants to kill him. So does Vlad. Ashton wants to paint him naked and then there's the Contessa. Suzy isn't certain they've broken up. One thing's for sure: Sam's life has been turned upside down.

'Newton's Balls'

Martin is dying and he has one wish. He asks his daughter, Megan, to find a man. But not a normal man, he is the product of Martin's quest, and obsession, for higher intelligence. A man made from the finest genetic material, a cocktail of stolen DNA, including the forefathers of science. A super human who will solve the world's problems. At least that's what Martin hopes.
But Kevin is a man with a rampant hedonistic thirst, a talent for deception, and the centre of the ensuing

chaos that brings a city to a standstill. He is a man who knows how to throw a hell of a party.

‘The Hedonist’s Apprentice’

Travis’s life is perfection. He has the looks, the car, the apartment and the women. Lots of women. Debbie says the sex is revelatory, which doesn’t help Sheryl. And then there’s Colin.
Colin’s life is bleak and without hope, and his sex life is so inconsequential that it is hard to assign it a proclivity in any direction. All Colin’s dreams come true when, thinking he’s working for MI6, he shadows Travis’s life and goes on a journey of orgiastic debauchery. But things aren’t quite as they seem as the noose tightens on Travis’s perfect world.

‘The Calamitous Kidnap of Oodle the Poodle’

Bryan Brizzard, a notorious bastard, and owner of short haul airline company Bryanair, hates everyone. He hates his suppliers, his employees, his passengers and his wife and children. But, Dom Hazel discovers, he really loves his poodle, Oodle. And Hazel is an animal assassin. But this time it’s a kidnap and Brizzard’s mansion is set in the Essex Woods where Hazel, who’s trying to be faithful to Julie, finds temptation and confusion. And dogging. The plan threatens to fall apart as Hazel leaves behind more of his DNA than he intends.

‘The Badger and Blondie’s Beaver’

Madeleine misses her old life in Paris. Her work as a forensic scientist is going great, but now she's marooned in the country and her social life, or more accurately her sex life, is a disaster. When she's called upon to extract a severed head from a weir, she meets Sam. Sam is her perfect man, but murder, mannequins, cocaine, the drug squad, Customs and Excise, multiple arrests and the Mafia get in the way.

Sam, Oliver and William are three young graduates desperate to make a fast buck. The plan seems so simple, it just involves the not entirely legal business of transporting silver which, by way of a cunning disguise, has been fashioned into dildos. But the journey refuses to go to plan.

'A Very UnChristian Retreat'

Hugo has only himself to blame. The bookings in their holiday complex in France are few and Jan, his wife, is forced to organise a yoga week. She remains in Godalming, which leaves Hugo alone with the irresistible Suzanna, who gives off signals he has difficulty interpreting. Jan is talked into hiring a private detective to lure Hugo, but his problems have only just begun. Hugo meets Lenny and Doris who claim to run art parties, which turn out to be more of the swinging sort. Hugo's friend, Gary, books in his gay friends, who have a penchant for the feral. But wild is how Lenny and Doris like it. Hugo doesn't tell Jan, and an unpaid telephone bill means she can't tell him about the Christian Retreat group who are on their way.

And then the chaos really begins.

'It's All About Danny'

"How does he manage to go away for a few weeks and come back a Nobel fucking Prize winner?"

Kathy can't believe it. Nor can Danny, who has tripped through life gliding past responsibility, commitment and anything that involved hard work. But when he is rejected by all the women in his life: his girlfriend, landlord and his boss at 'Bedding Bimonthly,' he has no choice. His better looking high-achieving brother, whose earnest phase has taken him away from the big money in the city, invites him to build a school in Africa with him.

Danny discovers that all the flatpack battles he has fought have given him a talent for it, and it lends his life new purpose. But his life changes when, during a fierce storm, he saves the only child of an African chief, who claims to have mystical powers. The chief invites him to make a wish. Danny can't decide whether he should wish for world peace, a cure for cancer or to be irresistible to women. Shallowness prevails.....

Does the Chief have strange powers or has Danny changed? He misses Kathy his girlfriend, who realises she's made a mistake. And then the wish turns into a nightmare...

'Looking Bloody Good Old Boy'

Arthur Cholmondely-Godstone is in the business of pensions. He offers a unique pension, from a nonreturnable sum, and he introduces his clients to a new way of living. He encourages them to explore radical views, try extreme sports and to eat, drink and smoke as much as they can. Or put another way, Arthur does his best to kill them.

Born from an old family and gifted with the family gene, which ensures him an unbreakable constitution, he is also the last in line and the family need an heir. But the family gene is cursed with a minimal sperm count, and his dissolute ways don't help. He is certain there is a child in his past, all he has to do is search his back catalogue of women, while keeping his clients in bad habits.

Brayman is proving to be irritatingly indestructible and Eddie B, the rock star who used to be a rock god, is trying to kill himself, which would be great, but he needs to finish his gigs before Arthur can collect all the money.

And someone is trying to kill Arthur.

'The Wildest Week of Daisy Wyler'

Daisy had lived her life as if on a merry-go-round, and she'd never stepped on a roller-coaster. There had been a husband, children and even grandchildren, but things had changed. A change dictated by her fickle ex-husband, and which prompts a new life in London.

But Daisy wants more. A bigger life, a wilder life. An exciting life. She finds an unlikely friend in Sophie, her neighbour, and there is an imminent party planned for Sophie's 'sort of' boyfriend, the dissolute Lord Crispin. Crispin's parties are legendary and favour the excessive. And so begins the wildest week of Daisy Wyler.

Find out more on gilescurtis.com

Printed in Great Britain
by Amazon

46518453R00229